ACKNOWLEDGEMENTS

I want to thank Franco the Creator and Bobby Humphrey for encouraging me to let my words flow.

Thanks to My Favorite Tall Girl, Sharon Evans, for reading my manuscript and helping me to make sense of it.

You guys helped me to find my voice and I am eternally greatful.

A MODERN FAMILY

A Novel of Fiction by James D. Holliday

1

"Next!!"

Mr. Sam had just finished what seemed like his hundredth haircut of the day, even though the shop had only been open for a little more than a few hours. Before noon on a Saturday, any inner city Black barbershop would have a standing room only crowd jockeying for an open seat in a barber chair or the waiting area. This one was no exception.

The shop sat on Broadway at the corner of an indiscriminate block in the Midtown section of town. Broadway was the main north-south thoroughfare in town, dividing the east and west sides of the city. "Mr. Sam's Cutz" had been a fixture in the neighborhood since 1968 when the city elected its first Black Mayor. When it first opened, it shared the block with many other businesses owned by a burgeoning group of Black and immigrant entrepreneurs.

Blacks came north from the harshly segregated south during the period of the great migration and immigrants moved to the area from all over the world. The new residents were attracted to the good paying jobs that the hulking factories and oil refineries offered back in the day helping pave the way to their dreams of a middle class life.

The Midtown area and its surrounding neighborhoods used to be abuzz with crowds, traffic and retail activity. During the heyday for the steel mills and the booming industrial period when the city was rapidly expanding, Midtown's streets were packed with traffic and its sidewalks bustling with people. Cars would occupy every parking space at the curb and traffic would fill two lanes on both sides of the street.

The city, the neighborhood and this particular block had fallen on hard times. The decline of the steel industry and the loss of manufacturing jobs took their toll. When the jobs left, so did the majority of the white residents. When they moved, they took the stores, shops and most of the restaurants with them. What was left was vacant buildings, abandoned businesses and a neighborhood with few prospects. The barbershop was one of only a few businesses still open and operating on the block. The others were the Pawn Shop across the street and a Blood Plasma Donation Center on the other end of the block.

The soothing sounds of smooth jazz music floated through the shop emanating from an old AM/FM radio that was positioned on a rickety table near the front. There were always four or five folding chairs arranged around the table. Older patrons used the table to play a game of chess or pulled out a checkboard for a game of draughts. The younger customers preferred a rousing game of dominoes, spades or bid whist. When it wasn't being used for board games or cards, the table held an assortment of magazines including Ebony, Jet, Sports Illustrated, GQ and Black Enterprise. ESPN Sports Center was always playing on the big screen TV on the wall opposite the chairs in the waiting area. The din of the buzzing hair clippers and what seemed like a thousand individual conversations competed with the sound from both the radio and the TV.

There wasn't anything special or unusual about Mr. Sam's shop. Two large windows with an unobstructed view of the street were positioned on both sides of the lone entry door. Retractable steel bars offered protection for the windows when the shop was closed. Bulletproof plexiglass covered the top half of the reinforced steel door. Five barber chairs were aligned in a row along the right side of the large, open shop. The chairs were built for comfort. Each one covered with overstuffed dark burgundy leather with extra wide armrests. Steel footrests on each chair allowed the customers to find a comfortable position while they were being serviced. Huge mirrors standing eight feet tall were positioned behind each chair. The mirrors were framed with large bright studio lights and oversized white light bulbs. Taped to each mirror was the ubiquitous poster depicting every possible permutation of black haircut available. There were individual wash basins behind each chair as well.

Mr. Sam's was air conditioned and the setting was always on high. Several oscillating fans strategically placed throughout the shop were on and constantly blowing. The heat from the bright lights and the number of people in the shop were in a persistant battle with the air conditioning and the fans. The fans and the A/C rarely won. On days when the weather was unusually warm or particularly humid, neither the barbers nor the customers could be completely comfortable. The shop was warm and stuffy and the smell of cologne mixed with cigarette or weed smoke filled clothes. The slightest hint of Fine Italian Men's Citrus Barber Aftershave and a light fog of talcum powder wafted throughout and gave the shop a sweet and pleasant bouquet.

Three of the five barber chairs belonged to Mr. Sam, Signifying Ray and Oscar, the three senior or master barbers in the shop. The other two chairs were occupied by two younger barbers in training, June Bug and Kwame.

Mr. Sam's attracted customers from the local neighborhood, all over town and the surrounding area. Much of the clientele included guys who had grown up in Midtown but moved away and had not been able to find a reliable barber in the suburbs or nearer to where they lived. All of the patrons came to the shop because they knew it was a place to get a good haircut. They also came because they didn't want to miss out on the latest happenings or buzz. The shop was home base for all of the neighborhood chatter, scandal and conversation. It was a place where old childhood friends could catch up with one another. Fathers could bring in their sons to indoctrinate them into the legacy and tradition of the Black barbershop. Brothers could have a much needed respite from the stresses of being Black men in a country that still did not readily or eagerly welcome them. Every week someone would come up with a solution to solve all of the problems in the world. The running joke in the shop was that the only thing that was missing was funding.

Mr. Sam looked like he might have been born cutting hair. He was average height with solid white hair that he kept neatly trimmed every day. The other barbers and customers joked that the lines and cuts on his head were so sharp and tight that you could cut yourself. When he was without a customer, he was constantly snipping or trimming his own hair in the mirror at his station. He prided himself on keeping his hair freshly cut and neat. He wanted potential customers to look at him and know that they could get a great haircut at his shop.

Mr. Sam was lean but not skinny. He definitely was not muscular either but looked like he could take care of himself if the need arose. He always wore a black barber smock with pockets where he kept combs, brushes and clippers. His chair sat right in the middle of the shop. Everything was neat and in its proper place at his barber station. His chair looked like it had never been used. It was a point of personal pride for him to keep his area immaculate and in order. He didn't let anyone fuck around

7

his area because he said it was like "fucking with his money". Mr. Sam wasn't mean nor easygoing but everyone knew he was serious when it came to managing his shop and they behaved accordingly.

Next to Mr. Sam, but closer to the door, was Signifyin' Ray's chair. Ray was shorter than Sam but twice as wide. As meticulous as Mr. Sam was in keeping up his appearance and making sure his work area was in order, Ray was the exact opposite. His chair and workstation were a mess. He had papers and supplies in unmanageable jumbles all over the place. He spent as much time searching for his clippers, talcum powder, shears and anything else that he needed to do his job as he spent cutting each customer's hair. The only reason that his work space wasn't replete with freshly cut hair droppings or spent paper neck tabs was that every hour Mr. Sam, Oscar or one of the other barbers would sweep the floor.

The only tell tale sign that Ray was a barber in the shop instead of a customer was that he also wore a smock like Sam's. Ray's smock looked like it had never seen the inside of a dry cleaner or a washing machine. It held food stains from what appeared to be every meal that Ray had ever eaten. It was also thoroughly wrinkled and if Ray ever did wash it, he certainly did not take the time to apply the warm side of an iron. He had long ago lost the waist ties to his smock and used a black belt to hold it together instead. Ray had an easy, toothy smile and talked incessantly.

Ray talked about anything and everything that came into his mind and he also talked about anyone who came into the shop. If a young brother walked in and his pants were sagging, Ray would compliment him on how nice his ass looked until he pulled them up. If someone came in reeking from the smell of weed, he would ask them to stand in front of one of the fans near his chair so he could get a contact high. He saved his most biting commentary for anyone who came into the shop with a hustle or a scam attempting to sell something to the customers. The shop went crazy one Saturday when a peddler tried to hawk a pair of Air Jordan sneakers that had obviously been stolen. Ray told him that he had to be "as high as giraffe pussy" trying to sell stolen shit in the shop. Everyone in the shop roared with laughter. Mr. Sam even chuckled to himself at Ray's retort. The peddler was so embarrassed that he left the shop and has never returned. Any customer who entered the door of the shop or sat in his chair was fair game for Ray. The patrons in the shop put up with him because they knew he didn't mean any harm and he knew how to shape and trim beards and mustaches better than anyone in town.

Oscar, who at one time had been a promising basketball prospect, occupied the chair on the other side of Mr. Sam. He was six feet five inches and at 235 pounds had a slim, athletic build. He sufferend an injury to his leg and his knee in a pickup basketball game on the courts at Roosevelt High School and never fully recovered. An opposing player gave him a hard and unnecessary check that knocked him down. He lay on the court hurt and writhing in pain until an ambulance arrived. He was taken to the emergency room at Methodist Hospital for treatment. Unfortunately, no doctor was available to treat or see him for several hours. By the time he finally received care from a doctor, it was too late to completely repair his injury. Oscar's hopes for a basketball career evaporated with every minute he had to wait to be seen.

Oscar also wore a black barber smock like Ray and Mr. Sam. He kept his smock clean and neatly pressed and it always looked like it had just been returned fresh from the cleaners. He was the least talkative barber in the whole shop but was very courteous and addressed his customers with almost military respect. Oscar was the most productive barber in the shop moving his customers in and out of his chair with speed and efficiency. He completed more haircuts than any other barber and everyone respected the business-like way that he did his job.

June Bug and Kwame, the two young barbers, were both ex-offenders. Mr. Sam had known them from his church when they were young boys, before they got into trouble. Mr. Sam knew that in both their cases June Bug and Kwame took plea deals instead of going through lengthy trials that might have resulted in longer incarcerations. He also knew that both of them had not committed the crimes for which they had been accused.

Hanging with the wrong group of friends got June Bug in trouble with the law. The police stopped him and his friends during an area-wide sweep looking for the perpetrators in a robbery. The police interviewed everyone individually using harsh questioning techniques that eventually got one person to give them the story they wanted to hear. Not only did the informant implicate June Bug, but he also accused everyone else in the group except himself!!

June Bug's family was unable to afford a competent lawyer so they had to rely on support from an attorney from the Public Defender's office. The overworked and overwhelmed lawyer suggested that June Bug take a plea. He convinced June Bug and his family that the plea deal would force his trial to move along more swiftly. The Public Defender assured them that since this was June Bug's first offense, he would be able to get off with probation and no jail time. Even though June Bug was innocent, he followed his attorney's recommendation. The Public Defender's plea deal and hope for probation tactic did not work. June Bug was sentenced to five years in prison. He served three years and was released for good behavior. Mr. Sam was working with him to get the conviction overturned. Evidence surfaced after the trial that his Public Defender had mismanaged the case.

Kwame was accused of a domestic violence crime by a former girlfriend while he was in college. He ended their relationship but she lied and told authorities that he beat her up and he was accused of battery and abuse. He was seen leaving her apartment by several witnesses and admitted to being with her on the day she was hurt. The evidence against him was overwhelming.

After telling his girlfriend that their relationship was over, Kwame went out with his college roommate and several friends to celebrate his independence. While celebrating, Kwame and his friends got into an altercation with denizens of the local town. There was a perennial fued between athletes at the university and guys from the surrounding towns. Every year an incident erupted between the two groups. One of the locals involved in the altercation was the scion of the richest man in the town. Kwame had actually been trying to separate the opposing factions in the melee and was holding a couple of the combatants at bay. When the police arrived they arrested him and all of the other participants in the brawl.

Seeking to find anything he could to punish the athletes for fighting with his son, the rich patriarch learned about Kwame and his ex-girlfriend. He located her and paid her to testify that Kwame had attacked her. He also coerced her to say that she was actually the one who wanted to end the relationship. When called to testify, he told her to say that Kwame was upset when he went out with his friends and was looking for trouble.

Kwame's arrest violated the athletic code of conduct at his

school. Intense lobbying from the wealthy business owner convinced the University Athletic Department to revoke his football scholarship. Without the support of the athletic department, Kwame had no means to support himself and pay his own bills or pay for his college education. He was labeled as a troublemaker and seen as damaged goods by other schools and was unable to transfer. He faced a domestic violence charge brought on by his ex-girlfriend and a battery charge stemming from the fight. He was in dire straits and agreed to accept a plea deal in exchange for a much lower prison sentence.

Halfway through his sentence, Kwame's ex-girlfriend came forward to tell the truth. She admitted that another man that she had been seeing while also dating Kwame was actually the miscreant that assaulted her. She confessed that she was upset about Kwame ending their relationship and wanted to make him suffer. She conspired with the other man that she was dating to beat her up. She admitted that when she first met Kwame, she knew he was a promising professional football prospect. She wanted him to be her ticket to a better life once he signed a lucrative football contract. When Kwame broke up with her, all of the plans she had put in place were destroyed. She conceded that the story she told the police about Kwame assaulting her was a lie. She never confessed to the payoff that she received from the local nabob so he got away scot free.

After he was released from prison, Kwame stumbled around trying to decide what to do with his life. He contemplated returning to college but was ineligible to play football and had no way to pay for classes. He tried other jobs that didn't pay well and eventually his size and athleticism caught the eye of the local drug dealer who was looking for an enforcer or a bodyguard. Kwame had no desire to get caught up in the drug game and turned to Mr. Sam who offered him an opportunity to become a barber.

Mr. Sam promised them both chairs in his shop once they were released from prison. In return, he made them promise to keep their noses clean and not to return to the activities or situations that had gotten them in trouble. Mr. Sam liked the symbiosis of having younger barbers on his staff and keeping June Bug and Kwame out of trouble. He knew he needed younger barbers to attract new customers. He enlisted their support to make sure the shop was a safe haven in the neighborhood. He asked them to make sure that their friends knew that gang activity was to be left outside on the street.

June Bug's chair was the one closest to the front of the shop. He was fair skinned, a hair under six feet tall and would have to gain weight to be considered lean since he weighed less than 130 pounds. June Bug wore his hair in a very close fade cut. His head was bald down by his ears but the top was covered in dark, rich, thick tight curls. June Bug's fade transition from bald to thick hair was imperceptible and his style attracted many customers to his chair asking for a similar look.

June Bug wanted to learn everything he could from Mr. Sam because he wanted to own this own shop one day. He was easy going with his customers and the patrons who frequented the shop. He made sure to stay clear of the bad influences that had got him caught up and sent to jail in the first place. He normally dressed in jeans and a crisp, white t-shirt that looked like he had just taken it out of the package before he put it on. He was famous in the shop for cutting designs and patterns, that many of the younger customers liked, into their heads. He was a master at more traditional styles as well and benefited from an ever expanding clientele.

Kwame had the chair at the very back of the shop. Mr. Sam

purposely placed him there telling him to keep an eye out on what was going on in the shop in case any trouble started. He and June Bug couldn't have been more different. Kwame had a deep dark complexion with a head full of thick dread locks that he cared for assiduously. He was six feet three inches tall and still powerfully built from his football playing days. He had a quiet spirit about him.

Kwame was embarrassed about his former life and the loss of his opportunity to play football. He was very shy and barely spoke to anyone in the shop other than Mr. Sam or Oscar. Like Oscar, however, Kwame took great care of his customers. He made sure that they were completely satisfied when he finished a cut. He took extra time to ensure his clients were happy before allowing anyone to leave his chair. People thought Mr. Sam kept Kwame around in case any altercations erupted in the shop between customers or Ray if he said anything inappropriate.

The linoleum tile floor in the shop had a black and white checkerboard pattern. The three rows of metal folding chairs in the waiting area were arrayed in lines of ten to twelve across. Each chair had a small faux leather cushion in the seat and across the back. The cushion was supposed to provide a modicum of comfort and support, but no one would ever say they successfully achieved either objective.

Mr. Sam controlled the remote control for the television and convincing him to change the station to something other than ESPN required the negotiating skills of an ambassador. The TV played with the sound moderately low and only the customers lucky enough to secure a seat directly in front of it were able to hear what was being broadcast.

The next client jumped in Mr. Sam's chair and told him what

kind of cut he wanted. The barbers and the customers were satisfied that this Saturday was a good day. The barbers were working as fast as they could and the waiting area was turning over as expeditiously as possible. There wasn't anything of special interest on the television and no one had yet started a game at the magazine table.

As usual the discussions in the shop centered on solving the problems of the world and improving the plight of the Black man. Mr. Sam allowed any topic to be discussed in the shop except politics. On the day after the 2016 election several fights flared up as patrons struggled to justify the results of the election and several customers admitted to not voting for the Democratic candidate. In response, Mr. Sam posted a sign forbidding any political discussions until after the 46th President was inaugurated.

Silence fell over the shop and everyone directed their attention to the jet-black Tesla Model X that glistened in the bright sunlight as it parked at the curb directly in front of the shop. The windows in the Model X were tinted black. The 22" Pirelli Scorpion Verde tires and the Dub Dazr gloss black rims with milled accents look like they had just been mounted on the car. The vanity license plates shouted 'XERXES'. Everyone knew that the local football hero, Xerxes Scott had just pulled up and was about to come in to get a haircut. He was a hometown star and local hero because even with his success, he had never abandoned his hometown or childhood neighborhood.

Xerxes had funded a technology lab at his alma mater, Roosevelt High School, that was stocked with state-of-the-art computers, wireless access points, routers, digital cameras and high resolution video monitors. He wanted to ensure that science, technology, engineering, arts and math (STEAM) related courses were incorporated into the curriculum. He wanted to provide inner-city students with as much a chance at success as other kids in more affluent areas. He also built his Mom and Dad a brand-new home and supported his siblings and their children as well. He wasn't perfect but in the eyes of his neighbors, he could do no wrong. Whenever he was in town on the weekends, he would drop by the shop for a haircut and to catch up on what was happening.

Xerxes was handsome, tall and muscular. Imagine a combination of Idris Elba, Denzel Washington and Kofi Siriboe. His deep, rich, dark skin and nearly completely bald head was contrasted by a set of pristine white teeth. He sported a fully-grown beard much like the one worn by James Harden of the Houston Rockets basketball team. He smiled easily and made people feel comfortable when they were around him. His massive hands surprised people but they served him well as a wide receiver in the National Football League (NFL). He exuded an aura of perpetual happiness and the customers in the shop clamored for his attention. Xerxes took a seat and patiently waited for his name to be called. Other customers offered him their spot in line, but he refused not wanting to be perceived as receiving special treatment.

Signifyin' Ray yelled, "Hey Xerxes, let me borrow the car this weekend!! I'll make sure to fill it up with gas and get it washed before I bring it back to you!!" Xerxes didn't have the heart to bust Ray out and tell him that the car was totally electric.

Someone else in the shop saw an opening and yelled, "You old motherfucker the car is all electric." He continued, "It don't need no damn gas."

Ray seemed to be embarrassed for the first time that anyone could remember. He did not have a ready retort and replied, "Shut the fuck up!!"

The heckling customer sarcastically responded, "Ray, your stupid ass will fuck it all up trying to put gas in a Tesla." He went on, "You better stick to that old ass Model-T you drive and leave the new cars to us youngbloods." The crowd in the shop hooted and hollered because it seemed that Ray might have finally met his match.

Ray responded, "At least I got a car you broke motherfucker." He continued, "How many miles you get on those knock off Air Jordans?" The crowd in the shop laughed. They knew Ray was back to his normal form.

Xerxes told Ray, "Come pick it up whenever you want it. Don't worry about filling it up."

Another customer in the shop tried to persaude Xerxes to invest in a restaurant, night club or some other poorly planned or researched business venture. He told the supplicant that he would have to review their business plan before making a decision. He knew that the conversation would usually end immediately when he requested details and specifics like a business plan but never wanted anyone to feel like they were bothering him. Just as another customer was about to recommend another business venture for him to consider, Oscar called Xerxes to take a seat in his chair.

Xerxes jumped up and took a seat in Oscar's chair and told him, "Trim and shape up my beard and give me my normal shave. Make it smooth like you know I like it."

Oscar replied, "Sure man. I got you." He added, "How is the fine lady your dating?"

Xerxes replied, "Who, Precious?!? Oh, she's real good man. Thanks."

Oscar pulled one of the paper neck tabs out of the dispenser roll and secured it around Xerxes' ample neck. He placed his African print barber cover over Xerxes broad chest and leaned him back in the chair. Oscar heated the shave cream and filled his hands with a large dollop of the white cream and began to spread it all over Xerxes' head. He also carefully spread the shave cream under his nose, down his cheek and along his neck to carefully outline his beard. He took his straight razor and gave it a couple of scrapes across the barber strop to sharpen the blade. Xerxes liked his scalp to be baby's bottom smooth and preferred his beard to be neatly trimmed and perfectly and symmetrically shaped. Oscar had been his barber since he was a teenager and knew exactly what his special customer wanted. Oscar started the shave and before a few minutes had passed, Xerxes was sound asleep.

2

"Where do you want to go for breakfast this morning sexy?" Abel yelled to Cyrus over the steamy water running in the shower.

"I want to go to the little soul food spot near downtown" Cyrus replied. "I think it's called Miss Sharon's, but I know it is going to be crowded by now. I'm too hungry to wait," he yelled from the shower. "I want some homemade biscuits, eggs, sausage and grits, so anywhere that has that on the menu is fine with me," Cyrus said. He added, "I'm hungry from fucking this hot, old man all night last night. I need to build up my energy."

Abel replied, "I got your old man alright."

Cyrus was taking an extra-long time in the shower. He was hoping that Abel would get the hint and join him in the steaming water. He was yearning to have another hot sex session before heading out for breakfast. Cyrus had spent most of the night before inside Abel. He smiled broadly thinking about how much he enjoyed their sex together. They were both ravenous after their long night of continuous and recurring copulation and had just gotten out of bed. He knew Abel liked him because of his insatiable sexual appetite and his ability to be totally dominant, while simultaneously sensitive in bed. He was much younger than Abel and knew that he had a good thing going with this older man. Cyrus knew how to give Abel just enough attention to keep him interested.

Abel weighed 215 pounts and was a shade under six feet tall. He had a hazelnut complexion and deep brown eyes. He wore his hair shaved bald or very closely cropped. He kept his hair closely shorn to hide the grey that was making a debut on the top of his head. Abel worked hard in the gym to prevent the inevitabilities of age from taking hold and showing on his body. Though he was not blessed with six-pack abs, he didn't have a beer belly or gut either. His broad and pronounced chest was compliments of the dozens of pushups and bench press exercises that he did in the gym several times a week.

Overall he knew he looked good for his age and knew that the work that he put in at the weight room gave him more than a passing glance from many. However, he always wanted more definition in his arms. It seemed that no matter how hard he worked his biceps and triceps they never developed the ripped cuts that he longed for. His most impressive asset was a nice, plump, round bottom.

Before he passed away, his Dad would always tell him his Mom's butt is what intrigued him and piqued his interest in following through to get to know her. His Dad loved telling the story of the first time he saw his future wife on the campus of Jackson State College in Mississippi. She had been walking ahead of him on campus with a group of other girls but stood out from the crowd and he noticed her immediately. He would laugh at how he thought, "She is going to be my wife." Abel would always blush when his Dad would talk about his Mom that way but it was obvious how much he deeply cared for her so many decades after their first meeting. Abel's family and friends used to tease him when he was a kid, calling him "Bubble" because even though he was slim he had inherited his Mom's apple bottom. As he got older and grew up, the rest of his body caught up with his ample backside. Today, his body was more height and weight proportioned.

Abel did not look like a man in his fifties. He prided himself on looking healthy and younger than his actual chronological age. Cyrus told him that the first time they met, he noticed his nice and firm butt. He told him that it, more than anything else, was what kept him coming back to see him as often as he did.

Abel yelled, "If you don't get out of that shower right now, we ain't going to be able to get a seat anywhere for breakfast" as he poked his head into the bathroom.

Cyrus replied with a sly smile, "Why don't you come and help me wash all the soap off my back" as he looked down at his semi-hard penis.

Abel smiled while looking directly at Cyrus' dick. He replied "Let's go get breakfast first and I'll take care of your back and that when we get done."

Cyrus got excited about the thought of more sex with Abel. He quickly rinsed the remaining soap off his body, got out of the shower and asked Abel to dry his back. As Abel was toweling down his back and butt, Cyrus turned around to show Abel how pleased he was that he was assisting him. Cyrus was well endowed and he knew he was well endowed. He was blessed with the rare combination of both length and girth. The head was extraordinarily large and the shaft was broad and heavy. A thick, throbbing vein ran the entire length of the shaft along the top. He could have easily and successfully posed as a model in a pornographic movie or sex novel. When Cyrus was aroused or erect, the head swelled and resembled the cupola atop of a large athletic stadium. Cyrus became as hard as turning left in rush hour traffic as Abel dried his back.

Cyrus said, "You don't want to leave me hanging like this do you?"

Abel kissed the tip and whispered, "I will take care of you a little later."

While not satisfied, Cyrus got dressed so they could get to breakfast.

At six feet two inches tall, Cyrus was several inches taller than Abel. His caramel hued skin bore the countenance of someone who spent their entire life basking in the sun. He had deep, seductive grey eyes and visited Mr. Sams Cutz regularly to maintain his close-cut fade hairstyle. He was athletic and his toned and well formed muscles evidenced the time he spent in the gym. Most of Cyrus' admirers were attracted to his chest, biceps and triceps. If he had been bald, Cyrus might have easily been mistaken for a Black version of Mr. Clean. He had a toned, flat stomach and the ridges in his abdominal muscles were conspicuous when he wore fitted shirts, which he often did. He had the body of a twenty-something year old and delighted in the fact that both men and women admired how he looked.

Cyrus had a tiny wisp of a mustache that accentuated the full lips that he constantly moistened with an ample tongue. He wasn't cocky, but he was certainly self-assured and exuded that aura. Cyrus dressed in grey sweatpants that were cut off just below the knee and deliberately opted to forego underwear. He loved when people noticed his endowment as he walked down the street commando style and often became aroused and grew larger. He was never embarrassed or ashamed nor did he try to hide his erection even when it occurred in public.

Cyrus recalled the first time they met, remembering how Abel kept looking at the print in his pants then directly at him.

Cyrus' interest and intrigue heightened when Abel unembarrassedly refused to look away when he was discovered. Most scopophiliacs would divert their eyes rather than hold the gaze of the object of their amour. Cyrus was attracted even more and knew Abel was older and more self-confident by the way he assuredly maintained his stare.

Abel put on a pair of black, clingy Under Armour workout shorts with a black tank top adding a pair of black Under Armour tennis shoes to complete the outfit. Abel knew that Cyrus liked seeing him in clingy shorts because they fit his ass so well. Abel was embarrassed at how prominent Cyrus' manstick appeared in the sweatpants that he put on and wished he had also worn underwear. He didn't protest and let him go out commando style though, because he relished the fact that he alone had a first hand, personal relationship with Cyrus' endowment while everyone else could only imagine what it was like. Abel and Cyrus were a good-looking couple -- athletic, confident, Black and attractive -- and they knew the impact they had when people saw them out together and liked the attention.

They finished dressing and left the house. As they walked to the garage, Abel tossed Cyrus the keys to his BMW X5 SUV. Cyrus did not own a car and he rented an apartment downtown near the South Shore train station. Abel usually let Cyrus drive whenever they were together and Cyrus enjoyed letting people think he was in control of the relationship he shared with Abel. Abel never minded Cyrus taking charge in the car because he certainly let him take charge in the bedroom when they were alone.

People often thought that Cyrus owned the BMW SUV and he loved it. Abel had purchased the top of the line M model in a rare, dark brown color that was only apparent when it shone in the bright sunlight. He had accessorized it with chrome running boards and wide 20" Perelli Premier LTX tires. He had also tinted the rear windows in the SUV, but at Cyrus' request left the front ones untouched. Cyrus wanted people to see him when he drove around town in Abel's car.

Cyrus and Abel arrived at Miss Sharon's restaurant and as expected, the parking lot was completely full. Metered street parking in the surrounding neighborhood was full as well. They circled the restaurant a couple of times and finally found an open space on the street a couple of blocks away. Cyrus parallel parked the car into the available spot with ease while Abel paid for parking using the ParkMobile parking app on his cellphone. He and Cyrus walked the couple of blocks to the restaurant. Once inside, Abel went up to the receptionist and asked that their names be placed on the waiting list to be seated.

Most of the women who were at the restaurant were overtly jealous of Cyrus and Abel. They were not conspicuously gay nor feminine but it was readily apparent to the women in the waiting area that they were together and not paying attention to any of them.

An excessively obese woman, who for some reason thought that dying her hair an awful shade of green was a good idea, was standing right by the door. She turned to the two similarly sized women who were with her and said, "Damn, the hottest two muthafuckas in the whole restaurant, and neither one of them want no pussy." She continued, "Why do the finest brothers have to always be in jail or turn out to be punks?"

One of her girlfriend replied "I know what you mean girl. They do look good though," the friend continued.

They all laughed raucously.

The third woman chimed in, "I would suck on that tall one like a dog with a bone, girl. Shit, I would suck the life out of him" she added. Using her best impression of the Wanda character made famous by Jamie Foxx on the TV show "In Living Color", she said "I'd rock his world."

They laughed loudly and high-fived one another. They continued whispering while sneaking sly looks at Cyrus and Abel.

Cyrus leaned over to Abel and whispered "Even if I was into pussy, I wouldn't touch that thing with a ten-foot pole and a case of disinfectant." He continued, "I wouldn't even fuck them with Donald Trump's little ass mushroom dick!"

Abel shushed him and said "You better be careful." He added, "Those are some linebacker bitches and I think they can take the both of us." They both laughed and just before Cyrus could make another comment, they were called to their table.

The receptionist escorted them to a table that was in the middle of the crowded, noisy dining area. Miss Sharon's was a warm, welcoming and cozy place. The round tables which mostly sat four patrons had red and white checkered table cloths on them. There were booths along the wall near the kitchen on the right side of the restaurant. The booths had long rectangular shaped tables that could accommodate as many as six diners. On the back side of the bank of booths, about five feet tall was a continuous wall that allowed an unimpeded view into the kitchen. Patrons could see and hear the commotion and activity in the busy kitchen as the staff attempted to keep up with all of the orders from the full seating area. Opposite the booths and along the side of the restaurant that faced the window was a row of square tables. These table were designed to seat two but could accomodate four when the restaurant was full, like it was on this day.

Miss Sharon's was sunny and bright with smatterings of African

Art and memorabilia dotting the walls. Motown and classic R&B music played on the audio system throughout. The servers and staff wore pressed white pants and shirts with white tennis shoes. The restaurant was a throwback to the 1960s and 70s. Pictures of Black leaders and civil rights icons hung on every wall. Plaques with positive aspirations were visible throughout as well.

The restaurant was efficiently run and the welcome aroma of bacon cooking, biscuits baking, coffee brewing and sausage frying wafted throughout. There was a continuous procession of plates laden with omelets, pancakes, waffles and toast coming from the kitchen. The cacophony of conversations at every table and plates clanging from the kitchen competed with the music playing on the sound system.

Once seated, Cyrus noticed a former friend from high school that he had not seen for quite a long time out of the corner of his eye. He told Abel that he was going over to say hello and got up from the table. The friend was sitting at a table with a fair skinned, massively muscled man who had excused himself and left the table just as Cyrus approached.

Cyrus asked, "Excuse me man, didn't you graduate from Roosevelt?" He added, "Isn't your name Maurice or something like that?"

The friend replied, "Stop bullshitting C, you know I did and you know my name is Maurice! What's up with you?" He asked with a raised eyebrow, "Is that your Dad, you are hanging with this morning?"

Cyrus responded, "That's right Maurice. I see you got jokes this morning." He added tersely, "No, that's not my Dad. My Dad is home fucking your Mom!!" He added, "He's just an old friend that I hang out with sometime."

Maurice said sarcastically, "Yeah he definitely is old. I can see cobwebs forming around his head from here" and laughed aloud. He continued, "When you want to hang out with some-one your own age, holla at me."

Cyrus said, "I had no idea that you were in the game back in high school." He added, "You definitely were on the down low."

Maurice replied, 'Yeah, I didn't know who I was back then. My family was real strict and all I did was go to school and back home." He added with a hushed tone, "I used to always see you in the hall though. I knew that when I used to see you, I would get excited."

Cyrus replied, "Yeah, right man. I was born at night, but it wasn't last night." He went on, "So what is your boy going to say about you having a crush on me."

Maurice replied incredulously, "What boy?"

Cyrus said, "That big dude that just left your table."

Maurice replied, "Oh, he's not my dude. He is just a client of mine. I work with ex-offenders and I am preparing him for a job interview." Maurice told Cyrus, "Give me your phone."

Cyrus pulled his phone from the back pocket of his sweats and gave it to his newly reacquainted friend. Maurice took a selfie and added his name as a contact in Cyrus' phone. He also sent himself a text using Cyrus' phone before he gave it back.

Maurice told Cyrus, "I am going to send you a message and it might be in your best interest if you respond." He waved at the waitress to bring his check and told Cyrus he would be in touch.

As Cyrus walked away, the man who had excused himself from the table as he approached returned. He and Maurice got up to pay their check and left the restaurant. Cyrus returned to the table where Abel was seated. He told him "That was an old friend that I knew from high school and hadn't seen in a while." Cyrus added, "His name is Maurice, but I can't think of his last name."

Abel said flatly, "I am used to you having a fan club wherever we go." He continued, "How long will it be before you hear from him?"

Cyrus said, "You got jokes, Abel." He feigned innocence and said, "I don't know what you're talking about."

At that exact moment, Cyrus received a text from the newly reacquainted friend. The text included a naked picture of Maurice and the words "I SWALLOW" in capital letters. Cyrus felt the beginnings of an erection stirring in his sweats and told Abel "I probably won't ever see him or hear from him again."

Their breakfasts arrived and they leisurely dined over shrimp and grits and chicken and waffles. They shared ample portions and bites from one another's plates.

Abel had work to do but Cyrus wanted to distract him with a long afternoon sex session if he could. As a compromise, they decided to check out an early movie at one of the local cineplexes before heading home since it was just after noon when they finished eating. They purposely selected a movie that neither of them really wanted to see because they had an ulterior motive. They chose seats in the last row of the theater and were mischievously excited when no one else bought tickets for the same movie. They were in the theater alone.

Once the theater went dark and the previews commenced, Cyrus instinctively loosened the drawstring on his grey sweatpants and exposed his full erection. Abel knowingly crouched on his knees in front of him and began to thoroughly service him. The theater was completely empty and Cyrus had an all-encompassing view from their perch in case any late movie goers came in. They thought they were relatively safe so Abel was able to complete his job without interruption.

Abel began by slowly licking the stiff mushroom head. He caressed the foramen in the center and watched Cyrus squirm because he knew that it drove him crazy. He licked the entire length of the shaft first along the top and then again along the bottom. He devoured the entire rock-hard protuberance until it filled his throat while simultaneously gently massaging Cyrus' pudenda. Abel felt him grow and harden in his mouth as Cyrus' hand pressed his head further and further down on the shaft. Cyrus' legs stiffened and Abel knew by his excited breathing that a climax was imminent.

Cyrus delivered a continuous stream of thick, white protein into Abel's amenable fauces just as the main attraction began. Abel savored every drop. He rose from his knees and sat back in his seat. He washed the mouthful of man seed down his throat with the large soda that he had purchased at the concession stand. Abel watched the movie with a contented smile when he noticed that Cyrus had fallen asleep.

After the movie, Abel took Cyrus home and dropped him off.

3

Oscar gently nudged Xerxes to wake him after he completed his shave and offered him a hand mirror to see if his craftmanship met with his approval. Xerxes smiled broadly and nodded his assent. He winced as the barber shave cologne was liberally applied to his freshly cut scalp and around the edges of his beard. He blinked as the aromatic fragrance of talcum powder was generously brushed all over his athletic frame. Oscar removed the barber cover and Xerxes got up from the chair. He handed Oscar the fee for the shave and included a generous $20 tip. Xerxes bid farewell to the other patrons in the shop and before departing turned to Oscar and said, "Alright O!! See you next time."

Oscar replied, "Alright man, looking forward to it. Tell your girl I said hello!!"

Xerxes replied, "Will do. Out!!" He jumped into his Tesla, checked the time and called Precious. They had a date later in the evening to attend a charity gala event. He wanted to know how much time he had to get dressed before he had to meet her.

*　*　*

Xerxes had known Precious almost all of his life. When they

first met in elementary school he was drawn to her dark and smooth skin. He liked her because she was more serious than the other little girls in their school. She didn't whine, cry or get into fights with the other kids despite them calling her names like "blackie" or "tar baby". Her skin tone is what appealed to him most. Smooth and dewey soft, it was as rich as a cup of hot cocoa with chocolate shavings on top. She was unaffected by the taunts of her schoolmates letting their invective roll off her back. Even the children of "woke" parents can be cruel when they are young.

He also liked her because she called him "Z." When they first met, he told her that his name was Xerxes. He said that it was pronounced 'Zirks-sis' and that he had been named for a Persian King who ruled over a large empire before Jesus Christ was born. She called him "Z" because she thought the first letter in his name began with a Z instead of an X. He thought it was cute and she was the only person that he allowed to use that moniker.

They were inseperable throughout their adolescent and teenage years even though they never officially declared a relationship. As a young boy, Xerxes was skinny, awkward and uncoordinated. He grew to become a masculine and confident man and developed a firm, muscular body. He played and excelled at several sports in high school and college. He was best at football.

At the same time, Precious was blossoming as well. She grew to become a confident beauty and learned to wear just enough makeup to accentuate her dark features. The short, cropped hairstyle that she preferred brought prominence to her face and made her more attractive. She and Xerxes often studied together in high school because she told him that she refused to be with a simple-minded man, no matter how fine or athletic he was. She had one of the brightest minds in their school, constantly impressing him with her ability to think logically and analytically. She made it clear to him that he would not be able to coast solely on his athletic skills and be with her. Xerxes had to stay on his toes in school to keep up with Precious.

They separated for college but remained close. Precious attended Spelman College in Atlanta studying Liberal Arts. She used her degree to matriculate to a prominent Law School realizing her ultimate dream of becoming an attorney. She took her studies seriously and was among the top ten percent of her graduating class.

Precious prioritized her studies over a social life while at Spelman College in Atlanta and Xerxes often disappointedly learned firsthand how important her education was to her. He often invited her to his football games while they were in college, but she always declined. She opted to spend time on her studies instead. When they were home for breaks or holidays, she made up for it by devoting all of her free time to him.

Xerxes received a football scholarship to University of Michigan but made sure to focus as much effort on his studies as he did on his game. He eschewed the 'dumb jock' sobriquet and worked hard to make sure that Precious maintained her interest in and attraction to him. He gained national notoriety with his football prowess and as his fame grew so did the cadre of groupies and hangers on who sought his time and attention. Women on his campus found him to be irresistible and so did the women at the other schools that Michigan played.

Xerxes followed a different path than many of his teammates who got caught up in or trapped with multiple abortions, unwanted pregnancies and forced marriages. He made sure that he protected himself against the golddiggers and opportunity seekers who preyed on future NFL prospects.

Sex was easy for athletes in college. Too easy. Xerxes had many teammates who became fathers several times over. He made sure that he protected himself and did not rely on anything his courtesans may have told him. He aggravated them because he foiled any duplicitous plans they may have had for him. Xerxes assumed that Precious knew of the life he led as a top college football prospect. If she did, she never seemed to be jealous or show any concern. He was also attracted to Precious' self confidence.

Xerxes knew that Precious planned to go to Law School right after college. They had hoped that she would gain acceptance to a school near to where he would be playing professional football. They were euphoric when Xerxes was drafted in the first round by the Chicago Bears. It was nirvana when Precious was accepted at the University of Chicago Law School because it allowed the two of them to remain close.

Xerxes was the first person she called on the day she found out that she had been accepted. She told him that she had gotten her acceptance letter but didn't want to share the the news of where she would be going over the phone. She asked him if he could stop by so that she could tell him face to face.

Xerxes headed straight to Precious' apartment. He loved her place because it was meticulously decorated and made him feel warm and comfortable. She called her apartment the "G", short for ghetto, and described it as having "project heat" because it literally was warm like the small public housing unit where she grew up. If the heat was on the apartment was always toasty. Precious joked that she often had to perform a protracted strip-tease routine as she struggled to find comfort.

Her place was in a section of town that was experiencing a renovation boom. She had been lucky enough to get in before the new development had begun in earnest. She was thankful for her rent controlled building because the rents and leases in many of the surrounding apartments and condominiums rose along with the increasing number of construction cranes.

She lived in a big and airy apartment with large oriel windows in the front that faced east. The bright, open living room was on the left just inside her front door. Precious had decorated the living room with a dark grey sectional sofa with large, over-stuffed cushions. Brightly colored pillows accentuated every cushion. A large, black leather reclining chair sat adjacent to the sofa. The sofa and the recliner faced a wide, woodburning fireplace with a decorative marble façade. The hardwood floors throughout the apartment were covered in African theme printed area rugs. The slightest fragrance of incense floated throughout the apartment.

An archway on the right side of the entry foyer led to a long exposed brick hallway. Precious had hung large black and white photographs of prominent African American women -- Rosa Parks, Dr. Johnetta Coleman, Oprah Winfrey, Maya Angelou, Madame C. J. Walker on the right side of the hallway. The photographs hung in large black frames with white borders. Recessed lights in the ceiling above shone down on each photo.

Four doors opened into the hallway on the wall opposite the photographs. The first door led to Precious' master bedroom suite. The second was the door to her guest bathroom. The third door opened into a large walk-in closet. The last door on the left side of the hallway was the door to the guest bedroom.

A large dining room with an ornate chandelier stood at the end of the long hallway. A small, open kitchen was on the left through an open archway in the dining room. The recently renovated kitchen had a large island in the center of the room.

The island served both as a storage area for pots, pans and other items as well as an eating surface. Two barstools sat on each side of the island.

Precious opened the door for Xerxes. Before he greeted her or said hello, Xerxes asked excitedly, "So P, did you get into one the schools that you really wanted to go to??" She already knew that he had been drafted by the Bears but wanted to tease him before letting him know they would still be close together.

She replied pretending to be somber, "It's one of the best schools in the country, but I hope you will be able to deal with me being on my own."

Xerxes knew that she was about to tell him that she had been accepted at Stanford or some other school that was far away. He steeled himself to hear her bad news. When she finally told him she would be attending University of Chicago, he grabbed her and hugged her. He told her how excited he was that they would still be close. She told him that she was excited too.

Xerxes and Precious kissed, delighted by the thought that they would still be together. They kissed again and lingered in embrace. Their emotions, the mutual excitment that they would be in the Chicago area together and the heat of their conjoined bodies confirmed that it was time to take their relationship to the next phase. They both knew and felt that it was time to finally consummate their bond as their bodies moved to a rhythm that neither of them had ever experienced before together.

Xerxes whispered, "I love you P. I am so glad we will still be together."

She cooed, "I know Daddy, its a dream come true!!"

Xerxes replied, "You are my dream baby!!" He added, "I don't know what I would do without you." He kissed her again and said, "I need you."

Precious stood five feet ten inches tall and had a slim build. Her body was disciplined and toned. She had the bearing of an athlete, a dancer or someone who worked out regularly. She did neither. In fact, Precious did everything she could to avoid exercise. She worked and studied incessantly. The only exercise she ever got was walking to and from the law library and carrying the large legal tomes that she used for her studies.

Precious had a flat stomach and a broad and perfectly round bottom. Her thighs and calves resembled those of a dancer. She thanked her Mother for forcing her to take ballet and tap dance lessons as a child. She was so serious and studious as a child, that her mother suggested the dancing classes as a welcome respite from her bookishness. Her legs were long and lithe and still retained the flexibility and agility that she had gained from dancing. She used yoga as a means of stretching, meditation and focus and every step she took exuded grace and purpose.

They kissed again and enjoyed the taste of each other's tongues. They sensed the heat of mutual attraction and explored each other's bodies with their hands and mouths.

Xerxes begged, "Please baby!!"

Prescious nodded her assent.

Their first encounter was not clumsy nor awkward. Xerxes gently placed Precious on the island in the center of her kitchen. He carefully unbuttoned her sheer, silk white blouse and smiled slyly when he saw the bright red bra that she wore. She grabbed him around the neck and he lifted her up from the island to remove her sweat pants. She wore a matching red G-string. Xerxes thought the red underwear offered a perfect contrast to her deep, dark skin. He kissed her delicately while he opened the clasp on the front of her bra and effortlessly removed it.

Precious had generous breasts, not large or small but a perfect fit for her frame. Her breasts were firm. They protruded directly and perpendicularly from her body. Her nipples were large and very sensitive. Her areola was a shade lighter than the dark skin on the rest of her body and formed perfect circles in the exact center of each breast. When Precious was alone, she found that by gently massaging her nipples she could easily become aroused. On the rare occasion that she found someone to assist her with her stimulation, Precious would go wild.

She felt Xerxes' warm, wide tongue exploring hers. His large hands held her. He picked her up and cupped her right buttock in his massive right palm and slowly slid the G-string down her left leg. He repeated the same motion with her right leg. She held him tightly and matched his gaze. She felt his large hands probe between her thighs. He lightly kissed then sucked her hard and firm nipples. She gasped as his tongue lingered over her breasts. He tenderly bit her nipples. She squealed as his fingers found the moistness between her thighs.

He put his damp fingers up to his nose and inhaled the aroma from her treasure. He placed his fingers in his mouth and relished how sweet her essence tasted to him. She giggled embarrassedly at the thought of him enjoying her. All of her.

She gently crooned in his ear, "I've been waiting for this for so long. Be gentle Z."

He pulled his hoodie off over his head and untied and dropped his sweatpants to the floor. His muscular frame stood directly in front of Precious. His protruding member pointed directly at the sensual spot that he had just discovered.

Precious whispered in his ear as she bit down hard on his ear lobe, "Let me see it!!"

Xerxes stepped back so that she could see his entire nakedness. He could see the admiration in her eyes. His erection grew firmer with the thought that what she saw was pleasing to her. She pulled him toward her and positioned her hands around his protruding appendage. It took both of her hands to completely surround him.

He gently whispered in her ear, "Baby, are you ready for this?"

Precious nodded her head and said, "Yes, Daddy, take your time" and lay back with anticipation.

Xerxes slowly and gingerly eased his bulging manhood inside Precious. She tensed slightly when she felt the tip touch her pudendum. She exhaled loudly as he slid his entire phallus inside her. He waited until he felt that she was comfortable with his length and girth before he began to slowly push and thrust inside her.

While not a virgin, Precious had never been with anyone as endowed as Z. She had never felt such pain but succumbed to a pleasure so overpowering that it allowed her to move to the same beat as Xerxes' thrusts. Their bodies were in tune and in perfect harmony as they moved to a rhythm and a dance that they had been building up to since childhood. The intensity of their dance grew heated and became excited. They breathed and panted excitedly. When the dance was done, they both let out a carnal scream. They held their passionate embrace as their breathing returned to normal. Xerxes lifted Precious and carried her to the bedroom. They fell asleep together locked in a tight embrace all night long.

Precious and Xerxes would be in the same city and close to both of their families. They decided to live, where they grew up, in northwest Indiana instead of Chicago.

* * *

Xerxes called Precious and said," Hey, Lupita, it's me."

She responded, "I think you have the wrong number, Sir." She continued, "There is no Lupita at this number."

Xerxes chuckled, "Oh, Hey Baby, I must have dialed your number by mistake."

Precious responded, "Hey sexy man, how are you?"

Xerxes replied sarcastically, "Sexy man? This is Z. Who were you expecting to call you?"

Precious replied, "Oh, this isn't Boris?" "It must be Shemar Moore then."

Xerxes said, "Nope. Strike two. You got one more shot and I'm hanging up."

Precious responded, "Oh, Z is that you? I guess if I can't be with my fantasy man, you will have to do."

They both laughed.

Xerxes said "I am done in the barbershop and wanted to know what time we were getting together tonight." He continued, "I also wanted to know if you needed or wanted anything."

She told him that he should plan to pick her up around 6:30 and they had to be at the event by 7:00. She also said that the only thing she needed was him.

Xerxes smiled as he heard Precious' reply. He loved the sound of her voice. It was sultry but articulate. She spoke so eloquently, enunciating every word so clearly and distinctly, that she reminded him of Maya Angelou. Her voice always sounded like it was full of joy or possibility and had an erotic lilt that aroused Xerxes every time he heard it. She had a hint of excitement in her voice everytime they spoke and she sounded like she had never had a bad day in her life. He wished that he could talk to her all day and all night long. They still made one another laugh and their relationship remained exciting and fresh.

She told him what she planned to wear and suggested that he accessorize his outfit with colors that accented hers. They wanted everyone to know that they were at the event together. He let her know what time he planned to pick her up and that she would be so impressed with his look that she would forget about Idris, Boris or anyone else. She laughed out loud and told him that she loved him.

Even thought they were committed to each other they maintained separate residences. More often than not, they ended up spending the night at one or the other's homes. They both liked the independence and freedom that the relationship afforded them, even though they had been exclusive with one another sexually for several years.

4

Cyrus couldn't wait for Abel to drop him off at home. He was anxious to reply to the text message that he received from Maurice. As soon as he walked into his apartment, he texted, "WYD" and waited for a response. He was discontented when there was no immediate reply.

Cyrus lived in a studio apartment in a newly renovated building just east of downtown. The city had begun a major redevelopment effort to entice people to return to the inner city. New buildings that housed popular restaurants and shops were being built all around. Apartments, condominiums and lofts filled with professionals and young singles dotted the

neighborhood. He liked being downtown and saw all of the new single men who were moving into the new residences in his area as potential sex partners. He wanted to meet as many as he could and craved having sex with anyone that was willing. Cyrus envisioned a career as a male escort and fantasized that he could make enough money charging men for his sexual favors to have a good life.

When he first met Abel and found out he was a business-owner, Cyrus devised a plan that he hoped would lure Abel into becoming enamored with him. His plan for Abel worked out much better than he hoped because Abel bought things for him when he wanted, gave him money when needed it and he let Cyrus drive his car whenever he asked. The denouement in his cabal was to devise a way for Abel's support to become a steady and ongoing source of income.

Cyrus loathed the thought of living with Abel because it would have prevented him from pursuing and engaging in coitus with anyone else. His sole objective was for Abel to become his primary benefactor while he was free to pursue other men for sex and financial support. He wanted to replicate the financial relationship that he was developing with Abel with as many other guys as he could.

Cyrus wanted and needed a steady flow of income to accomplish his dreams. He dreamt of moving into a condo, a loft or one of the new, luxury apartments under construction in his neighborhood. Cyrus' body and what he could do with it was his passport to the good life that he wanted to live.

He grew up in the foster care system and had little discipline or structure in his life, but learned that he could make money using his body as a teenager. He discovered that wealthy, white men would pay him handsomely to let them perform fellatio on him. Downlow Black and gay men would compensate him as well when he favored them with his time.

Cyrus had to settle for his small studio apartment until he could make his fantasies come true. His entire apartment was visible from the jamb of the front door. A round, four-top dining room table and chairs set sat near the back wall on the left side of the apartment. The table was constructed of metallic, slate gray material with a clean, efficient and modular appearance. Cyrus had seen the dining table set on display at the local Ikea and convinced Abel to buy it. They spent one afternoon assembling the entire set before making love.

A long, leather sofa sleeper occupied the middle of the room, just inside the front door. Cyrus and a friend labored to bring the heavy, oversized settee into his apartment when he first bought it. He often fell asleep on the sofa with its plush, black leather cushions without pulling out the mattress for the bed. A large matching lounge chair sat perpindicular to the sofa facing the door. A faux leather coffee table was positioned in front of the sofa and lounge chair. An 82" 4K high definition, flat screen television was mounted on the wall in front of the sofa. Cyrus had persuaded Abel to buy the TV for him on his birthday. He used it to watch porn when he was unable to connect with Abel or arrange a date with anyone else.

There were two doors in an alcove on the wall to the left of the large TV. The door on the left opened into a modest bathroom. The bathroom contained a singular wash basin, a toilet and a shower. It was not large enough for tub. The door on the right opened to a closet which extended directly behind the wall that held the television. A waist high counter extended from the alcove outward toward the dining room table. The small kitchenette with an undersized stove, refrigerator and sink sat just behind the waist high wall. Cabinets hung from the ceiling above the stove and to the left of the refigerator. The kitchen couldn't accommodate its own table. The back door to the apartment which led to the alley and the apartment's parking garage was on the back wall, directly opposite the entry door. If Cyrus owned a vehicle, he would use this entrance to get to his car and the apartment's parking garage.

Cyrus had done no real decorating in his apartment. Except for the big screen TV, he had not added artwork or any decorations to his walls. There were no plants, greenery or other adorn-ments to enhance his living space. His extensive collection of colorful sneakers were arrayed against the wall along the floor beneath the television. The vivid and colorful collection of shoes resembled a decorative art display. The unit's most appealing amenity, however, was its white walls which were ablaze in sunlight when the sun shone brightly outside.

Cyrus immediately undressed. and jumped in the shower. He washed off any lasting residue from his night with Abel or their encounter at the movie theater. He finished his shower and decided to dress in an old, beat up tank top and loose-fitting gym shorts. He decided he'd just watch porn and jack-off and wanted to be comfortable because he had no plans to go back out. Just as he settled in and began to relax, he noticed that he had received a text message. Cyrus picked up the phone and couldn't contain his excitement. The message was from Maurice.

> Maurice: I saw you when you came in the restaurant this AM. Woulda came over but didn't want to interrupt you and your Dad from having breakfast together.

He ended the message with an emoji with a devilish grin.

> Cyrus: You got jokes. I told you he was not my Dad. He's just a friend I hang out with from time to time.

> Maurice: You don't consider your Sugar Daddy to be your Dad?

Cyrus was perturbed by Maurice's implication that he had a Sugar Daddy. Abel often did support Cyrus financially but he chafed at the thought of people telling him directly to his face that he was only good for being kept by a man. Even though it was true, Cyrus did not like people to think that he was only good at sex and nothing else. He wanted to put Maurice in his place but did not want to piss him off and ruin the possibility of a new hook up. Instead, he replied:

> Cyrus: Abel and I are just friends. That ain't got nothing to do with what you are I are trying to do.

> Maurice: Oh, really, so how can I find a friend like that?

> Cyrus: Whatever man. What the fuck are you trying to do right now!?!?

> Maurice: I'm just chilling and trying to stay out of trouble.

Cyrus knew that Maurice had given him the opening that he wanted.

> Cyrus: So what kind of trouble are you trying to stay out of if you don't mind me asking? I bet I got some trouble you would love to get into you.

> Maurice: Yeah, I saw it today in those sweats you had on. It looked like a snake that was trying to get free when you were talking to me at the restaurant. Are you finally tired of pussy with cobwebs on it and ready for some new ass?"

> Cyrus: Fuck, yeah!! It would be good to see a nice ass in something other than Depends. LOL.

> Maurice: ROTFLMAO

> Cyrus: So what are we doing man? I don't host. I only travel?"

> Maurice: I can host tonight. Do you want my address? How long will it take you to get here?

Once he got the location, Cyrus replied that he could make it to Maurice's apartment in about thirty minutes. Maurice responded "Cool" and Cyrus got up to get ready to leave. He requested an Uber and while waiting for it to arrive, went to his bathroom and moisturized his entire body with Palmer's Cocoa Butter skin cream. He went to his closet and found a pair of oversized basketball shorts and an Under Armor fitted t-shirt that he put on. He found a Houston Astros baseball cap that he wore turned backwards. Just as he finished dressing his ride arrived.

Cyrus couldn't remember clearly whether Maurice was a wrestler or a member of the track team back in high school. Maurice was five feet seven inches tall with an athletically lean body, not muscular, but with no visible body fat at all. Cyrus liked guys that were built trim and tight like Maurice because he could easily overpower them and have his way during sex.

Maurice's complexion matched the color of the caramel in a Hershey's Kiss. His head was completely bald along the sides and at the back but he had Medusa-like dreadlocks growing out from the top. His full lips revealed a wide, toothy smile and he had a genuine laugh that made you want to laugh in return. Maurice was clean shaven but his eyebrows and eyelashes were full and bushy. Cyrus' erection and his excitement grew as he remembered more about his high school friend.

All Cyrus could think about on his Uber ride to Maurice's apartment was fucking someone new. He prided himself on being successful at keeping his side activities hidden from Abel. He was careful to always conduct his escapades with someone new after he had spent time with Abel and satisfied him sexually. Cyrus enjoyed the fact that Abel was mature and secure enough that he never questioned where he was when they were apart.

Cyrus was a player and he kept his body tight and in shape. His body was a valuable asset and the men that he dated or who craved to spend time with him wanted a chance to experience it and him. He could have been as dumb as a box of rocks but as long as he performed sexually, his partners were satisfied.

He loved sex and he knew that he was good at performing it. He loved the excitement of having a new sexual encounter. He was committed to meeting his goal of having sex with as many men as he possibly could. His doctor had prescribed the Pre-exposure Prophylactic (PreP) regimen for him to prevent the posibility of contracting HIV or another STD and he took his medications diligently. He thought that he had eliminated any obstacles that could prevent him from accomplishing his plans and could be as promiscuous as he wanted.

He never hosted or invited any of his sexual conquests to his apartment. Abel was the first and only man that he had ever allowed in his space. When he broke off a relationship, which he usually did when he got bored or when he met someone new, he did not want any of his former paramours hounding him at his apartment. Cyrus was always the one that ended his relationships. He stayed with Abel as long as he had because Abel could be counted on to support him financially if any urgent situations arose. He had also grown comfortable with Abel and liked the fact the he did not pressure him for a more committed relationship. Abel would not hesitate to treat Cyrus to a trip, a night out on the town, or a fancy dinner at a great restaurant. Cyrus knew that Abel would treat him to almost anything he wanted.

As usual, Cyrus did not wear underwear. Even in the oversized basketball shorts, when he walked you could see the outline of his firm manhood flopping back and forth. He thought that the look gave him a bit of a 'hood edge, which also turned guys on. He sprinted out of his front door and texted Maurice that he was on the way.

The Uber driver tuned the radio to the the Quiet Storm radio program and Cyrus was serenaded by smooth jazz during the ride. Just as they arrived at Maurice's apartment "This Woman's Work" by Maxwell was playing on the radio. Cyrus loved the song, which Maxwell sings almost entirely in a high soprano tone, because it made him think of the love scene from the movie "Love and Basketball". In the scene, the lead female character played by Sanaa Lathan was making love to her long-time neighbor and love interest played by Omar Epps for the first time. When Sanaa saw how well endowed Omar was, in the movie, she gasped. Cyrus liked that scene because most guys reacted that way to him when they saw his erection for the first time.

Cyrus jumped out of the car and approached the front door of his friend's apartment building. The building was in a neighborhood that had long since seen its heyday. The front door to the building was a fortified metal double door. The bottom on one side had been replaced with a large wooden board as if the glass had been knocked out or broken. At one time, a canopy covered the entry door. The canopy had fallen down but the frame for it still remained. An electronic directory listing the names of all of the apartment's tenants hung on the wall just to the right over the door. The light above the directory flickered off and on making it difficult to see or read the names.

A chorus of barking dogs competing for the lead in a nocturnal musical permeated the night air. The wailing sirens from approaching or receding police cars and fire trucks created a cacophonous symphony as well. Music blared from passing cars and televisions played with volume levels turned up to their extremes. A new sign announcing that the building was "Under New Management" hung to the side of the directory. It was apparent, however, that the new management had not yet begun to make any substantive or positive changes.

Cyrus texted Maurice to let him know he had arrived. Maurice texted him back to let him know which code to select on the building directory. Cyrus followed the directions on the large screen until he found the correct code. He entered the code and Maurice pressed the button that allowed Cyrus access to the building.

The entry doors opened to a large foyer with tenant mail boxes along the back wall of the open space. A large window facing an outdoor patio in the center courtyard of the building was just to the left of the mailboxes. Cyrus thought to himself that the patio would be a really quiet place to chill in the summer time if the landscaping had been kept up and the seating areas maintained. The patio clearly had not welcomed any guests for quite a long time. Cyrus' sneakers emitted a cadenced squeak with each footfall on the linoleum floor as he crossed the foyer toward his friend's apartment.

Maurice's apartment was on the first floor down a long hall to the right off of the main foyer. The hallway was carpeted in an indistinguishable gray color. It was also clear that the carpet was sorely in need of a cleaning. Cyrus could hear conversations emanating from the various other units as he walked down the hall. He could tell which tenants chose fish as their meal of choice for the evening and he could also discern the pungent smell of marijuana wafting out of more than one unit as he passed. A small light, which barely provided enough illumination to see the apartment numbers, shone over the top of each door.

The apartment numbers were painted verticially on the heavy metal doors. The dimly lit hall made it difficult to see the numbers which were painted in black. Cyrus remarked to himself how the building could be made to look to like an upscale hotel in a funky art deco building instead of an apartment building with the right updates and modifications.

When Cyrus reached Maurice's apartment he reached out to knock on the door. His knuckles met the metal barrier but he noticed that the apartment door was slightly ajar. It creaked loudly as he slowly pushed it open and stepped directly into Maurice's dimly lit studio unit. Cyrus mentally compared the size of Maurice's unit to his own and surmised that he liked his place better.

Maurice's apartment was smaller than Cyrus' and it did not have a separate dining area adjacent to the living room. His dining area and kitchen were combined. Maurice's bathroom was on the right as well but, unlike Cyrus' apartment, it was directly beside the kitchen. A stream of smooth jazz music emanated from a stereo system or radio playing somewhere in the apartment.

Cyrus detected the slightest hint of incense floating in the air along with the distinct aroma of recently smoked marijuana. He could also tell that Maurice had enjoyed fried chicken for dinner. The smell of the chicken caused Cyrus to make a mental note to have the shared ride driver take him by one of his favorite take out restaurants to grab some food on his way home. He remembered that he hadn't eaten anything since having brunch with Abel.

As he stepped into the dark space, Cyrus was startled by the sound of the heavy metal door closing behind him. Maurice never uttered a word as he tapped Cyrus on his back. Cyrus turned around and felt his basketball shorts being pulled down around his shoes. Maurice grabbed and gently massaged his ever-stiffening pole and Cyrus felt the gentlest kiss on the tip of it. He enjoyed the warm, moist tongue that licked his manhood and began to tremble. He had not expected this session with Maurice to commence so abruptly. Cyrus had imagined a long foreplay session where he wanted to tease and torment Maurice to get back at him for the disrespectful comments he made about Abel. Instead, Maurice initiated the carnal connection instantaneously which caught Cyrus completely off guard. Maurice was an experienced sex partner and introduced Cyrus to pleasures had had not expected. He went wild when he realized that Maurice had a cube of ice at the back of his throat as he swallowed Cyrus entire manhood. Cyrus shuddered when he felt the combination of both the hot and the cold sensations simultaneously.

"Shit!!!", Cyrus exhaled.

He became totally erect from Maurice's manual and oral stimulation and followed him to a sofa in the center of the apartment. Maurice, who was already naked, lay down on his back on the edge of the sofa. Cyrus knelt on the floor beside the sofa and faced Maurice. Maurice positioned his legs so that they rested on Cyrus' shoulders. Cyrus took his index finger, moistened it with his tongue and placed the wet digit inside Maurice's ass. Maurice moaned with ecstasy and delight as his body moistened from the thrill of his imminent penetration. Cyrus continued to stimulate and massage the welcoming, ever wetting orifice and removed his finger and tasted it. He was surprised that it too tasted like cocoa butter.

Cyrus chuckled and asked, "Palmers?"

Maurice replied knowingly, "Yeah, Palmers."

Cyrus asked seductively, "So, you ready for this big dick?"

Maurice replied breathlessly, "Yes, but take your time. I heard how big you are from dudes you hooked up with back in high school and need time to get used to you."

Cyrus placed the tip of his rigid manhood against the welcoming opening and held it there for several minutes. Maurice squirmed as Cyrus rubbed the tip back and forth against the moist fissure but hesitated before sliding it in. He placed the bulging head at the tip of Maurice's receptive sphincter and carefully and gently slid inside. The moisture from Maurice's ecstasy eliminated any resistance or friction and Cyrus was able to probe further and deeper with every stroke.

Once they both got comfortable, Cyrus pulled out a bottle of amyl nitrate, Poppers, that he had brought with him. Cyrus loved the affect that Poppers had on him during sex. It made his heart pound and his senses more accute. Poppers increased the intensity of his ejaculations and made his body feel warm all over. He took two long whiffs of the stimulant and held it up to Maurice's nostrils so he can take a whiff as well. They both felt affects immediately and the passion and excitement of their first encounter gripped them.

Cyrus felt Maurice's warmth accepting him and his tightness capitulating with every thrust. Cyrus panted and moaned as he pushed harder and deeper inside Maurice. Maurice begged and pleaded for more as he succumbed to Cyrus' dominance.

They took a second whiff of the Poppers and the excitement of sex with a new person had Cyrus throbbing and thrusting with increased intensity. The stimulant had a similar affect on Maurice and he rode Cyrus like a bucking bronco. Cyrus was pounding Maurice at a feverish pace and he looked at him and said, "I'm about to nutt man!!!" Maurice replied, "Make me pregnant Daddy!!"

Cyrus leaned in close and kissed Maurice on the lips as he made one final forceful thrust. The eruption came so quickly and was so intense that it scared and surprised both of them. Maurice gasped as a single tear formed in his right eye. He lay still and accepted Cyrus' fullness. Cyrus whispered "The pussy is warm and tight" Maurice replied "And it's yours whenever you want it."

Cyrus maintained his conjoined embrace with Maurice and continued to pulsate and deposit semen with each paroxysm. Maurice's muscles clinched and tightened around Cyrus with each contraction. He milked every drop of man juice that Cyrus delivered.

Cyrus finally extracted himself and sat down on the floor beside the sofa. He had planned to chill for a few minutes and rest for a while hoping Maurice would be up for a second hot, steamy sex session. He knew that he would last longer the second time and wanted to give Maurice a reason to invite him back another time.

Abruptly and inexplicably, Maurice bounded up from the sofa and went into the batchroom to retrieve a wet wash cloth.

He handed it to Cyrus and suggested that he use it to clean himself up. Cyrus was surprised by his quick and unexpected movement and accepted the moist rag. He cleaned himself up but was shocked when Maurice politely but sternly ushered him to the door. Cyrus pulled up his basketball shorts and was smoothing out his fitted t-shirt as Maurice unceremoniously rushed him out of the apartment.

Cyrus was caught off guard when Maurice ushered him out into the hallway so quickly and he still needed a few minutes to arrange his clothes before heading out to call for a Uber. He had never been ushered out of someone's home. He was always the one to determine when a sex session was over. He vowed that Maurice would beg him to stay the next time they got together.

5

Abel drove straight home after dropping Cyrus at his place. He had work to do before getting dressed to attend an event later that evening with his attorney, Precious Thomas. He gave Precious two prerequisites before accepting her invitation. He told her that he absolutely would not wear formal attire and that he had to be seated at her table. He didn't want to have to feign interest in or be forced to have banal conversations with people that he thought were boring. Abel could be painfully shy when he first met new people socially.

He lived in a newly constructed home on the west side of town. His house was bright and airy with large windows on the front and the back. On bright, sunny days, his house was awash in warm, cozy light. The ceilings on the main level of his home were ten feet tall which gave his place an aspect of spaciousness. The wide double-door entryway opened onto a white tiled foyer. Accordion doors on the right side of the foyer just inside the front door opened to a small coat closet. The large, open living room which was the centerpiece of the main level was on the left. A warm, woodburning fireplace which offered a welcome respite on frigid nights was the focal point of the wall in the living room. The fireplace had no mantel, but white porcelain tile formed the hearth. Black and white photographs from the Harlem Renaissance Era filled the walls throught Abel's home.

The kitchen was adjacent to the living room but situated near the back of the house. The open kitchen had new stainless-steel appliances and dark grey marble counters. A waist high, island of dark wood separated the kitchen from the dining room. A bright, airy morning room stood directly behind the dining room. Sliding glass doors led from the morning room to the finished deck that spanned the entire width of the back of the house. Stairs led down from the deck to a perfectly green and manicured backyard. Wrought iron patio furniture on the deck was visible through the sliding glass door. There was a round table with four chairs and a bright red expandable umbrella standing in the center of the round table. A bright red Weber barbeque grill sat off to the left adjacent to the round table.

A wide staircase that led to the second floor and a hallway to the bedrooms was directly beyond the coat closet on the right. The two guest bedrooms that overlooked the back of the house and a shared bathroom were on one side of the hallway. The master bedroom suite which stretched across the entire front of the home was on the other side.

The master bedroom suite which included a custom designed, walk-in closet was just inside the bedroom door. There was ample storage for Abel's ties and underwear. His shirts, shoes, slacks and suits were arranged by color and fabric and arrayed based on the season of the year when they would be worn. His closet rivaled the display area in any expensive men's haber-dashery.

The door directly across from the walk-in closet led to an expansive master bathroom. A large jacuzzi tub sat directly behind the bathroom door. On the same side of the wall, but beyond the jacuzzi tub Abel had installed a steam shower with water jets and outlets that produced steam at three levels -- eye level, waist level or shin level. There was a wide bench for seat-ing on three of the four sides of the shower. Abel liked to lux-uriate in the steam shower on days that had been particularly exhausting or when Cyrus was over and they spent the night making love.

Beyond the closet and the bathroom was a large open sleeping area. On the wall to the left stood an oversized king bed. A decorative mirror that spanned the entire width of the bed covered the wall behind the bed. The reflection of the room in the mirror made everything appear to be twice as large. Cyrus and Abel often marveled at the reflection of their lovemaking in that mirror.

Abel walked into the large closet to decide what he wanted to wear to the gala. His signature look was bow ties and the multiple shelves in his closet with his wide assortment of colors and styles showed his affinity for them. He selected a particularly brightly colored bowtie to match the brilliantly colored sox he had put on. He had recently purchased a particularly outlandish pair from an online website that featured outrageous designs and decided tonight was a perfect night for their debut. He matched the sox with a pair of navy-blue, pleated dress slacks and found a dress shirt with thin horizontal blue pinstripes. He knew that the horizontally striped shirt would help him stand out at the event. The matching bow-tie and sox gave the entire outfit a look of business with a hint of fun. Abel laughed to himself thinking that he would count the number of men who showed up at the event in boring white or blue shirts with the generic long business striped tie. Abel matched his shiniest black shoes with a black belt and topped his ensemble off with a Diesel watch with an extra wide black wrist band. His collection of watches nearly rivaled his collection of bowties. He took one last look in the full-length mirror before walking out the door. He thought he passed inspection and grabbed his keys and jumped in his car.

Abel tuned the radio in the X5 to the Watercolors channel on Sirius/XM radio. The contemporary jazz allowed him to clear his mind and just relax. He liked jazz because it allowed him to face any drama that might come his way during the day. The soothing fusion of instruments and complex melodies into one harmonious chorus becalmed him. As he drove along he opened the panoramic sunroof to welcome in the coolness of the early evening and thought about Cyrus.

Abel liked Cyrus a lot but he knew Cyrus didn't have the same feelings or emotions about him. He knew that he enjoyed sex with Cyrus but when he was honest with himself, he did not see a long-term relationship developing between the two of them. He stayed with Cyrus, he thought, because such a long time had passed since his last relationship with anyone. He knew that finding a compatible partner, or someone, anyone that he thought he could have a serious relationship with at his age, would be hard. He chuckled because even though Cyrus wasn't an ideal partner, he wasn't ready to give up the good sex that they had until he found someone he wanted to commit to.

The museum was one of the most popular in the area partly because there was always a new exhibit or event being held there. A long, wide set of stairs led to the main entrance from the parking lot. The entrance featured large ionic columns giving the building the resemblance of a neo-classic or beaux art temple. The series of main entry doors were broad and tall making it readily apparent that this building had an important and vital purpose. Inside the main doors and down six stairs was a huge main hall with white marble tile floors. Several large, ornate Swarovski crystal chandeliers hung over the center of this main foyer bathing the lavish entryway in bright, welcoming light. Precious' event was being held in one of the exhibit areas inside of the museum.

Abel pulled into the parking lot and drove straight up to the valet stand. He jumped out of his car and surrendered his keys to the valet attendant. He jokingly said, "Bring it back washed, detailed and full of gas."

The attendant replied, "Sure Pops, if you let me borrow it this weekend."

Abel looked back incredulously and said, "Pops!?!?" Both he and the attendant shared a laugh.

As he climbed the long staircase heading toward the entrance to the museum, he heard a female voice scream, "Denzel? Denzel is that you?" Abel smiled broadly as Precious ran up to greet him and embraced him warmly. She planted a huge kiss directly on his lips. Abel nuzzled her back and replied "Madame, I beg your pardon!! I think you are kissing the wrong man." They both laughed.

Xerxes followed closely behind Precious but wasn't quite sure what to make of this display of affection between Precious and Abel. She had never given him a reason to be jealous before in their relationship, so he decided not to jump to any conclusions this time.

Precious put her arm around Abel's waste and said, "Damn, Abel, you are looking good enough to eat tonight!!" She continued, "Who helped you pull this drag together?"

Abel exclaimed, "Drag?!?" He feigned indignation and added, "Don't come for me tonight!! Just because we're dressed up don't mean I won't beat you down right here."

Precious said, "No, baby!! I'm serious boo! You look good tonight."

Abel replied, "Well you know how I do."

She responded, "Well you did well tonight." She continued, "Let me introduce you to my childhood friend and long-time partner, Z, I mean Xerxes."

Xerxes looked Abel directly in his eyes while giving him a firm handshake. He pulled Abel toward him for an embrace and said "What's up man?"

Abel, was caught off guard at how big Xerxes' hands were and how tightly they embraced him. He stuttered a response "H-h-hey M-m-man. I'm A-a-a-bel."

Precious laughed and told Abel, "And don't you be trying to take him from me either."

Her joke broke the tension between Abel and Xerxes and both men laughed. They chatted easily as they went inside the venue and found their table at the gala.

The gala was being held in a large room that had been decorated in black and gold bunting. The room had been festooned so well that it was impossible to tell which exhibit area was being used for the event. No traces of exhibits were apparent or exposed. The room had about 50 – 75 round tables with eight seats at each one. At the front of the room was a stage with a large table spread across it. There were 20 chairs at the table which provided seating for the emcee, dignitaries and other honorees. A large banner stretched across the back drop of the stage and two big-screen TV monitors were on each side.

Precious had arranged to sit next to Abel as she promised. She placed Xerxes on his other side so they could act as buffers for him from the other guests at their table. They were seated at a table near the front of the room just to the left of the main stage.

Abel was surprised at how comfortable he felt talking to Xerxes. They both laughed easily as they talked about college, fraternities and sororities, football and Abel's business. They also talked about how Abel met Precious. Abel took advantage of meeting Xerxes and questioned him about exercising and building muscle. Once he saw how interested Abel was, Xerxes offered to provide him personal training if he was open to it. Xerxes gave Abel his telephone number and suggested that he call him if he was serious about working out. Xerxes even invited Abel to a strength training session at the Bears' training camp. Abel wondered if he would be able to control himself in a gym with all of those muscular bodies around but he agreed to take Xerxes up on his offer.

The meal came and the program started so the trio had very little time for small talk during the event. Once the program was over, Precious excused herself to press the flesh with some of her other existing and potential clients before they all got away. She wanted to have a night cap prior to heading home so she asked Xerxes and Abel to be hang out at the table until she returned.

Xerxes told Abel, "I should be jealous of you. My girl talks about you all of the time. She says she enjoys working with you."

Abel replied, "There's definitely no need to be jealous man. She is great to work with and she is taking my business places we never thought we would go." He continued, "She has great strategic vision. I often think that she could be doing so much more to help herself and the community."

Xerxes said, "Yeah, man. I know what you mean. I wouldn't be surprised if she didn't step out on her own or something like that." He continued, "I don't ever want to be the reason that she doesn't realize her fullest potential."

Abel said, "So what about you man, other than being the Bears star player, what are you into?"

Xerxes responded, "Yeah, right!! Star player. I do some community work through the team and I am trying to position myself for what happens after football. But right now I am not sure what that is or what I want it to be."

Abel asked, "So what kind of things are you interested in? What do you want to do when you grow up?"

Xerxes said, "I'm not sure, man. Something in the business world probably." He added, "Hey, maybe you can give me some tips. Maybe be like a mentor."

Abel said, "So you help me build my body and I help you build your business, huh?"

Xerxes responded, "Yeah man, you scratch my balls and I'll scratch yours."

Abel was caught off guard by Xerxes directness and nervously asked, "What?"

Xerxes said, "Sorry man. That's something we say in the locker room. I hope I didn't offend you."

Abel replied, while looking Xerxes directly in his eyes, "No man, I'm not offended at all. I can handle anything you throw this way."

Xerxes had a perplexed look on his face and said, "You sure?"

Abel joked, "Don't come until I call for you" and laughed slyly.

Xerxes said, "Alright man, we will see."

Precious returned to the table and draped her arms around both men. She said, "Let's get out of here. I want to do something fun and can't imagine two other men that I would want to do it with."

Xerxes looked at Abel and Precious and said, "Oh, so we're into threesomes now?"

Abel tried to hide the excitement he felt at the thought of that prospect.

Precious responded, "The two of you couldn't handle all of this anyway." They laughed and left the gala.

They went to a late-night café called Donna's that was a short walk from the museum. Only three tables were occupied and the rest of the intimate cafe was empty. A middle-age couple sat at one table and the other two tables were being used by students who appeared to be pulling all-night study sessions The trio had their choice of the remaining tables and selected one near the front of the restaurant. They ordered coffee and a light dessert when the server came to their table.

Abel was surprised at how comfortable he felt around Precious and Xerxes, but their playful banter and badinage made it easy. It was obvious by their persiflage that they clearly cared for and liked one another. Abel wanted to know how they met and how long they had known one another.

Precious said, "I first met Z in third or fourth grade." She continued, "He was all feet and hands and was skinny as a rail."

Xerxes interjected, "A soon to be formidable rail."

They all laughed.

Precious went on, "I was drawn to him because he saw me and who I was and wasn't turned off." She said, "I was a dark skinned, nappy headed girl before it was popular and some of those little bitches in school were brutal to me." Precious continued, "Z never shunned me or treated me funny."

Xerxes said, "She was more serious than the other stupid little girls who were focused on being pretty or being popular." He added, "She took my breath away because she was so serious and so focused on what she wanted to do and become."

Precious said, "He quickly became my best friend, not just my best friend who was a boy, but my best friend." She added, "I knew that I could trust him and I knew he would be a part of my life forever." Precious went on, "Then he started to get muscles and turned out to be kind of fine."

Xerxes interrupted, "Kind of!?"

Precious continued, "I told him that I knew he would be a football superstar and would probably go pro at some time, but I said that I would kick him to the curb if he didn't develop his mind along with his body."

"I told him to put as much effort into developing his brain since that was the most important muscle in his body."

Xerxes interrupted, "Yeah man, she told me she wouldn't be with a stupid motherfucker, no matter how fine he was." He went on, "I appreciate her so much for that."

Abel said, "You guys seem to be so good together." He added, "Why did you not ever get married?"

Realizing that he may have brought up a subject that was too personal, Abel said, "I'm sorry if I am getting in y'all's business." He added, "Forget I asked that."

Precious and Xerxes looked at one another. Precious said, "Abel, no we will answer." She added, "I don't think we ever saw the need to get married. We realized that we would be in one another's life for the rest of our days one way or another."

Xerxes jumped in, "We didn't think we needed an official ceremony. We are committed to each other."

Abel said, "I can see how close y'all are and you make a good partnership. But what if someone else comes along?"

They looked at one another and Xerxes nodded to Precious as if to say, answer him.

She said, "We are life-long friends so if we meet and end up with someone else, they will have to know that Z is my best friend and I am his." She went on, "Hopefully there won't be any drama or jealousy bullshit because I'll beat a bitch down if she's crazy!!"

They laughed.

Precious continued, "I would never hurt Z and the person he ended up with and he feels the same about me."

Xerxes said, "We don't stand in each other's way either." He added, "But so far I haven't met anyone I like or want to be with more than Precious."

Precious responded, "I know a lot of guys I want to be with more than Z – Idris Elba, Denzel, Rick Fox – but they ain't smelling me like that so he will do until they change their mind."

They all laughed loudly.

Abel said, "I love you guys' energy and how you interact."

They both said, almost simultaneously, "We love it too."

Xerxes said, "It works for us."

Precious said, "Yeah, he'll do in a pinch."

They laughed more and drank their coffees.

A little after midnight, they got up and walked out of the restaurant. They went back to the musem and waited for the valet to retrieve their cars. While waiting all three of them engaged in a long, tight group hug. Precious pecked Abel on the cheek and he got into his car and headed home.

Precious and Xerxes watched him drive away and Xerxes said, "I like him." He continued, "He seems to be a good dude."

Precious smiled.

6

Cyrus was agitated. He had texted Maurice several times but gotten no response. He wanted another no strings attached sex session with his recently reacquainted high school friend and was hoping that the sex would be as raw and exciting as it was the first time. He did not remember any rumors or gossip about Maurice being on the "DL" from back in high school. He knew he was an athlete, but other than seeing him in the hallways going to and from classes, he couldn't remember very much more about him at all.

Cyrus was surprised because he thought he knew all of the "in" brothers at his school. As he remembers it, they all were trying to get with him back in the day. He had never, ever been in a situation where he hounded anyone for sex and always had an abundance of potential suitors pursuing him. He never had to worry about where he would get his next nutt and knew he did not savor chasing after Maurice to get it. He was thirsty for Maurice and craved him. He wondered if Abel felt this same unease and discomfort about him when he was not around?

He texted Maurice again and this time added a picture of his full erection. The text message read "He is anxious for another round and can't wait to see you again." A few minutes later, he sent another text asking "WYA?" He got no response to any of

his messages. When Abel let him borrow his X5 or he was able to use someone else's car, Cyrus cruised by Maurice's apartment building hoping to catch a glimpse of him. He knew he was out of control because he wanted Maurice so badly but was power-less to do anything to make him respond. He persuaded Abel to return to Miss Sharon's for brunch several weekends in a row hoping to catch sight of Maurice in case he returned to the place where they reconnected. Maurice seemed to have vanished into thin air however and still refused to respond to Cyrus' entreaties.

Cyrus decided it was time to move on and gave up thinking he would ever hear back from or see Maurice again. He stopped cruising by his place and refocused his energy and efforts on meeting someone new. He was flabbergasted when he discovered that Maurice had sent him a text message when he picked up his phone one evening intending to call Abel. The message showed the Kirsten Dunst character from the movie "Interview with a Vampire" saying very lustily, "I want some more." Cyrus instantly became erect and couldn't hide his excitement. He replied instantly, "When? Where?"

Maurice texted back "I'll hit you when the time is right."

Cyrus went out of his mind anticipating the coveted text. He couldn't wait to find out when he and Maurice would connect again. Reflecting back on their initial encounter aroused him. The two of them set no unrealistic expectations and they had no discussions about further commitment. There was no illusion or intimation about a potential relationship. They shared nothing but pure lust and unadulterated sex and Cyrus yearned for more. Cyrus really only wanted two things from his random encounters. He wanted sex and he wanted money. His sexual partners always wanted more and they usually wanted more of a connection with him than he was able or willing to give. By contrast, the relationship he was developing with Maurice was animalistic and carnal and he loved it.

Cyrus had been so focused on chasing after Maurice that he left little time to connect with Abel. Abel kept trying to arrange a rendezvous so they could make up for lost time. Cyrus made it difficult to settle on a date and time because he wanted to keep his schedule open in case he heard from Maurice and continuously rebutted Abel's entreaties. Cyrus' recurring proroguing displeased Abel who began to loudly complain about being unable to see him. Cyrus finally relented and they arranged to have an intimate dinner at one of their favorite restaurants. They also decided that Cyrus would spend the night at Abel's after dinner so they could share a night of raunchy sex and steamy lovemaking. They texted and sexted throughout the day of their planned tryst in excited anticipation of their meeting later that evening.

Cyrus lingered in the shower and took an uncharacteristically long time to decide what he wanted to wear. He hoped to tease and entice Abel while they dined and wanted to wear something especially sexy that would allow him to accomplish this goal. He decided that he would sit close so that Abel could secretly massage his manhood under the table while they ate. He hoped to arouse Abel so much that he would beg for sex by the time they got back to his house.

Cyrus chose a sheer, tight-fitting black t-shirt and black jeans. As always, he neglected to wear underwear and the bulge in his jeans was particularly evident and well pronounced. He knew what awaited him at the end of the night and couldn't hide his excitement. He finished dressing and headed out of his apartment to jump in the Lyft that he'd arranged to take him to his meeting with Abel. He settled into the back seat of the car and his phone buzzed indicating an incoming text. He thought it might be a message from Abel letting him know he was on the way, but was excited to find out that it was the text that he had been waiting on from Maurice. The text was simply a picture of Maurice's naked ass with The Supremes classic hit song, "Come See About Me" playing in a loop.

The excitement that had been building all day between Cyrus and Abel with their texting and sexting evaporated immediately. All Cyrus could think of was seeing Maurice again and didn't care who he had to shit on to make it happen, even if it was Abel.

He couldn't understand why the carnal desire to be with Maurice was so overwhelming and intense. He had never been in this situation with anyone before and couldn't control it no matter how much he wanted to. He was unnerved because Maurice exclusively directed when, where and how they hooked up. Cyrus wanted and needed to gain some kind of control of his wanton relationship with Maurice, but desire overpowered him and forced him to forsake the plans he had made to spend time with Abel. Cyrus was agitated because his thirst for Maurice was taking complete control of him.

He hastily sent a text to Abel.

Cyrus: Sorry. Can't make it tonight. Not feeling well.

Abel saw the text and was extremely disappointed.

Abel: Damn!! Need me to come check on you. Need anything?

Cyrus: No I'm good. Took some meds. Gonna chill. Was hoping to feel better by the end of the day, so we could still connect. Sorry for the last minute change in plans. Raincheck?

Cyrus' sole objective all day long had been to see Abel until he received the text from Maurice. He had no willpower to resist his hankering to see Maurice again so his texted lies to Abel flowed easily.

Abel: I hope you feel better, I will check on you tomorrow. We can reconnect whenever you want.

Cyrus smiled because he could hook up with Maurice and catch up with Abel at another time. He surmised that Abel would want the dick even more when they finally did get together.

Cyrus updated the drop off address for the Lyft driver and when he arrived at Maurice's apartment building, jumped out of the car and entered Maurice's code on the directory at the entrance. Maurice hit the buzzer to let him in and Cyrus walked to Maurice's door. Cyrus tapped lightly and found the door ajar again. The door creaked familiarly as he slowly pushed it open stepped into the dimly lit unit.

Cyrus was already erect as he excitedly anticipated a tap on his shoulder like he had gotten before. As he carefully inched further and further into the dark space, he loosened the belt on his jeans. They fell to the floor just as Cyrus felt Maurice's warm mouth envelop his bigness. He felt the sensual moistness along the tip and on the underside of his member. Maurice's tongue trailed the thick, throbbing vein on the top of Cyrus' phallus as he gently cupped and caressed his balls. He tenderly kissed them causing Cyrus' man juices to ooze from the tip of his granite-like manstick. Maurice moaned with pleasure as he gently licked each droplet of the building fluid.

Cyrus breathed hard and was already so erect that he couldn't wait to slide inside Maurice's warm, thick and welcoming ass. Maurice directed Cyrus to the sofa in the middle of the room and removed his jeans from around his ankles as he knelt in front of him. He immediately began to work furiously servicing Cyrus. His rhythmic slurping sounds were so loud that Cyrus was certain the neighbors could hear them and knew what they were doing. He grew more excited as he watched Maurice's head go up and down engulfing more and more of his shaft each time. Cyrus was surprised that Maurice could handle his entire endowment and reveled each time he felt the back of Maurice's throat. His legs began to twitch and he started to squirm as Maurice swallowed him.

Maurice brought Cyrus to the point of explosion and, as he felt his body tensing up, slowed down and decreased his urgency. Cyrus regained his composure and the impending explosion passed. Maurice repeated this several times and every time he brought Cyrus close to completion, he would moan and beg and warn Maurice that he was ready to cum. Each time Maurice slowed his pace and would not let Cyrus shoot. Cyrus grew increasingly frustrated and shouted disgustedly "Shit man, I was almost there. You gotta let me give you this nutt. I can't take this shit much longer." Maurice started up again and brought Cyrus just to the point of ecstasy but stopped. Cyrus' knees shivered and he writhed and begged his friend to let him finish. He knew he couldn't take much more and needed to explode his juices as soon as possible.

Maurice still had not said a word as he pushed Cyrus down on the sofa. He knelt between his legs on the floor in front of him and grabbed his balls and began his work all over again. His hands went from Cyrus' balls to his nipples, around his navel and back. He worked at a frenzied pace. Cyrus' knees jerked and he was sweating profusely as he begged Maurice not to stop this time.

Maurice went about his task as if he was on a mission. Cyrus grabbed him by the back of his head and forced him down on the wet, juicy, throbbing appendage. He knew he couldn't take this pleasure much longer and had to explode soon. Cyrus held Maurice's head down as he repeatedly and more rapidly thrust inside his mouth. He whispered "Please baby, you gotta let me cum this time." Maurice did not respond or react. He knew Cyrus was close to exploding and wanted to make sure he got every drop of the building load.

Cyrus' legs shot straight out and locked hard. He shivered

and then grabbed and massaged his hard nipples. Maurice ferociously sucked Cyrus' shaft and felt an incredible explosion of warm fluid flood his mouth. Cyrus yelled "Oh, Shit!!" and repeated it several times.

Cyrus pulsated inside Maurice's mouth and each pulse delivered more of the thick, white man juice down Maurice's throat. Cyrus' hardness subsided with each pulse. Maurice did not release his grip on Cyrus until the throbbing had stopped and the liquid protein ceased to flow.

Cyrus calmed down and his breathing returned to normal. His erection disappeared and he returned to a flaccid state. Just as before, Maurice abruptly rose and went to the bathroom to retrieve a warm wash cloth that he handed to Cyrus to use to clean up. Cyrus took the warm cloth and complied with Maurice's instructions. He readjusted his clothes and as soon as he was intact and composed again, Maurice walked him to the door and quickly closed it behind him.

7

Abel had been very busy since the gala event. His company was successful and growing. He had been working very closely with Precious on sales agreements, patents and real estate contracts and had not had much time to cash in on his rain check with Cyrus. There was palpable tension between the two of them when they did get a chance to communicate. Abel did the best he could to try to stay in touch but Cyrus felt he was being crowded. He felt that Abel's constant attempts at checking in and asking what he was doing were invasive. Abel knew they needed to reconnect and did everything he could to get things back on track.

He hoped to surprise Cyrus with a more muscular and toned body whenever they were able to meet again so he had begun working out with Xerxes. Unfortunately, they missed several scheduled sessions because of their hectic and busy schedules. Abel wanted to get back on track with his muscle building regimen so he sent Xerxes a text asking if they could revive their workouts. He wanted to arrange sessions that they both could commit to and did not interfere with his work schedule or Xerxes' practice schedule with the Bears.

Xerxes was perplexed and embarrassed by the broad smile that brightened his face when he received the text from Abel. He knew that he really liked Abel and grew more comfortable with him everytime they worked out but couldn't understand why the text delighted him so much. He learned that Abel had a wicked and wry sense of humor and grew comfortable teasing and joking with him.

He was pleasantly surprised how toned Abel's body was when they first began working out together and joked that, with a little more consistent time in the gym, Abel would be as popular as he was if they went out together for a night on the town. He teased Abel saying, "The attractive honeys will be all over you and won't give me the time of day." Abel reminded Xerxes that "the attractive honeys" would be safe from him, but that he might not be.

Precious was so enamored with Abel that Xerxes couldn't resist growing fond of him as well. She praised him every chance she got and delighted in the work they collaborated on and the successes they accomplished. She raved about how intelligent and knowledgeable Abel was and even suggested that Xerxes solicit his advice on a financial proposition that he had been offered. Xerxes followed her advice and sought Abel's input and realized a significant financial windfall as a result. Xerxes' trust in Abel grew and he slowly let him into the small inner circle of people he called friends. Precious, so far, had been the only other member of that group.

After asking for Abel's address, Xerxes agreed to pick him up so they could go to the training facility for their workout session. Xerxes wore a pair of oversized red Nike workout shorts that looked like they had been poured over his thighs. He paired them with a black Champion tank top whose seams struggled to restrain his massive muscles. Coincidentally, Abel had donned a pair of black Under Armour shorts and a bright red t-shirt. They laughed when they realized they had spontaneously dressed in matching colors.

Xerxes said "Great minds" when Abel climbed into his Tesla. Abel responded, "Yeah, I know right. What's up with you?!" Xerxes replied, "Chillin'" and drove the quiet, electric chariot away from Abel's home.

Abel told Xerxes that he liked the Tesla and had contemplated purchasing one for himself. He asked Xerxes what he thought about the car. Xerxes raved about the savings and benefits of the electric vehicle and how upgrades and modifications are delivered to the vehicle like downloading an app or updating the software on a cell phone. He told Abel that he was welcome to test drive his Tesla anytime he wanted. Abel gushed his thanks and told Xerxes that he would take him up on his offer.

Xerxes opened the panoramic sunroof to allow the bright sun to shine on them as they drove along. He had an eclectic stream of music playing on the Bang and Olufson premium sound system. Abel said, "Damn man, this sound system is tight? Thanks for helping me with this workout thing again. I hope our schedules don't get busy and we can keep it up this time."

Xerxes replied, "Thanks. No, problem dude. I'd do anything for Precious." He went on, "She told me that she thinks she saw a muscle when y'all were at a meeting or something the other day and she told me to keep up the good work with you."

Abel feigned indignation and said, "Oh, so Precious saw a muscle, huh? She told you to keep up the good work with me!! You're only doing this for her, huh?!? So, you don't want to work out with me. Well, I can go work out with her then and you can drop me off back at home."

Xerxes wasn't sure if Abel was joking or serious and stuttered, "No-no-no man. I want to work out with you. This ain't just for her. I-I-I-I'm sorry man."

Abel grinned widely and said, "I'm just fucking with you man. No worries." He continued, "So how long is it going to take for me to look like you?"

Xerxes thanked him for the compliment and said, "Let's get you looking like the best you first. Our body styles are different and we just need to make sure you are the best Abel that you can be."

Abel responded, "That's cool man. I'm at your disposal. Just use me and don't abuse me."

They laughed and bantered comfortably as they drove to the training center.

Xerxes arranged a rigorous and exacting training regimen for Abel and also recommended modifications that he might make to his diet. He committed to working with Abel as often as he could during the football season and offered to continue during the off season to ensure Abel accomplished his goals.

He pushed Abel like he had never been pushed before during their workout. He spotted him while he bench pressed and encouraged Abel to lift heavier weights and complete more repetitions. Abel liked the bench press exercise best, not only because it was his favorite exercise but, when Xerxes spotted him he could surreptitiously examine and appreciate his endowment. Xerxes was totally unaware how much of a motivation and incentive he was for Abel. Abel liked doing squats almost as much as he did bench presses because he could feel Xerxes' hot breath on the back of his neck and feel his firm body press against him from behind when he completed a set. Working out with Xerxes vicariously excited and stimulated Abel and he was glad that they were connecting again. If Xerxes noticed the persistent bulge in Abel's shorts during their work-out, he hid his displeasure and did not protest.

Xerxes invited Abel to join him for a bite at the training facility restaurant after their workout They found a table in the center of the cavernous training center dining facility and settled in. Xerxes said, "You did good today man for your first workout in a while. I wish we had not had this break. I see a lot of potential in you." He asked, "I didn't push you too hard this time, did I?"

Abel responded, "Thanks man. No not at all. I have never been stretched or stimulated like I was today."

Abel blushed when he said stimulated.

Xerxes said, "Precious thinks very highly of you, man. How did you guys meet?"

Abel recounted how he had been seeking an attorney to help him with his struggling business and wanted an attorney that could help him reach his strategic and long-term goals. Unfortunately, he said, he had only been introduced to older, white, male attorneys who represented large, corporate law firms. Abel didn't think that he would get the attention and level of support he needed from the candidates that he had met. He asked friends, neighbors and people at his church if they had any recommendations for a good attorney and one of them knew Precious and arranged a first meeting with her.

He told Xerxes that he still remembered the navy blue business suit and pastel pink blouse that she wore at their first meeting. He told him the tailored business suit suggested a woman who cared about the way she looked but was not a slave to fashion. He mentioned how polite she was and how she exuded confidence.

Xerxes interrupted, "Yeah man, that's her. She's got enough confidence for about fifteen people. She's always been that way."

Abel agreed and added that she was so poised and had so much self-determination that he knew he had to work with her. He told Xerxes that at the onset of their relationship he gave Precious small tasks to complete to get a sense of how she worked. He told him she punctually and successfully completed every task she had been assigned and that he rewarded her with more duties and responsibilities. He finally began to ask for her input and suggestions on strategy and long term plans as his trust and reliance grew.

Abel said. "She's like family now and I don't think I would be where I am without her."

Xerxes' next question completely surprised Abel. He said, "You seem to be a good dude. Down to earth. How long have you known you were into dudes? I mean with your income and success, you could probably have any lady that you wanted." Realizing that he may have offended Abel or been too forward, Xerxes said, "I'm sorry dude. Did I go too far too fast?"

Abel replied, "No man, it's cool." He asked, "Are you sure you got enough time?"

Xerxes said, "Sure man. Tell me."

Abel tacitly revealed, "I was molested as a child by a neighbor. It went on for several years."

Xerxes, touched Abel's shoulder and said very soothingly, "I'm sorry man. You don't have to talk about it if you don't want to."

Abel felt comfortable talking to Xerxes and went on, "I'm good. When I was about six years old my next door neighbor, Mr. Coleman, used to cut my hair. He had been cutting my hair for as long as I can remember and like clockwork about once every other week, I would go and see him."

As Abel opened up to Xerxes, the memories of his childhood violation played like a bad movie. He described how the front door of the Coleman's neat and cozy apartment opened directly into the living room. A large archway that opened to the kitchen, bathroom and two bedrooms was just to the right inside the entry doorway. One of the bedrooms belonged to Mr. Coleman's daughter, Olivia and the other belonged to his son, Ira. The apartment's only bathroom was behind the kitchen and across the hall from Ira and Olivia's bedrooms.

The Coleman's living room stretched across the entire front of the apartment. An old black and white television, which was the primary focal point in the room, sat on a table along the same wall as the archway to the kitchen. The door to Mr. and Mrs. Coleman's bedroom was to the left of the television. The living room was filled with comfortable chairs, tables and a large sofa that all faced the TV. The sofa and chairs were covered in the ubiquitous plastic that was fashionable in living room decor during the 1960s.

Abel recounted that when Mr. Coleman cut his hair, he would bring a chair from the kitchen into the living room. He placed a towel under the chair to catch any hair that might fall and positioned the chair right in front of the television so that I would have something to focus on and not squirm or fall asleep while he performed his job.

Abel said, "One of the times I went over to get my hair cut, Ira let me in." Abel told Xerxes that he had been to Mr. Coleman's apartment many times and did not think anything unusual when Ira invited him in. Abel said, "Ira told me to sit in the chair in the living room. He said his father would be back soon." Abel continued, "I sat there and remember watching the TV. I don't remember what was on, maybe Perry Mason or something like that." He went on, "One show became another which became another and I got bored or tired or both. I knew Ira was somewhere in the back of the house and I was wondering what time Mr. Coleman was going to arrive so I decided to go and check with him. "

Abel spoke in a whisper as he described how he discreetly rose from the chair and walked through the kitchen and went to Ira's bedroom door. He told Xerxes that instead of knocking on the door he just pushed it open and was shocked to discover Ira stroking his large, erect penis. Abel recounted how he was frozen with fear because had never seen anyone else's penis, and certainly not an erect one. Abel startled Ira who clumsily and unsuccessfully tried to conceal the erection inside his underwear. He yelled at Abel, "What do you want!? Get the fuck out of my room!! You're in trouble Abel!!" Ira continued, "I am going to tell your father!!"

Abel described how scared he was and admitted that he did not know what he should do. He told him how he wanted to run but knew that he had seen something that he shouldn't have and believed Ira when he said he was going to tell his parents. Ira said, "If you don't want me to tell on you, you have to do something for me."

Abel knew that he did not want his father to know what he had seen and he would do anything to get Ira to keep the secret. He was afraid, in tears and begged Ira not to tell what he had seen. He asked dejectedly, "What do you want me to do?"

Ira said, "Come here."

Abel said, "Ira told me to get down on my knees and to put my mouth on him. He told me to suck on him until he told me to stop." Abel told Xerxes that Ira was still clad in his underwear and all he remembers tasting was a mouthful of cotton. He described how much Ira seemed to enjoy what he was doing and how the tip of his underwear eventually got really sticky and wet.

When Abel had finished Ira told him, "Now don't ever tell anybody what you just did and I won't ever tell on you."

Abel told Xerxes that he and Ira continued their clandestine relationship for several years. Abel remembered how Ira continued to wear his underwear for their first several encounters but eventually convinced him to perform fellatio without the white cotton barrier. Ira savored the oral stimulation much more without the underwear and instructed Abel to "lick the tip." Abel admitted that he didn't know what he was doing and why Ira enjoyed it so much but Ira never told his parents what he had seen so he decided he would keep up his end of their bargain.

Abel described how his skills improved so well that he learned how to satisfy Ira without ever gagging or choking when his explosion came. He explained how he grew to eagerly anticipate Ira's orgasmic utterances each time his juices flowed into Abel's mouth. Ira's legs stiffened and his breathing accelerated and Abel knew that he had successfully accomplished his objective. Abel had a special power and liked the way that he could use it to control and satisfy Ira.

Abel told Xerxes that his trysts with Ira continued until he went away to college. When Ira came home from school for breaks or holidays, they would continue their dalliances. Abel accepted the fact that he liked performing oral sex and when Ira was no longer available, he sought other partners.

Abel described how he began searching the telephone directory to get the phone number for random guys that attracted him. He called them up and asked if they would let him perform fellatio on them. If they were hesitant or reluctant, Abel would offer to compensate them. He told Xerxes how surprised he was that so many guys were receptive to his proposition and that the majority of them refused his recompense. He told him that most of his inamorato enjoyed what he did and were even more ecstatic because he loved to swallow.

He described how he was always selective and circumspect when choosing a potential paramour but found himself uncontrollably drawn to a classmate during his senior year of high school. He recounted how shocked he was when his classmate, who had a reputation for being a tough guy, assented to his request for oral sex because he had overheard him disparaging homosexuality saying he "wouldn't be caught dead doing no gay shit!!" Abel described how once their illicit relationship began, he and his classmate connected regularly.

Xerxes interrupted, "You must be damn good at what you do!!."

Abel replied confidantly, "Yeah man. I got skills."

Abel told Xerxes that ultimately his classmate wanted more than just oral sex and pressed him to try something new. Abel eventually relented and intercourse became a part of their repetoire. He admitted to Xerxes that he detested copulation with his friend because he often ejaculated too quickly and was abusive and insulting during sex. Abel's embarassment and dread that his classmate would divulge the details of their liaisons at school froze him in their clandestine amour.

Xerxes was ashamed because the details of Abel's past and the ease with which he discussed them aroused him sexually. He did his best to conceal the reaction that Abel's story was having on him.

Abel's tone grew quiet and he talked much more slowly. Xerxes leaned in closer as he described how he had arranged to meet his classmate for sex one Saturday morning while his family was away. Abel had ridden his bike across town to his classmate's house. As soon as he arrived and his classmate welcomed him inside, he knelt and immediately began to perform. Abel took a deep breath and spoke as if he was watching the event play out all over again. He told Xerxes that without his knowledge, his classmate had told several of his neighborhood friends what Abel was coming to do. He had covertly schemed to have his friends sneak in and watch Abel as he serviced him and deliberately left his front door unlocked. Abel was oblivious to their stealthy entrance and was shocked and mortified when they began to hoot and jeer as his friend ejaculated and he rose to depart. When he realized that the neighborhood friends had been silently watching him the whole time he was despondent and dejected. He noticed a self-satisfied smirk on his classmate's face and realized that he had arranged the whole nightmare. The classmate and his abettors forcibly seques- tered Abel in a separate room and held him until he orally ser- viced them all one at a time.

Abel finally finished the despicable chore, after what seemed like forever, and was finally allowed to leave. He bolted from the house, jumped on his bike and sped away in a daze.

He admitted to Xerxes that as soon as he got free from his ordeal that he contemplated committing suicide. He cringed at the thought of what his classmates and friends would say when they found out what he had done and dreaded returning to school. He was certain the word would get around about what he had done but was even more afraid of committing suicide. He only had to make it through the rest of his senior year so Abel decided he would have to face any fear, embarassment or shame that might come his way. He dreaded exposure everyday for the rest of the year and refused to allow anyone to get close to him.

Xerxes was mesmerized by the detail that Abel provided and amazed at how easily he talked about his troubling past. He was sympathetic about what Abel had experienced but was more concerned because the explicit descriptions that Abel provided aroused him. He said to Abel, "Damn man!! I'm sorry that happened to you."

Abel told Xerxes, "I had a problem with it for a long time. Wondering what I did to cause it to happen. It took a long time and counseling for me to understand that it wasn't my fault and that I didn't do anything wrong." He added, "I have come to terms about it and I own my shit. It wasn't Ira's fault that I hooked up with all those other dudes after him."

Xerxes said, "Yeah, but imagine what you might be doing if he had never made you do it in the first place."

Abel responded, "I like the man that I have become. I had to develop self-confidence, because I was always on my own. I didn't have a lot of friends in school because of rumors about what I liked to do. Back then, no one knew what molestation was or understood what I had been through, so I learned to rely on myself." He said, "Who knows what I might have turned out to be if I had taken a different path. Hell, I might not have met Precious and might not have gotten to know you."

Xerxes responded, "I never looked at it like that man."

Xerxes dropped Abel back off at his house after their long almost completely silent ride from the Training Center. They both were thinking about the story that Abel had shared. Abel wondered if he had shared too much about his life and Xerxes felt like he needed to protect him now that he knew more about his story.

Abel said, "Thanks for the workout man. I can't wait for the next time" and jumped out of the car and headed toward his door. Xerxes turned the car off and got and went after Abel. He grabbed him just as he was about to walk up his walkway and gave him a long, hard embrace. Abel was surprised how long and hard Xerxes held him. Xerxes whispered in Abel's ear as he released him from the bear hug "I love you man and I am always here for you." Xerxes got back in the car and drove off.

Abel stood on the street in front of his place for a long time, not sure of what to think about what had just happened.

8

Cyrus was troubled when he woke up because he was unable to eradicate the memory of his assignations with Maurice from his mind. Sex with Maurice was lewd and unabashedly carnal and he couldn't control how much he coveted more. He didn't have to talk, feign affection or pretend that he wanted anything other than to surrender the load of semen that he delivered. Maurice was a more than willing partner in the raw and unadulterated sex that they mutually savored.

He was more frustrated because he had no way to determine when or how frequently he and Maurice would connect. He also had no control over whether they would actually ever hook up again at all. Maurice was in the driver's seat and Cyrus was entirely at his mercy.

Cyrus' disquiet was exacerbated because he also had not heard from Abel for several weeks despite repeated attempts at reaching out to him. Cyrus had never played the role of the pursuer, he was always the prey, and he did not relish the awkward spot in which he found himself. He was perturbed because Abel was always his constant and faithful inamorato and he had been unsuccessful in his attempts to connect. Now he had two men who were unresponsive to his entreaties and he lay awake most nights wondering what he needed to do to regain control of both situations.

Cyrus continued to text Maurice but still received no response. He was determined to find a way to persuade him to acquiesce to his pleas for another rendezvous. He was past caring whether Maurice would think he was "thirsty" because of his incessant texts and constant begging. He tagged supplicants who badgered him the way he was hounding Maurice with the "thirsty" label and quickly eliminated them from his roster of paramours. He was distressed because he was obsessed with wanting to see and be with Maurice again but was powerless in his ability to control the efficacy of making that happen.

He decided he needed to take control of his predicament with Maurice and concocted a ruse that he hoped would end the ambiguity about their relationship. He decided he would surprise Maurice with an unsolicited visit and confront him. He loathed the thought of someone showing up at his apartment unannounced and vowed that he would end a relationship with anyone that did. But decided he was willing to accept whatever consequences arose from his spontaneous and impetuous act. He knew the current status of his relationship with Maurice was unsustainable.

Cyrus noticed an attractive, heavily muscled man walking down the street as his Uber neared Maurice's apartment. He knew that he had seen this man before but couldn't recollect the specific circumstances of their encounter. He mused that he would have pursued this stranger and attempted to add him to his list of sex partners if he wasn't so fixated on resolving his agita with Maurice.

Cyrus relished the repartee and excitement of meeting a new sex partner before they actually indulged in intercourse for the first time. He was always on the prowl for his next new sexual conquest and chuckled that he needed to visit Maurice's neighborhood more often if guys like this one frequented the area.

Cyrus got a call from Abel just as the Uber arrived at Maurices's apartment. He finally had a hiatus from his jam-packed day working on his business expansion efforts with Precious and wanted to let Cyrus know he was thinking about him. Abel had expected to leave a message but was caught off guard when Cyrus answered. Cyrus yelled, "So where in the hell have you been? I've been trying to call your ass for weeks. What the fuck is up with you?"

Abel replied cautiously, "I've been busy with work man. You know this expansion is taking a lot of my time. Me and Precious..."

Cyrus interrupted, "That bitch Precious!! It's always about that bitch. Are you fucking her!?!?"

Abel tried to calm him down. "Cyrus, you know me and Precious are just business associates. It's not even like that."

Cyrus yelled, "I don't know what the fuck it's like. I can't catch up with your ass no more to find out what it's like. You're always doing something with that bitch!! Y'all are always together!!" He added "The both of y'all can kiss my ass!!"

Cyrus knew that he was going off and needed to reign himself in but he was unable to control his temper. He was exasperated and frustrated at his inability to control his situation with Maurice and Abel and took all of his resentment out on Abel.

Abel had never known Cyrus to be so agitated about anything and wanted to know what was causing it. He tried his best to diffuse the situation and said, "I'm sorry man. All of this madness will be over in a few weeks then I will be all yours."

Cyrus bellowed, "A few weeks!!! You can suck my dick!!! I will have found me a new man in a few weeks. I want someone who is there for me when I want them to be and clearly your lame ass ain't up to the job."

Abel tried again to appease Cyrus, "Hey man, I'm sorry. What can I do to straighten this situation out with you?"

Cyrus replied, "You can go fuck yourself and that bitch Precious too. That's what you can do!!" and hung up the phone.

Cyrus knew he had gone too far with Abel as soon as he hung up the phone. He wanted to call him back to apologize but detested the thought of displaying any signs of weakness. Maintaining supremacy in his relationship with Abel was paramount and he knew he needed to protect his dominance and position of control. He decided he'd wait several days and send Abel a text apologizing for his crudeness. He knew Abel's anger would evaporate if he feigned contrition and told him he was upset because he hadn't heard from him for such a long time. He would pretend to be remorseful and plead with Abel to allow him to atone for his crudeness. He was confident that given the chance to be alone with Abel, he could inveigle him with the pleasure of a good fuck and everything would be okay again.

He was so mad and frustrated after his altercation with Abel that he was no longer in the mood to confront Maurice. He didn't want to strike out with him too so he decided to return home so he could cool off. He updated the destination with his Uber driver and they drove away.

Cyrus woke up the next morning and was more frustrated than he had been after his call with Abel. He knew that he couldn't make it through another day without resolving his plight with Maurice. He was determined to find a way to gain entry to Maurice's apartment building and, once inside, confront him. He planned to tell Maurice that he was visiting another friend who had recently moved into the building and decided to stop by to see him since he was in the building.

Cyrus took a Lyft to Maurice's apartment just before noon and gained access to the building by pressing several apartment buzzers until someone let him in. He correctly surmised that the tenants in Maurice's building weren't overly concerned about tight security and knew that someone would let him in. He entered the building and followed the same path to Maurice's door that he had taken twice before. He attempted to knock on the door, but again found it to be ajar. The creaking door announced his presence as he quietly and carefully stepped inside. He was nervous, his throat was dry and he quietly announced himself saying, "Hey sexy, I was in your building visiting another friend and thought I would stop by to see if you wanted some more of this big ass dick that you like so much."

Cyrus assumed that Maurice must have been in the bathroom or somewhere else in the building but was startled when the door loudly slammed shut behind him. A deep bass voice replied, "I was wondering who was creeping up in my camp when I heard the door opening. I thought you were trying to steel my shit so I hid behind the door. But, nah, you didn't come to steel my shit did you? You came to steal my man!! You're the motherfucker that's been fucking my boy behind my back!! You don't know how much I've been hoping to meet your ass." He licked his lips and continued, "And look here, you walk your ass right up into my fucking house! Thanks!!"

Cyrus was startled because he had never heard anyone speak above a whisper in this small space before and the deep voice reverberated all around the apartment. He turned around to face the sonorous bass and recognized his outraged antagonist to be the same muscular man that he had admired on the street the day before. He also realized that he was the same man that he had seen at breakfast with Maurice several months before at Miss Sharon's.

Cyrus' bald, sepia-complexioned adversary was several inches taller and outweighed him by at least thirty pounds. His heavily muscled chest, triceps and biceps were massive as well and he had a flat stomach with clearly defined abdominal muscles. His thighs and legs were broad and thick and it was evident that he spent as much or more time in the gym than Cyrus. Thick silver hoop earrings hung from each ear lobe and matched the hoops that hung from piercings in each nipple. His fit frame evinced not one single ounce of body fat and he resembled a bald replica of Dewayne the Rock Johnson. Cyrus felt a sickening feeling in his stomach because it was clear that this antagonist could protect or defend himself and he appeared to be readying himself for an attack.

Cyrus desperately attempted to convince his assailant that he was in the wrong apartment. He said, "I'm sorry big man, I think I'm in the wrong spot."

The heavily muscled foe was not fooled and replied, "Hold the fuck up!! I got my boy's cell phone right here. Let's see if your ass got the wrong spot or not!!"

He slowly typed in the cell number of the phone that had left multiple text messages on Maurice's phone. Cyrus felt a growing dryness in his mouth with each number that was pressed. When his assailant entered the final digit, Cyrus' phone beeped indicating that he had just received a message. Cyrus looked around searching for an escape route and despaired when he found none. His brawny adversary stood like an impenetrable wall between him and the only exit.

The powerfully built man sarcastically and rhetorically asked, "Now what would you do if you knew somebody was fucking your boy and you found out who it was?" He continued, "What would you do if you knew someone was kicking it with your man and you found him in your fucking spot hoping to get with him again. What the fuck would you do?"

Cyrus apologized, "Hey man, I didn't know Maurice had a man!!

He never told me." He stuttered, 'He-he-he invited me over and kicked it with me!! I didn't even know he was with nobody. It ain't my fault man."

The muscled man asked, "So what did y'all do together? Did he give you head? I know he loves to give head. Did he let you fuck him too!?!?" He continued, "I want to know because whatever you did to him, I am going to do to your punk ass!!"

Cyrus surveyed the apartment again. He was hoping that an escape route had miraculously materialized but saw none. He decided he would go down fighting if that was his only option and indignantly replied, "Yeah, motherfucker!!! He sucked my big ass dick and swallowed a mouthful of my nutt." He taunted, "I came back another time and fucked the shit out of him." Cyrus chided, "He left skid marks on my dick because I fucked him so deep. In fact, when y'all are fucking, he is probably thinking about me!!" He added, "It was some good bussy too."

The man attacked Cyrus before he could get the last words out of his mouth. The fight, such as it was, didn't last very long. Cyrus tried to land one or two punches but quickly realized that he was no match for his burly foe. He felt a blow to his cheek before collapsing to the floor. He wasn't unconscious but Cyrus lay on the floor in a state of catalepsy. He was able to see everything that was happening but was powerless to move, speak or offer any substantial resistance.

He was lifted off the floor and his body draped over the back of the sofa in the middle of the living room. He heard his attacker say, "I am going to bitch you out like I used to do my cellmates back in the joint. After I bust your ass wide open, nobody is ever going to want to fuck with your ass ever again."

He pulled Cyrus' sweatpants down around his ankles and admiringly said, "That's a nice thick ass you got. I hope it's ready for this big raw dick!!" This was one time that Cyrus regretted not wearing underwear. He felt a tortuous and agonizing pain and heard a loud grunt as the man entered him with one savage thrust. Violating Cyrus without preparation or lubrication was painful for him as well but he wanted retribution and punishing Cyrus was his way of getting it. He continued his thrusts, each time pressing harder and going deeper.

Cyrus wanted to scream or cry out but couldn't find his voice. He knew that he wouldn't be able to take the excruciating pain from this assault much longer. He was in agony and surmised that his attacker had to be even more well endowed than he was.

Cyrus was a top and had never been penetrated before in his life. The pain he felt was intolerable and grew more intense and acute with every powerful thrust. Cyrus prayed for unconsciousness. He felt dampness at the point of penetration but couldn't discern whether his assaulter had ejaculated or if he was bleeding. Unable to withstand his pain any longer, Cyrus lost consciousness.

He awakened in the hallway on the floor outside of Maurice's apartment with his sweatpants still down around his ankles. Blood covered his shirt and pooled inside his sweatpants as well. A lump had begun to form above his left eye that was tender to the touch. He slowly stood, rearranged his clothes and began to walk toward the building exit. His first steps were halting as he struggled to regain his equilibrium. He tasted blood and probed his teeth with his tongue to ensure that none of them had been knocked out.

Cyrus wished that he could call Abel and ask him to come and get him. He felt vulnerable and afraid and wished that Abel could help make him feel better. After his diatribe the day before, however, he wasn't sure whether he would even take his call. He also had no good explanation for his disheveled condition and rumpled appearance so he wouldn't be able to plausibly respond to any questions that he knew Abel would pose.

He collected himself and slowly and painfully walked out of the apartment building. He called for an Uber so that he could get home as quickly as he could. He was anxious and impatient because all he wanted to do was get away from this apartment building as fast as he could. He knew that he had been violated and would need to get checked for sexually transmitted diseases (STDs). He needed to confirm that he was intact as quickly as possible.

When he got home, he took a long look in the mirror in his bathroom. He had a black eye and a large bruise over his left eye. His mouth was bloody because one of the blows caused his teeth to cut his upper lip. It was apparent that he had gotten the worst end of whatever altercation he had been involved in. He slowly undressed. The adrenaline that carried him through the fight and got him home left his body and was very quickly being replaced by aches and pains all over.

Cyrus took a long, soothing shower. His body welcomed the water and he stood in the constant stream of warmth as long as he could. After his shower, he grabbed his cell phone hoping to text Maurice to let him know what had happened and to see if he had been involved in arranging the ambush. Maurice's information had been deleted from the contacts in his phone so he no longer had any way of getting in touch with him.

The aches and pains from his encounter gradually subsided as he dried himself. He generously moisturized his entire body in soothing, healing shea butter. He found his stash of marijuana and rolling papers and meticulously formed a nice, fat blunt. He searched through the music library on his iPhone until he found "Love Serenade" by Ramsey Lewis' and let it play over and over again in repeat mode.

Cyrus lit the spliff and took a long slow drag. His pain subsided and tensions eased with each pull on the oversized joint. By the time Ramsey Lewis had played three time times, Cyrus was relaxed and no longer felt any pain. He extinguised the blunt and lay back on his sofa bed. Before long, he was enveloped in the comfort of sleep.

At least he knew that his unsettled situation with Maurice was resolved, even though the outcome was not what he had hoped for.

9

Precious had earned a reputation as a competent and capable attorney. A solid and growing group of supporters had initiated discussions with her about pursuing a career in politics. She had not ever seriously considered public office as an avocation but grew receptive to the aspirations that these potential backers had for her. She weighed the odds of making such a monumental move and saw no down side. Once her decision to move into politics was made, the only outstanding task she had was to determine the best way to break the news to Xerxes.

She had established a constant presence in Washington, DC successfully securing federal grant funding to help Abel expand his business. She developed a reputation for being a skilled arbiter and gifted negotiator and successfully garnered support and commitments from liberals and conservatives alike. She built a directory of contacts that included influencers and power-brokers from all over the country that she planned to rely on to support her political aspirations.

Many people that she contacted were initially surprised about her planned career change, but as the idea settled in and they thought about it more, they realized that she was just the right person for the job and were committed to supporting her.

Her timing was perfect. The incumbent from her district had abruptly decided not to seek re-election. Precious had worked with her before and immediately sought her endorsement. She knew garnering the incumbent's statement of support would assure her a win in the primary election. Winning the primary in the democratic leaning district guaranteed her victory in the general election.

Even though she had no prior experience in politics, Precious began to think about all the things that she wanted to accomplish once elected. She would leverage her vast legal experience in combination with community organizing work that she had done to develop a list of issues most important to her likely constituents. Her supporters and potential staff members knew that with her well-heeled connections, wide-ranging experience and winning personality, they could easily and successfully position her to be the next representative.

Precious initiated the necessary and required political filings to register her candidacy for the soon-to-be-vacant position and officially established a campaign committee. She kicked off her fund raising efforts in earnest and was elated when financial backers reached out to offer their support. She decided how and when she wanted to officially launch her campaign but needed to break the news to Xerxes before she went public. She knew he'd never forgive her if he heard about her career change from anyone else but her.

She decided to invite him to dinner at his favorite restaurant to break the news. She would arrange to have his favorite meal prepared to make sure he was in the right mood. She hoped he would be happy for her and supportive of the changes she was about to make in their lives. She called him on the phone, "Hey Boo!! How is your day going so far?"

Xerxes responded, "It's good now that I have heard from my favorite girl. What's up?"

She replied, "Can you meet me tonight at Deborah's? I want to take my favorite man to dinner at his favorite restaurant."

Xerxes answered sarcastically, "Well I know Idris Elba is your favorite man and he's making a movie in England. So if you are OK with sloppy seconds like me, then I can do my best to fill in for him, if that is cool."

Precious said, "Shut up fool. I've made a reservation for 7:30. Wear something sexy."

Xerxes replied, "I will if you will."

He smiled because he had something to look forward to now that he would be seeing her later that evening.

Precious rivaled Lupita Nyongo or a cover model from Essense magazine in the form-fitting, black leather dress that hugged her lithe frame as if it had been painted on. She contrasted the ebony hue of the dress with a pair of fire engine red Christian Louboutin stilleto pumps and a matching red bracelet and necklace set. Her hair was fashioned into tight twists and pulled back and away from her face highlighting impeccably done maquillage. She wanted to look her best because she and Xerxes would have a conversation that would determine their friendship and relationship for the rest of their lives.

Xerxes dressed in a pair of fitted black slacks that he matched with a body hugging black knit mock turtleneck sweater. He added a red leather belt that was a perfect match with a pair of red leather Hermes shoes. He added a perfectly tailored grey and black herringbone sports jacket. Xerxes always dressed smartly but when he knew he was seeing Precious he stepped up his game to match hers. They were always to best dressed couple wherever they went.

Precious had arrived at the restaurant about ten minutes before Xerxes. He pulled up to the restaurant in the shiny jet black Tesla and surrendered his keys to the valet attendant. He saw Precious through the window of the restaurant and smiled warmly when her eyes met his. He bore the countenance of Shaka Zulu or some other African deity as he stood in the diffused lighting of the entry foyer to Deborah's.

Deborah's was a quaint, romantic hideaway that kissed the shores of Lake Michigan in the Miller Beach section of town. Miller Beach was a secluded enclave characterized by large, expensive homes with expansive views of the lake. Most of the homes were situated on winding streets that meandered their way up hills in the area that at one time was barren sand dunes. Miller Beach Road, the main business thoroughfare in the area, zigged and zagged along as it paralleled the whimsical shore-line of the lake. A pristine, sandy beach that imperceptibly disappeared into the lake sat on the north side of Miller Beach Road and bustling restaurants, shops, diners and cafes sat on the south.

Deborah's was situated on the corner of Miller Bearch Road at it's intersection with Marquette Boulevard, the primary thor-oughfare that allowed egress and ingress to the neighborhood. It was famous for it's succulent cuisine and breathtaking views of the Chicago skyline in the distance. The restaurant had five small booths that accommodated two or four diners arrayed along both walls. Two rows of five tables each were situated in the middle of the restaurant between the rows of booths on both sides. Large floor to ceiling windows that offered unob-structed views of the lake formed the front wall of the restaur-ant. Lustrous ebony, hardwood floors added to the elegant and dignified ambiance. Black linen table cloths paired with grey napkins and a single burning taper were positioned atop each table. Subdued lighting provided by dimly lit recessed fixtures throughout enhanced the romantic milieu.

Double swinging doors in the right corner of the back wall offered access to the kitchen and the restroom area. An intim-ate bar and waiting area with comfortable chairs sat just behind the Maitre'd stand at the front of the restuarant. Soft instru-mental R&B music played on the sound system throughout.

Precious had selected the middle table along the front wall of the restaurant with a clear view of the beach and the lake. Xerxes joined her as soon as he entered. The clear, cloudless sky provided a unimpeded view of the sun as it danced across the sky and hid behind the shimmering Chicago skyline on the horizon. The restaurant was far from crowded so Precious and Xerxes were able to speak freely.

Xerxes gave Precious a soft peck on the cheek as he sat down and said, "Damn girl, you're looking good tonight!"

Precious replied, "Thanks, sexy man. So are you. I was just trying to live up to your standards."

They laughed easily as they ordered appetizers.

Precious told Xerxes that she had already arranged for a special entree for him and asked, "How was your day Boo?"

Xerxes responded, "It was good baby." He continued, "Practice was good today and I think we are ready for the game on Sunday."

Precious said, "I know y'all will do well." She added, "I have been keeping up with you this season. My baby is having a good year!!"

Xerxes said, "It's a contract year and I have to bump up my stats so I get that incentive check. It will help me be able to ask for big money on my new contract." He smiled and added, "I know this gold digger with expensive tastes."

Precious smiled.

She ordered a house salad and Xerxes wanted the lobster bisque, a dish for which Deborah's was well known. Their appetizers arrived and Precious took a serious tone. She said to Xerxes, "Baby, there is something that I need to tell you and I hope you won't be too upset, but it's very important that I tell you before you find out some other way."

Xerxes wasn't sure what Precious wanted to tell him but grew nervous because of her somber tone. He asked, "Damn baby are you good!?! What is it!? You're sounding serious as shit!! Are you OK?"

Precious said, "Yes, baby. I'm OK." She went on, "I have a chance to do something in my life that I never expected I would be able to do because I never knew that I wanted it at least until just now." She added, "You know all I ever wanted to do was to be an lawyer, right?"

Xerxes, replied, "Yes and you are a damn good one too."

She said, "Thanks." Precious went on, "I just heard about an opportunity and a lot of people that I've talked to think it would be perfect for me. And the timing is just right. It's perfect in fact." She apologized, "I know this is something that you and I would normally have a discussion about first, but I didn't want you to do or say anything that would change my mind."

Xerxes replied, "You know I would never do anything to keep you from reaching your goals. What is it baby?"

Precious said excitedly, "I'm running for Congress." She added, "There is a seat that is about to be open because the incumbent is not running for re-election. She just made the announcement so there is no favored candidate to take her place. I think I would be perfect for it and have already asked for her endorsement. I've also talked to some folks that are willing to support my campaign with serious dollars. It would be a chance to do some really good shit for the neighborhood."

Xerxes interjected, "You are already doing some good shit, Baby."

Precious said, "Thanks sexy. That means a lot." She continued, "Well this Congressional seat will give me a chance to do good on a much bigger scale and I hope you will understand and support my decision."

Xerxes heard her words, "Support my decision". He knew that he would have to be on board to support Precious' plans. Especially since her mind was clearly already made up.

Their entrees arrived while Precious continued to assure Xerxes that she was making the right decision for her. She told him how her work with Abel and her other clients had given her a really strong network of contacts in Washington, DC. She explained to him that a group of her potential supporters had already done exploratory work. She told him how they convinced her that she had an excellent chance to win the seat.

While she continued to make her case, Precious noticed two things. First, that Xerxes had been listening for several minutes without saying a word. Second, that he had barely touched his food. Xerxes knew from as far back as when he and Precious first met as kids that she would go a long way. He always hoped they would make their life journey together and he certainly did not want to be the one to ever stand in her way.

Precious asked, "Xerxes!? Babe!? Z!? Are you alright? You are barely eating. I have never known you not to be hungry and especially when I requested your favorite meal. What do you think?"

Xerxes replied, "P Baby I'm good. It must be that I am so excited about your news. I'm so proud of you. I know you will be successful!! Will I be able to carry your bags for you when you get to DC?" He continued, "Should I call you Madame Baby?"

Precious laughed.

She asked, "Daddy, are you sure? It will mean that I am in DC a lot more if, I mean when, I win." She continued, "I will have to be on the road a lot for the campaign too."

Xerxes said, "Baby, I would never stand in your way. You know that. Just let me know what is the limit to how much I can contribute to your campaign." She hugged him and whispered, "I love you."

He hugged her back.

Precious launched into more of the details of her planned campaign. She told him who some of her financial backers were and how much they committed to her and her campaign. She talked about what she wanted her platform to be and the areas on which she wanted to focus. She outlined her whole strategy and he could see how excited she was about this new possibility in her life.

Xerxes tried to hide that he had completely lost his appetite and he feigned interest in what she was saying and all that she planned to do but he knew their relationship had changed forever.

10

Xerxes joyously celebrated Precious' landslide victory with her on election night but had to turn around the next day and divert his attention and focus to the critical divisional football game coming up on Sunday. Precious would immediately leave for meetings in Washington, DC so they wouldn't have time to further discuss the seismic changes occurring in their lives. He had enthusiastically supported her throughout the campaign and was glad that she won and was living out her dreams but was torn because their life together was disintegrating.

He was uncertain what the massive changes would mean for them. Xerxes had two years remaining on his new contract with the Bears and was unable to pick up and move to DC to be with Precious. He knew the players and the rosters for both the Washington NFL team and the Baltimore Ravens and, even if he wanted to be traded, didn't see a open position available for him to join either team. Instead, he decided to focus on helping Precious transition to the next phase of her life and deal with his concerns about them and their relationship later.

Xerxes usually followed a standard weekly practice regimen and a pre-game ritual but Precious' election win and immediate departure for DC threw him off his normal routine. All week at practice, his timing was off with the quarterback or he dropped passes, missed assignments and fumbled the ball. He got into a shoving match with a teammate when he accused him of missing an assignment. Xerxes had never had a bad week in practice before and concluded that Precious' move was affecting him more than he had anticipated.

The Bears were facing their divisional rival, the Detroit Lions, and the game had playoff implications for both teams. The Bears needed a win to clinch a wild card berth in the playoffs and Detroit needed to win to keep their hopes of securing the final wild card berth alive. The team expected Soldier Field to be filled to capacity and were looking forward to the hype from the raucous crowd and the excitement of playing at home to spur them on to victory. The teams were evenly matched and the game was expected to be tight. The Lions won when the two teams played ealier in the season in Detroit, but the Bears were the odds-on favorite to win at home.

Xerxes customarily delivered his "A-game" in critical and important matches like this one. He was normally and reliably the Bears "go-to-guy" because he consistently delivered when victory was uncertain and the game was still on the line. He reveled in his role and not only enjoyed getting the ball in the game when the stakes were high, but demanded it as well.

Since his rookie season, he had faithfully and consistently delivered for the Bears, but in this game against the Lions, he struggled. He dropped a screen pass that should have resulted in a first down for the Bears and extended a third quarter drive. He missed a reception on a two-point conversion try later in the game that would have given the Bears an almost insur-mountable five point lead. The five-point cushion would have forced the Lions to drive the length of the field to score a touch-down to win. Xerxes' muff gave the Lions a shot at a field goal that could have forced the game into overtime. Fortunately, the Bears defense held and they eked out a win.

Xerxes' mediocre performance against the Lions broke his ten-game streak of 100-yards receiving and abrogated an incentive clause in his contract that would have resulted in a six-figure bonus at the end of the year. He was so infuriated with his performance that he faked an injury and pulled himself from the game. Even though the Bears won, Xerxes did not feel like he contributed anything to the team's success and was inconsolable when his teammates tried to cheer him up.

Abel watched the game from home and could tell that Xerxes was not performing up to par. As soon as the game was over, he sent him a text to check on him. Xerxes showered, dressed and participated in the obligatory post-game press conference before he got Abel's text. He jumped in his car and left the stadium as he read the message.

Abel: Hey man, saw the game. You, OK?"

Xerxes: Not my best effort, but I'm good.

Abel: Where are you headed?

Xerxes: To the crib.

Abel: Want some company?

Xerxes: Sure. But I might not be the best company.

Abel: Be there in a few. Anything you need?

Xerxes replied no and continued his drive home.

Xerxes arrived home and undressed removing everything except his fitted boxers. He filled a large decanter with Jack Daniels and Coke, pulled out his cache of weed and meticulously rolled a blunt. Precious would normally be available to help console him and buoy his spirits when he performed poorly, but she was in DC. He needed something to expunge the memory of his subpar performance from his mind and bring him out of his funk. He had finished about half of his snifter of Jack and Coke and was about to fire up the blunt when Abel rang the buzzer. He had forgotten that Abel was coming over and pressed the access button to let him in.

The muted lighting in Xerxes' massive condominium disoriented Abel but the soft sounds of smooth jazz emanating from the Bose premium surround speakers and Xerxes' warm embrace welcomed him. Abel had seen Xerxes in gym shorts, sweat pants or a tank top when they worked out together in the gym, but he had never seen him in form-fitting boxer shorts without a shirt. He struggled to conceal his disquiet and amazement at how completely toned and perfectly proportioned Xerxes' body was. The snug-fitting briefs did a mediocre job of obscuring Xerxes' endowment and clearly displayed the length and thickness of his manhood.

Xerxes smiled slyly as he caught Abel covertly admiring him. Abel respected his friendship with Xerxes and never tried to proposition him during their workouts together in the gym. Xerxes was amused however because it was evident to him that Abel was struggling to conceal his interest in and attraction to him. He offered Abel a drink but he declined. He guided him to his den with its oversized leather, reclining sofas and offered him a seat.

Abel complied and asked, "How you doing big man? I watched the game...."

Xerxes interrupted, "I just couldn't get on track today. I was way out of sync."

Abel asked, "So what was up? What was the problem man?"

Xerxes replied, "A lot of things man. I'm about to lose my girl and can't even fight to keep her. She's the only woman that I have ever loved and I don't want to hold her back. I just gotta find a way to deal with this shit and not let her know it's fucking with me like this."

Abel said, "You are not losing her man. She is just doing something that she has gotta do right now." Abel asked, "Can you at least let her know how you feel?"

Xerxes yelled, "Hell no, and don't you tell her either!! She's got to want to be with me as much as I want to be with her or it won't work. I'm proud of her and want her to do her thing, but politics wasn't a part of what we ever talked about. I love her and will always love her, but she's got to want to get back to me on her own." Xerxes said, "I'm not feeling sorry for myself, but this shit has me all turned around. Do you mind, if I fire up this blunt? You can hit it too, if you want."

Abel was aghast and asked, "You're smoking weed during the season? You must be fucked up!!"

Xerxes replied, "I'm good man. I just had a pee test last week. The team doctors don't ever repeat drug tests that soon and I need something to get my head together."

Abel had very limited experience with weed but felt like he needed to be a good friend and agreed to smoke with Xerxes.

He told Xerxes, "Sure man I will try some but I'm a virgin with weed. Don't take advantage of me." He added, "I have to warn you, weed makes me hungry, horny and sleepy, so I hope you got food and a place for me to sleep if I get too high."

Xerxes smiled slyly.,"I got you dude." He joked, "I won't do anything to you that you don't let me."

Abel laughed nervously.

Xerxes fired up the blunt and took two long drags on it before he passed it to Abel. Abel took the joint and barely took a pull before motioning to return it to Xerxes. Xerxes protested, "Unh-uh man. The cadence is puff, puff, pass. You gotta hit that shit one more time." Abel took a second long drag on the oversized spliff and passed it back to Xerxes. He inhaled too much of the smoke and began to cough and gag violently.

Xerxes took another hit of the blunt and asked, "Are you OK? You want something to drink?"

Abel's coughing spell subsided and he replied, "Yeah man, I'll take a small one of whatever you are having on the rocks."

Xerxes rested the blunt in an ashtray on the table in front of them and headed to the kitchen to prepare Abel's drink. Abel marveled at the perfect symmetry of his body and how grace-fully he moved as he walked away. He was equally mesmerized by the huge bulge in the front of his shorts that drew his focus when he returned.

Xerxes offered the aperitif to Abel and retrieved the smoldering joint from the ashtray and took another long drag. He told Abel to take it easy on his next hit before he passed the blunt back to him. They relaxed and grew more comfortable as the effects of the drug and the drink engulfed them.

Xerxes asked, "Have you ever had a shotgun?"

Abel replied "No. What's that?"

Xerxes looked him directly in his eyes and asked, "Do you trust me?"

Abel answered hesitantly, 'Yeah man. Sure."

Xerxes said, "Bet!! Let me show you."

He took the lit blunt and rotated it so that the burning end was inside his mouth. He situated his mouth close to Abel's and directed him to open wide. Abel complied and Xerxes blew a rush of smoke directly into his mouth. Xerxes sat back as Abel inhaled a mouthful of the vapor and began to choke and retch again.

Xerxes laughed and asked Abel if he was OK. Abel regained his composure and admitted to Xerxes that he was not expecting so much smoke. He said incredulously, "I thought you said you had me!!"

Xerxes replied, "Sorry man. I forgot that you were a virgin." He added, "I'll take it easy on your next time."

Abel was already light headed from the weed and offered little rejection when Xerxes cajoled him to take more. He liked the calm and blissful feeling that was permeating his body as a result of the shotgun and asked Xerxes if he could have another.

Xerxes had a more devious and lascivious objective in mind when he asked Abel, "Are you sure you want it?"

Abel completely missed his double entendre and replied, "Sure, I think I am used to it now."

Xerxes turned the blunt around in his mouth again and faced Abel. This time, their lips accidently touched as Abel moved closer and opened his mouth. He ingested another mouthful of smoke but did not cough or gag. Xerxes leaned back and said, "I'm proud of you. You took that like a pro this time." He asked, "Do you catch on with everything so quickly?"

Abel was intoxicated from the weed and the drink and Xerxes' innuendo completely eluded him, but the erection that was developing in his fitted boxers was patently conspicuous and impossible to miss. Abel was emboldened by his inebriation and held his gaze and did not look away when Xerxes caught him checking him out. Xerxes met his stare and said, "You told me the affect that weed has on you. Let me show you what affect it has on me."

Xerxes stood up and pulled down his form-fitting boxers revealing a full erection. Abel admired it for its beauty, magnitude and perfection. Xerxes was blessed with a quintessential combination of extreme length and massive girth. The end of his ideal protuberance was fashioned in the shape of an enormous mushroom head. Large throbbing veins on both sides and along the top extended the entire length of his phallus. It had a slight curve to the right and aciculated toward Abel, beckoning him to taste it.

Abel swallowed hard and asked, "Are you sure you want to do this?"

Xerxes said, "I'm fucked up man and my dick is hard. Of course, I want to do this."

Abel knelt directly in front of Xerxes and gently kissed the side, the tip, the bottom and the head of his dick. Xerxes reflexively pulsated each time Abel touched and licked his sheath. He was precumming and Abel, not wanting to miss a drop, licked the wet juices that oozed from the tip. Xerxes moaned as Abel orally caressed his length and shuddered when he swallowed it whole. Abel initially strained and struggled until he got used to Xerxes because he was longer and thicker than Cyrus.

Abel grabbed Xerxes' firmly muscled ass and forced his manhood further down his throat. Xerxes was in complete ecstasy as Abel went about his task. Abel developed a consistent rhythm and continued to service the long, thick shaft. Xerxes' excitement grew and his massive gluteal muscles tensed as he approached his climax. He warned Abel, "Shit!! I'm about ready to bust man."

Abel was on a mission and ignored the warning. His excitment grew and his rate increased as he devoured more and more of Xerxes' massive, rock hard human dildo. Xerxes shuddered, his legs quivered and he yelled, "FUCK!!!!" as he exploded in Abel's mouth.

Abel continued until he had swallowed every drop of seed that Xerxes dispensed. He sat back on the sofa with a satisfied smile and took a long sip of his cocktail. He looked over at Xerxes and asked if he was OK. Xerxes smiled and said, "I'm not down in my feelings no more."

They laughed.

Abel was embarrassed and felt as if he had betrayed Precious' trust. He said to Xerxes, "I'm so sorry man. This is going to fuck up my relationship with you and with Precious."

Xerxes replied, "Chill man. Didn't nothing happen tonight that both of us didn't want to happen." He added, "Who knows where me and Precious are right now anyway and if you don't holler, I won't scream. Let's just see how this plays out. It's a one-time thing. You helped me get through some shit I was going through. Let's just go back to being boys."

Abel agreed and stood up to leave.

Xerxes said, "You can chill here if you ain't ready to drive yet."

Abel said cool and Xerxes showed him to the guest bedroom.

Abel fell asleep as soon as his head hit the pillow. When he awakened the next morning, he was surprised to find Xerxes curled up in bed with his arms around him.

11

Precious quickly settled into her new role in Congress. She lobbied successfully to be placed on several influential sub-committees. She developed a close personal relationship with the Speaker of the House while simultaneously ensuring that her colleagues didn't perceive her to be overly aggressive. She joined the Congressional Black Caucus and became one of their most influential members while steadily developing important and strategic contacts in Washington and across the country.

Precious immediately executed the strategic plan that she devised when she made the decision to run for office. She quickly learned, however, that she could put all of her energy and effort into her new role in Congress or she could devote her time to nurturing her relationship with Xerxes, but she could not do both. Her hectic schedule did not allow her to get back home to see him as frequently as she hoped. When she did get back home her schedule was filled with political events, fundraisers or activities with her constituents and she felt guilty because it left very little time for her to spend with Xerxes.

Their last few attempted trysts in Washington were unavoidably interrupted by last minute changes in Precious' schedule. The Congressional Black Caucus (CBC) made a show of unity and support against the proliferation of assault weapons after a mass shooter killed several parishioners at an African American church on one occasion. The entire time Xerxes was in town, Precious was preoccupied with coordinating the messaging for the CBC, preparing statements for the media and conducting interviews with journalists. Another time, Xerxes was enroute to visit her but before he arrived, she had to be spirited away to a secure location along with the other freshman African American Congresswomen after the FBI uncovered a credible plot to assassinate one of them. The FBI whisked her away so quickly that she was only able to let Xerxes know she was safe. She couldn't tell him where she was or how long she would be sequestered and by the time she was released from protective custody, Xerxes had left town.

Precious lived in an apartment in the Anacostia section of Washington, DC. The gentrification and development that had for years invaded the rest of the city had finally crossed the Anacostia River bridge. She explored every quadrant of the bustling and popular city looking for accommodations but was unable to afford the exorbitant rents in the neighborhoods west of the river. She had initially avoided prospecting in neighborhoods east of the river because that section of the city had a reputation for being impoverished and crime-infested. Precious visited the area and discovered for herself a diamond in the rough and leased an apartment in the recently renovated building.

Crossing the bridge and leasing an apartment in Anacostia saved Precious several thousand dollars a month in rent. Her building was directly adjacent to the Minnesota Avenue Metro Station on the Orange Line and offered the flexibility and convenience to get to anywhere she needed to as quickly as possible. Several staffers and other people who worked on Capital Hill followed her to the area once they learned how economical it was. Precious welcomed the influx of new neighbors because she always had company going to or coming from her office on the subway.

Precious expected Xerxes to join her in Washington to accompany her while she searched for a new place to live but their schedules never matched and she had to move ahead on her own. She admired his taste and valued his opinion and sought his stamp of approval that she had found a place that he considered safe and secure. She was disheartened when they were never able to synchronize their schedules. She opted not to buy a house or a condominium because she knew that congress and politics was extremely unpredictable. One scandalous news story or bad election outcome could result in her having to leave office.

She adored her building and the block where she lived but spent very little time furnishing or decorating her new apartment. The sturdily constructed, 1890s-era building originally housed a convent but the nun's quarters had been refurbished, combined and converted into one-, two- and three-bedroom apartments. Extra thick walls and heavy insulation insured quiet and privacy for each unit. Bright, modern lighting, enhanced security and impeccably maintained hardwood floors belied the devout origins of the building. Abundant sunlight overspread apartments facing east in the morning while brilliant afternoon and evening sunsets saturated the units facing west. Oversized doors and towering ceilings gave each apartment a cavernous feel.

Precious' two-bedroom, corner unit on the top floor of the south end of the building was bathed in sunlight all day long. Her front door opened into a huge foyer with pristinely polished hardwood floors. A large, spacious living room with a small dining room behind it was on the left just beyond the foyer. New stainless steel appliances, marble countertops and strategically placed hanging track lights adorned the large kitchen behind the dining room. An island that included the stove, sink and three barstools for seating formed the central focus of the modern kitchen. A door leading to the back stairs and fire escape was centered on the back wall of the kitchen.

The bedrooms and bathrooms were situated on the right side of the apartment off the foyer. Two of the former nun's quarters were combined to form the large master bedroom and bathroom suite. A large walk-in closet spanned the entire wall opposite the entry door to the room. An oversized bed was arranged against one wall of the room and a sitting area that Precious transformed into a home office space was on the other. A smaller guest bedroom and bathroom was further back on the right side of the apartment next to the master bedroom.

Precious loved her place because her rooms were larger than anything she had seen west of the Anacostia River in DC, she paid much less in rent and it was furnished. She knew her hectic congressional schedule wouldn't allow time to shop for furniture to fill a new home. The grey slate leather sofa and matching love seat were functional and comfortable. When she found a moment to relax or unwind, the overstuffed pillows and cushions that adorned the sofa and loveseat embraced her. African print area rugs enhanced the floor in the living and dining rooms. Wall mounted smart TVs hung on the walls in the living room and both bedrooms. Precious added pastel colored throw pillows, pictures of Xerxes and decorative plants to make the apartment feel like home.

The majority of her neighbors were retirees who loved the large, spacious units that the building offered. Most were long-time tenants who cherished the privacy and solitude offered by the extra thick walls and over abundant insulation that muted noises and sounds emanating from individual apartments. Prospective tenants with small children and smoking were prohibited in the building but small pets were allowed. Precious knew that she had found a treasure and thanked her aide profusely for telling her about the apartment as soon as it became available.

She used the office she had set up in her master bedroom to

work from home when insomnia or relestness caused sleep to escape her. She conducted research, authored legislation or drafted correspondence to her supporters and constituents. Her home office connection proved to be invaluable and allowed Precious to dedicate her all to her congressional job. She was more accessible and responsive to voters and her staff as well. She worked more hours in Congress than she ever did her in law practice back at home.

Precious had to postpone any dreams or plans that she had ever envisioned with Xerxes to focus on attaining the goals she set when she ran for Congress. She was still committed to Xerxes and wanted him in her life but wasn't in a position to make any more definitive plans with him at this time. She knew that she wanted to have children and she expected that Xerxes did too but they had never had a real discussion about parenting or starting a family. They had always had too much fun and been to active to make a concrete plan and assumed that when the time was right, they would both know it and begin to build a family together. She knew that any plans she had for motherhood would have to be put off until after she completed her her first term in congress.

She had just begun her life in politics so it was too early to start to think about what she wanted to do when she was done. She decided she would give her all to her role in congress and do everything she could to support her constituents. She knew that she would run for a second term and decided to wait until then to focus on the other things she might want to do in her life. She hoped that having a baby and becoming a mother would endear her to her constituents and help her to be more committed to making a change for her children and their children as well.

Precious knew that Xerxes only had a few years left to play in his pro football career and hoped that he would be supportive of her revised life plan. She knew he wanted to start a business or fund a non-profit foundation and become a sports analyst on a television show after he retired. She prayed that when she was ready he would want to and be ready to start a family and their schedules would harmonize perfectly.

Xerxes was very proud of Precious and her accomplishments in congress. People who knew the two of them and would congratulate him and tell him proud they were of her and the work she was doing. He still needed to work through the changes that they were going through and what it meant for him, but he knew that they would always be friends. Even if they ended up growing apart as a couple he needed to give her the freedom to reach her fullest potential. He was sad though because allowing her to realize her fullest potential might mean there was no longer any room in her life for him.

Precious and Xerxes tried to stay in touch as much as possible by text or FaceTime whenever they could. They usually started the day or ended the night by talking or texting one another. They knew that their love had not waned or diminished but were beginning to realize that, unlike the old AT&T television commercial, long distance was not the best thing to being there.

While they remained best friends and shared everything, they felt themselves moving in different directions.

12

Precious and Xerxes had always been able to rely on one another but their new life apart brought challenges for both of them. Their schedules were in persistent conflict and they both relied on Abel to be their dependable intermediary.

Precious had become somewhat of a celebrity and regularly appeared on MSNBC, CNN or other liberal-leaning political commentary programs. She was gaining a reputation as an important voice for the Democratic Party. Her popularity soared even higher after she appeared on the FOX Morning News program and held her own against the cadre of argumentative and antagonistic hosts. She became an audience favorite and frequent guest on "The Daily Show" with Trevor Noah after he described her as fresh, innovative and well informed. Her Twitter followers exploded exponentially and she was constantly in demand. Precious and Xerxes' time together was already constrained and her newfound notoriety and burgeoning popularity diminished it even more.

Xerxes was embarassed by the frustration and resentment he felt regarding Precious' move into politics and redirected his focus into his game. He was performing at an All-Star level and led the league in pass receptions, yards gained and received an Offensive Player of the Year MVP nomination. He was a beast in practice, in the gym and on the field and was having his best year ever.

Abel advised him that if he left football at the pinnacle of his performance he would substantially improve his chances of garnering a lucrative endorsment deal or becoming a television sports analyst on one of the pre-eminent sports shows. He reminded him that there were a myriad of profitable opportunities for players after football if they were lucky enough to get out of the game at the right time in their careers. He told him that he could improve his marketability and increase his chances of being a part of that exclusive club.

Unable to maintain contact with one another, Precious often called Abel after her television appearances and Xerxes would call him after his games. Abel cherished his role as emissary and trusted friend and judiciously relayed messages between the two of them. He had become their communications conduit and accepted and embraced his role as confidant. He was also glad that Xerxes had not told her about their indiscretion and damaged his friendship with her.

One morning, after an appearance on "The Daily Show", she called Abel to clap back at him in response to an acerbic text he sent. His text read, "The correct foundation for a bitch as black as you is not Light Egyptian #7!!" A subsequent text chided her for appearing "shiny and oily" and berating her for having "enough grease on her face for a two-piece and a biscuit." When he answered the phone Precious pretended to be annoyed and greeted him, "Good morning Motherfucker!!" Recognizing her voice, he laughed at her off-color sobriquet and reasoned that she wouldn't be so upset if his text had not hit the mark so appropriately. Precious agreed with Abel's assessment of her appearance and confessed that all make-up artists are not skilled in successfully blending the foundation of women with melanin kissed skin tones. She promised to consult her own make-up artist in the future about what skin tones to demand and pledged to never embarrass herself that way again.

She asked Abel what he thought about her appearance on the

show and whether she succeeded in imparting her message effectively. He assured her that she was eloquent and articulate and communicated her perspective quite well. He told her that she clearly communicated the democratic priorities and party message. Precious assured him that she had received the blessing from the Speaker of the House before accepting the invitation to appear and parroted the Party talking points.

Their conversation eventually turned to Xerxes and Precious lamented how badly she missed talking to him after his games during football season. She described how they would analyze and reassess every play as she critiqued his performance. Abel joked that he had replaced her as Xerxes' post-game psychiatrist and was surprised how much he had grown to love the game and had become an avid football fan.

He described how sorely Xerxes missed her, how much he loved her so deeply and how badly he wished they could be together. He conceded that Xerxes actually wanted to talk more about her than he did about his performance in the game. She thanked Abel for looking out for Xerxes and for being such a good and loyal friend. She promised to find time to hang out with him on her next trip to town. He called her a liar and told her that he loved her and hung up the phone.

Xerxes and Abel usually talked after every game and their conversations always began with his performance and ways he could improve his game. Prior to her move into politics, he and Precious had designated Sundays as their intimate and exclusive day together.
During the off season, they deliberately lounged or canoodled all day in bed, waking or rising only to perform ablutions or to get sustenance.

On game days, Xerxes followed a standard pre-game regimen that Precious had learned over time never to interrupt. While he prepared himself for battle and put on his game face she made arrangements to watch the game as if she were a professional sports scout. Xerxes expected her to intently watch the game, impartially critique his performance and disspationately offer suggestions for improvement. After the game, they would make contact and he would solicit her unvarnished assessment. Now that she was into politics, her Sunday political schedule made it impossible for her to watch his games and provide input. Xerxes still needed someone to critique his performance and he supplanted Precious with Abel.

Like most other professional football teams, the Bears normally played on Sunday afternoons. In her new role, Precious routinely used Sundays as a time to travel to or from DC. When she was not travelling, she used Sundays to meet with her staff and catch up on congressional and legislative activities. She tried to have a television airing Xerxes' games on near while she met with her staff, but realized that she couldn't focus on his performance and her legislative duties simultaneously. She was relegated to sending a generic text congratulating him when the Bears won or a message offering encouragement if they lost. Precious didn't have enough bandwidth to stay abreast of how Xerxes was performing so she had no way of knowing he was having a break out year.

Xerxes knew that Abel and Precious talked much more frequently than the two of them did so instead of fruitlessly reaching out to her, he began to communicate and convey messages to her through Abel. He gradually began to expand their discussions beyond Precious and what she was doing in DC and found himself enjoying their conversations as well.

He eventually persuaded Abel to watch his games and offer any suggestions that he thought would help him improve his game. Abel was very attentive and surprised and impressed Xerxes with his attention to detail and focus on his performance in the game. Xerxes began to rely on Abel's input and found his meta-morphosis into a hard core football fan sensual.

 After the Bears mid-season loss to the Seattle Seahawks in a particularly hard-fought contest, they talked at length. Abel said, "I thought they had you on that 2nd and 15 play when you caught that screen pass behind the line." He continued, "I didn't think you were going to turn that into a gain, let alone make the first down."

Xerxes replied, "Yeah, me too. The right guard opened up a lane when he caught one of the safeties blitzing."

Abel asked, "So how long did you have to sit in the sauna after the game today?" He continued, "You took some good hits today."

Xerxes responded, "I was in the tub for about an hour. The Seahawks have a great defense and they hit really hard," There was a long pause before Xerxes added in a serious tone, "I don't know how much longer I can take this shit, A" using his new moniker for Abel. He continued, "I hear a lot about CTE and try to avoid head collisions as best I can, but this shit is starting to take a toll." Xerxes went on, "After the season, I am going to have an independent doctor, not one of these NFL assholes, take a look at me." He added, "I want to get out of this game with my mind and my body. I look at some of the players from back in the day, and they all need canes or walkers and can barely speak." He continued, "They can't think straight." Xerxes said, "I want to be able to enjoy my post football days."

Abel replied, "I hear you man." He added, "You gotta do what you gotta do."

They spent the rest of their time talking about Precious. Xerxes asked what he and Precious talked about and how she was doing. He wanted to know what legislation she was working on and how it was progressing. He asked what television shows she was going to be appearing on. He wanted to know how her staff was working out and if she really enjoyed her new life in DC.

Xerxes had never been a political junkie but tried to catch Precious whenever she was on TV or record her appearance to watch later. He was never able to see her when she appeared on the Sunday morning shows because they interfered with his game day preparations, but he made an extra effort to watch when he knew in advance she was going to be on TV.

Abel updated Xerxes on everything related to Precious and told him how much she missed him. He told him how she wished they were able to talk more and how much she missed the sound of his voice. Xerxes thanked Abel for being the go between for the two of them and told him how much he appreciated him for being such a good friend. Xerxes was happy to hear that Precious missed him but saddened to know that there was no easy resolution to their disharmony anytime soon.

Xerxes tone turned serious. He said, "I'm tired of talking about me and P, man. What's up with you A?"

Abel replied, "I'm just going with the flow man." He went on, "Work is going well, thanks to help from Precious. She is still helping me to make the right contacts to continue to grow."

Xerxes asked, "So what are you doing besides working and being a liaison for me and Precious?" He asked, "Who are you trying to get next to?" Xerxes added, "That body is getting pretty nice and tight now. I know somebody is reaping the benefits, right?"

Abel blushed. He was glad Xerxes was on the phone and couldn't see him and replied, "I'm Jack."

Xerxes said, "What!?"

Abel replied, "You know, Jack. All work and no play, Jack."

Xerxes said, "Well, we got to do something about that don't we?!?" He added, "We can't let all of that go to waste."

Abel laughed and said, "Don't nobody want none of this." He said, "Shit, I can't even give it away."

Xerxes responded slyly, "You can give it to me." He added, "It was pretty good the last time."

Abel said, "Man, you better stop fucking with me. I'm going to think you are serious......."

Xerxes interrupted, "That sounds like a good idea."

Abel asked, "What sounds like a good idea?"

Xerxes replied, "Fucking."

Abel was caught off guard and hurried off the call because he wasn't prepared to take their conversation where it was going.

13

Xerxes and Abel were becoming best friends. Xerxes needed someone to fill the void left by Precious. He was ashamed because he resented her for entering politics and moving to DC and wanted to find someone to take her place in his heart. He tried dating but quickly discovered that, like back at Michigan, his football status only attracted women of a certain pedigree.

Perhaps being with Precious for so long spoiled him and established a bar that was impossible for any of the women he pursued to reach. He couldn't envision a life or long-term relationship with any of them. He shared his multiple dating misfortunes with Abel but admonished him not to tell Precious. He didn't want her to know how much he was struggling without her and didn't want to create an awkward situation between the two of them. What if Precious forced Abel to choose between her and Xerxes and he chose her? Xerxes would have lost the two most important people in his life.

He grudgingly realized that finding another woman to replace Precious was not likely to happen. He had known since childhood that she was the one and only female that he wanted in his life and he sadly and reluctantly acquiesced to this reality.

Abel enjoyed his workout regimen with Xerxes. The sessions were tough and grueling but he had finally begun to notice significant development in his muscularity. His physical progress was complimented by a boost in his self-esteem and he began to admire the visage that reflected back at him when he looked in the mirror. He was euphoric when Xerxes suggested they continue their workouts during the football season as well. They worked out four times a week during the off season and Xerxes arranged for Abel to join him and the team for strength training sessions during the season.

Usually when they worked out, Xerxes' primary topic of conversation was what he wanted to do with his life after football. He liked to get input from Abel because he valued his opinion. He'd say, "You know man, I'm not trying to do this football shit for the rest of my life. I'm trying to figure out what the next phase of my life should be."

Abel completed his set and asked, "So what is it that you want to do with Xerxes 2.0?"

Xerxes laughed, "2.0 huh?"

Abel said, "Yeah man, so what are you thinking about?"

Xerxes said, "If I manage it right, I should have enough skrilla from football to last. I haven't been running through my money like a lot of these assholes. I don't bling and I don't floss!!." He added, "I ain't got no posse, entourage or gang of niggas sniffing my jock either. I mean other than you and Precious, I don't hang out with nobody."

He continued, "I spoke to a Financial Advisor early on in my career and he set up all this trust and mutual fund shit so I am covered financially after football. I want to do something good for the 'hood and for the schools. I want to do something that will have a long-lasting impact, even after I am gone."

Abel smiled, "That's impressive man."

Xerxes said, "When I came into the league, the NFL matched players up with financial advisors. It wasn't good PR for NFL players to be broke soon after they retired. Back in the day, lots of old players used to have to hock their Super Bowl rings and shit to survive. They would end up having to do all kinds of bullshit to make money -- stupid ass TV commercials, personal appearances and lame ass endorsements for shit they didn't like. The NFL set up this program hoping to help brothers not go broke."

He added, "Most of these motherfuckers never had no real money before football and when they finally got some a lot of them went crazy. They told us shit like we make a lot of money, but it ain't enough for us, Mamma, Daddy, your cousins, your baby mommas and all the homeboys in the 'hood. We can't be drivin' Bentleys, Benzes, BMWs and all that other bullshit either. They said we had to learn that we could live like we were professional athletes and have a plan for after we stopped playing."

Xerxes said, "What stood out for me most was when they said most players don't have a career of more than maybe five to ten years if we're lucky. They told us they could help us put together a plan to stretch our playing money to last 40 or 50 years after we stop playing."

Xerxes said, "I already knew that shit, right, but hearing it the way they said it and with real life examples of former players made it seem more real. Other than buying my folks a house and looking out for fam, the only thing I have splurged on is my camp and my ride. I should have a good base after retirement. My coins should last a long time and keep me comfortable. Now that fam is good and I am taken care of, I want to do something for the community."

Abel said, "That's what's up man. What you got in mind?" Xerxes told Abel that he wasn't sure yet but knew he wanted to make a difference. Abel confessed, "I have a similar goal. I built this business so I wouldn't have to work for anyone else and now that it is moving along on inertia, I can focus on my legacy as well. I wanted to build a building and put my name on it or something like that, but all that does is stroke my ego." Abel continued, "Maybe I can do something else that has a bigger impact on our people instead."

Xerxes said, "This is some of what I was hoping to do with Precious man. I am not mad that she is pursuing her dream in DC. But I had hoped that we could build this legacy together."

Abel said, "I know man, I had hoped to get her input into what I was developing too."

They both realized how much a part of their lives she was and laughed. Abel said, "OK, let's work on a plan and see what she thinks about it."

Xerxes said, "Cool, I like that."

Xerxes stared blankly ahead for a moment and slowly turned and looked directly and sternly at Abel and asked, "So what are we doing man?"

Abel matched his gaze but looked perplexed and asked, "What do you mean what are we doing?"

Xerxes said, "Don't get new on me." He continued, "Lately we've been spending all this time together." "What the fuck are we doing?"

Abel replied, "I thought we were working out and getting to know each other. I like hanging with you." He looked directly into Xerxes' eyes and asked, "What do you want us to be doing?"

Xerxes replied, "I have only been this close to two people in my life. Precious and you. Precious has made a decision about what she wants the next phase of her life to be. While her decision ain't what I thought it would be and we may not end up as a couple like I thought, I have finally come to terms with the fact that she and I will always be best friends and that may have to be enough."

Xerxes continued, "And you know I have been trying my damnedest to find another bitch to take her place and had zero luck with that. I refuse to spend the rest of my life fucking somebody new every other week. I don't want to be the Wilt Chamberlain of football. I loved Precious because she knew me and loved me before the money came. I don't know if I will ever be able to find or trust that anyone would want me for anything else but the money." He whispered, "I also don't want to spend the rest of my days alone."

Abel responded, "That's funny man. I'm dealing with the same shit in my lifestyle. I can't trust that anyone would ever want me for just me." Abel said, "Hell, the motherfucker that I have been kicking it with for the past few months is only with me because of what I can do for him financially. He probably thinks that I don't know or that I'm just stupid. Shit, he probably thinks I am mesmerized by the dick!! It's good dick, but I ain't dick-matyzed!! I ain't never found no one I can trust or who wanted me for just me and I had gotten used to the idea that I would never find a partner."

Xerxes whispered, "I know what you're talking about A. I know exactly what you mean."

Xerxes and Abel spent more and more time together outside of their workout sessions. They discovered a mutual affinity for Sci-Fi and Action movies and met once a week to catch the latest releases. They were both foodies and sought new restaurants that they explored together. Abel learned to appreciate Xerxes' love of shopping because he could stealthily but lustily enjoy watching him try on clothes during their shopping forays. He even accepted Xerxes' invitation to join him and several teammates at a local night club during the Bears' bye week. They both laughed when, as Xerxes predicted, Abel attracted his share of the "good looking honeys". Their comity was growing organically so they mutually agreed to abstain from sex or intimacy because they didn't want concupiscence to taint their budding friendship. Secretly, however, they both found it increasingly difficult to resist the attraction growing between them.

Xerxes told Abel about his childhood and how he became a football player. He talked about his large family and how they often struggled financially. Both his parents worked but food was oftentimes a luxury they did not always enjoy. He was the middle child with three older siblings and two younger ones. Xerxes oldest brother was born while his parents were still in high school, so they quickly married. The other children came in rapid succession so his parents were unable to extend their education beyond high school.

Xerxes' older brothers and sister followed their parents example and married young and sired families as adolescents. None of them graduated high school because unexpected pregnancies forced them to drop out and care for their own lives and families. He saw up close and personal how their lack of education and premature parenthood vanquished their dreams and supplanted them with struggle and challenges. Like his parents, they accepted jobs beneath their capabilities and struggled to provide for their burgeoning families. He vowed he would not replicate their disheartening destinies.

Xerxes experienced a monumental growth spurt in middle school and discovered an affinity for athletics. He played several sports including basketball and track, but was best at football and earned an athletic scholarship to the University of Michigan. He was the first person in his family to go to college and started a tradition that was followed by his younger siblings, his nieces and nephews.

Xerxes beamed when he described how he used a portion of his first round draft pick signing bonus to build brand-new homes for his family. He teared up when he told Abel he paid college tuitions for his younger brother and sister and for his older siblings' children as well. He held up his massive hands and told Abel that he used them to completely change the trajectory of his life and the lives of his family and he wanted to do the same for other families.

Abel opened up and told Xerxes about his childhood beyond his experiences with Ira. He told him about his only sister and the fact that they were estranged. Abel said that she devoted all of her time and energy to her marriage and her family which left little time for him and their parents. He described how un-attached and distant she was and that she only returned home for funerals or family weddings.

Abel told Xerxes about his father who died from a heart attack when he was a teenager and his Mom, who met and married a new man. He told him he respected his stepfather because he cared for and treated his Mom so well but, that he didn't go out of his way to be overly affectionate. He talked about his lone adult nephew who lived on the west coast and how they were developing a closer relationship since he had become an adult and moved out on his own. Abel smiled when he talked about trips and visits he had shared with his nephew. He told Xerxes he wanted to treat his nephew to a Bears' game on his next visit to town and asked if he could arrange it. Xerxes assured

him that he could. Xerxes liked the fact that Abel felt com-fortable opening up to him and was beginning to rely on him a lot. When Xerxes got down himself or complained when he struggled in a game, Abel would not let him wallow in self-pity but would tell him to work harder. Xerxes liked the fact that, like Precious, Abel could be brutally honest and not pull any punches.

Xerxes was becoming Abel's best cheerleader and he liked that. If Abel expressed any uncertainty in a potential business deci-sion, Xerxes would help him weigh the pros and cons. He would ask Abel what he thought Precious would recommend that he do in that situation. Abel would share expansion plans, self-esteem concerns and other insecurities with Xerxes. He was pleasantly surprised at Xerxes' business acumen and ability to see a situation from several different perspectives.

Xerxes liked the fact that he had someone that he could hang out with and talk to. Abel was really helping him move beyond Precious' move to DC and Xerxes appreciated it. They were becoming best friends and enjoyed the relationship they were developing.

14

Abel didn't want to damage his relationship with Precious as she was gaining status and power in Washington and he didn't want to destroy the budding friendship he was developing with Xerxes. He couldn't expunge the memory of their amourous encounter from his mind and regretted that he was unable to resist Xerxes' animalistic allure.

He was attracted to Xerxes like an addict who is seduced by a crack pipe but was disheartened because he allowed himself to succumb to his enticements so easily. He still had the image of Xerxes' perfect nude body in his mind and it was as clear as if he was standing directly in front of him. Abel knew, as he suspected so did Xerxes, that their encounter was more than a one-time, weed-induced quickie. He smiled slyly as the details of their indiscretion replayed in his mind and he remembered how good it was. Xerxes made him feel much better than Cyrus ever did and he reveled in it.

Xerxes' question about what they were doing danced in Abel's mind. He knew what he wanted to happen between the two of them and decided it was time to get clarity on whether Xerxes had similar desires. He sent Xerxes a text to see when they could talk.

    Abel: Morning man!! HYD?

Abel lay in bed thinking about Xerxes while he awaited a response and finally admitted to himself that he was falling in

love. He tried hard not to capitulate to his emotions but realized he was quickly losing the battle. He found it more difficult
to maintain his composure whenever he was around Xerxes and
decided he needed to find out if Xerxes could possibly feel the
same way about him. If Xerxes didn't reciprocate Abel's feelings, he needed to know so he could pump his brakes and rein
in his emotions. If they needed to revert back to the friendship
they enjoyed before having sex, Abel needed to find out right
away. He was falling too deeply too quickly and had to find out
where they stood before he was too far gone. Abel felt a growing sexual tension whenever he was around Xerxes and needed
to control himself before doing or saying anything to alienate
him and prevent them from remaining friends.

Abel had not spoken with Precious in a while because her
congressional and television appearance schedule was always
booked. He had also been distant with her because he was
ashamed and embarassed about his encounter with Xerxes and
was sure that she would be able to osmose his guilt when they
spoke. He decided to contact her anyway and sent a quick text.

Abel: Morning Madam President, how is DC?

Precious: Boo!! In a meeting. Let me get back 2 U.

He had never closed the loop with Cyrus after their last call
when he berated him. After reading Precious' reply, he sent a
message to Cyrus.

Abel: What's up sexy Daddy!?!" "HYD?

He struck out with Cyrus as well and did not get a response.

Abel was unlucky with Xerxes, Precious and Cyrus so he
decided to get out of bed and get ready for work. He arose and
walked into his bathroom and turned on the shower and the
steam. He thought a long, hot luxurious steam shower would
be a refreshing and energizing way to start his day. He stepped

into the steaming deluge and let the water and vapor wash all over him. The soothing stream of water and hot mists of steam enveloped him and he stood motionless under the rainfall showerhead for several minutes basking in the warmth. He finally grabbed the container of shaving gel and lathered his head to begin his shave. He heard Cyrus' ring tone on his phone from the bedroom just as he completed his first razor stroke. He thought about bolting from the shower to take the call but opted to complete his shave and luxuriate in the shower. He let the call go to voice mail and planned to respond to it once he completed his ablutions.

Abel caressed his smooth head to assess the quality of his shave and was content that his dome was as clean and smooth as a baby's bottom. He liberally applied body wash all over his naked frame and commenced his shower. He loved warm showers and took extra care this morning to perform a thorough job. He lingered under the warm cascading waters for a long time as his thoughts replayed every detail of his post-game nocturnal visit to see Xerxes. He remembered Xerxes' smell and could still taste his essence on his tongue. His body reimagined the pain and pleasure of Xerxes penetrating him and felt as if it was happening all over again. He relived the heat and passion of Xerxes moving inside him and craved to experience those feelings again and again. He was aroused, his nipples stiffened and he developed a steel-like erection. The steady stream of water felt like a liquid massage and he thought about pleasuring himself to satisfaction before getting out of the shower and heading to work. He knew if he fantasized about Xerxes any longer he wouldn't be able to control himself. He decided against it and switched the shower valve from hot to cold and allowed the burst of frigid liquid to expel his sensuous imaginings. The coldness of the water dismissed the memory of Abel's muscular paramour from his mind and he finished his shower so that he could begin his day.

Abel got out of the shower and grabbed his phone to retrieve Cyrus' message. He was surprised because the excitement and arousal that he normally felt when anticipating a message from Cyrus was missing. He also realized that he was disappointed because the message was from Cyrus and not Xerxes.

Cyrus' message began to play and Abel was aghast. In a belligerent tone, Cyrus said, "Where in the fuck have you been!?! I've been trying to call your punk ass for a while and you can't call my ass back!! Fuck you, you bitch ass muthafucka!!! You ain't never got to call me back ever!!! And don't never try to see me no more either! You ain't never going to get none of this dick again either!!"

Abel wondered what he had done to have his day start so badly. Xerxes hadn't replied yet. Precious was too busy for him and Cyrus had completely reproached him. He hoped that the start of his day was not an omen for how the rest of his day would go.

He finished dressing and walked out the door just as his phone rang. He gasped when he noticed Xerxes' name appear on his Caller ID. He needed to compose himself before hearing Xerxes' voice so he let the phone ring a few times. Just as the call was about to go to voice mail, he answered and heard Xerxes say, "Hey, what's up sexy? I just got your text and decided to call instead of texting you back. I'm glad you called because I wanted to spit about what happened the other night at my camp, if that's cool with you."

Abel said, "Sure man. Who should go first?"

Xerxes said, "Let me go first. First off, nothing happened that I didn't want to happen. It is not your fault and you did not do anything to cause it. I hope that it does not impact how we get down. I guess I had always been curious about that and I'm glad that my first time was with you. I can't blame it on me being high or Precious not being here with me, or anything else. I just want us to be cool man."

Xerxes continued, "I am going to tell you something." He went on, "The only other person who knew I had ever done anything like that is dead." He commanded, "You can't mention this to anyone, not even Precious!" Xerxes asked, "You cool with that?"

Abel replied, "Sure man, what is it?"

Xerxes told Abel he had an uncle that came to stay with his family when he was fourteen years old. His uncle had been in the military and came home for a short stint before moving out west to finish his enlistment. Xerxes told him that he and his uncle shared a bedroom because the house was not large enough for him to have his own space. He joked that his growth spurt made him too big to sleep in the bunk beds with his younger siblings and he had finally graduated to having his own room. His younger siblings shared a room with bunk beds and his older brothers and sister were no longer in the house. Xerxes was excited to finally have privacy, but since there was nowhere else for his uncle to stay, he reluctantly accepted the company.

Xerxes and his uncle got along well and he told him about all of the places he visited and the experiences he had while in the service. He told him about all of the exotic places he visited when he was on leave and made them all seem exciting and fascinating. He told Xerxes about his military assignments and what he got to do while in the service as well. They would stay up late into the night, well beyond the time that anyone else in the house was awake, talking. His uncle's experiences captivated Xerxes and he grew to like and trust him.

He told Abel that he once woke up in the middle of the night in a panic because his underwear was wet. He knew that he had not wet the bed but was not sure what was causing the moistness. He wanted to tell his parents but his uncle heard him stirring and woke up and asked what was going on. Xerxes was embarrassed but because he trusted his uncle and they talked about everything else, he told him what happened. Xerxes remembered how ashamed and perplexed he was when his uncle roared with laughter. His uncle composed himself and told Xerxes that he was OK and everything was going to be alright. He told Xerxes that he was becoming a man and what he experienced was a wet dream. Xerxes had never heard those words before.

His uncle explained that Xerxes' body was beginning to produce the fluids that would allow him to become a father. They stayed up until the early morning and his uncle told him all about the birds and the bees. He answered every question that Xerxes had and told him the next time he felt the moistness emerging to wake him up and let him know. His uncle promised to do whatever he could to help him get through it. Xerxes was relieved and thanked his uncle and went back to sleep.

He felt the wetness burgeoning a few nights later and woke his uncle as he was instructed. His disoriented uncle awoke and asked Xerxes what was going on. Xerxes confessed that he was having the "wet dream" and needed his uncle to help him with it like he promised. His uncle calmed him and asked him to show him what he was talking about. Xerxes pulled down his briefs to display his rock hard, bulging erection. Xerxes uncle admired his nephews bigness and told him, "You are going to make a lot of little girls really happy with that. You are bigger than me already and you're still growing." Xerxes did not understand what his uncle was saying and asked, "So how are you going to help me?" He added, "I'm scared!!"

Xerxes decribed how his uncle gently placed his mouth on him and began to suck his dick. He remembered the warmth and moistness of his uncle's throat and the titillation of his tongue as it fondled his phallas. It gratified him and did not take long before he flooded his uncle's mouth with semen. Xerxes described how much his uncle enjoyed this taste of his juices and after his erection subsided he went back to bed.

Xerxes said that after the first time, whenever he had a wet dream his uncle would service him and he looked forward to and enjoyed their secret liaisons for the entire time he stayed with his family. Before moving to the west coast, his uncle admonished him never to tell anyone what they had done. He confessed to Abel that he learned that his uncle had been killed in a car accident on the eve of his disastrous performance in the Lions game and the night before they hooked up.

Xerxes admitted that he had been thinking about his uncle all day long and couldn't concentrate in the Lions' game and performed so badly. He told Abel that when he came by to console him that night, he was thinking about his adolescent relationship with his uncle, what Abel told him about his experiences with Ira and Precious being in DC. He confessed he was feeling sorry for himself and wanted to find a way to feel better. His mind only allowed him to remember how good his uncle made him feel and how much Abel said he enjoyed servicing Ira. He naively concluded that if they hooked up, they could both feel better together.

Abel replied, "Wow man, sorry about your uncle, but thanks for telling me about him." Abel added, "I honestly have to tell you that I could have said no or pushed back but what we did together was something that I wanted to happen too. I wanted it to happen from the first time I met you but never thought it actually would ever happen because I would never do anything to hurt Precious. I would be lying if I said that I had not ever thought about it." Abel went on, "I also have to say it was as better than I imagined it would be too." Abel realized that he might have crossed a line and said, "Damn, man, I'm sorry about that last comment."

Xerxes laughed and said, "It's cool man. It was damn good to me too. I like hanging with you and working out with you and don't want that bullshit affecting us."

Abel said, "Man, you don't know how glad I am you told me that. I was starting to feel funny being around you and didn't want you to be feeling the same way about me."

Xerxes asked, "Funny!?! Funny how!?!"

Abel was embarrassed and said, "Don't worry about it. I'm just glad you let me know what was up. He had gotten his answer on whether Xerxes was feeling the same way that he was and was disheartened to learn that he was not. He asked, "So can we put this behind us and act like it never happened?"

Xerxes responded, "I'd like that man, but make sure you don't try and take advantage of me anytime in the future." He couldn't even finish the statement before he broke out into a loud, roaring laugh.

Abel hesitated for a moment and laughed as well. He felt much better now that he and Xerxes had cleared the air. It took his mind off of the call that he had received from Cyrus.

Xerxes asked, "So now that we got the bullshit out of the way, when do you want to hang out again?"

Abel replied, "Let me get to my office and check my calendar. I'll send you a text."

Xerxes said, "Cool man." "I'm glad to have you as a friend."

Abel said, "I am too. "Let me holla back at you later." "Have a good day."

Xerxes replied, "You have a better one."

15

Why is it that when something eludes you, you always seem to want it so much more? The one thing that was missing in Xerxes' life is what he coveted the most. While he felt that Precious deserved all of the success she was working so hard to attain, he hated the fact that he also sensed that every accomplishment she achieved forced him further into obscurity in her life. Her move into politics had become a wedge between the two of them and he was powerless to do anything about it.

Abel told Xerxes that the best time to try to connect with Precious was normally very early in the morning before she left for work or late in the evening. She and her staff were often so busy working to manipulate the wheels of our democracy that they regularly and frequently shared dinners together. More often than not by the time she was finally free from her day and ready to settle in for the evening, he was already well into his slumber needing the rest and recovery that sleep offered him to use in practice the next morning. Weekends might offer her a few more moments of free time but he was usually consumed with preparations for an upcoming game.

Her work was important and he knew it but it did not make him feel any better about the two of them. As much as he wanted her to succeed in this new phase of her life, it was exactly what was keeping them apart. He had become the jealous lover to her new suitor.......her job.

She had been his lover as well as his best friend but he wondered if he could actually talk to her about the new feelings that were invading his life. He needed to tell her about what he was experiencing but wondered if she would still want to be his friend once he allowed her into his new world. Would she even still want to be in his life once she knew? He needed to talk directly to her and couldn't use Abel as his go between for this conversation. He took a chance and sent her a text hoping she would be available to chat.

Xerxes: Hey P? Need to talk. U got a minute?

Precious got the message and decided to call him back instead of replying to his text. He picked up his phone and before he could greet her she said, "Hey Baby, how you doing? It's been a while. I miss you!!! What's up!?!"

He was surprised that she was actually available and was caught off guard by her call. He replied, "Hey Bae. I wasn't expecting you to get back to me so soon. Yeah, it has been a minute. It's good to hear your voice too. I got some shit we need to talk about. You got a few minutes?"

"Yeah Z, that's why I called. I'm free for you."

"Thanks baby. So, how are you really doing? How is DC treating you?"

"Honestly, I feel like my life is not my own anymore but I also feel like this is exactly what I am supposed to be doing right now. It's busier and faster paced than I thought. But, I'm really loving it and I think I am making a difference. So, how are you? How is your season going?"

He was disappointed that she was oblivious to the fact that he was having a breakout season and was on track to receive a nomination for an MVP award. He mused that normally she would know his statistics better than he did but hid his disappointment and replied, "I'm doing good this year baby. Real good."

"That's great baby, but what's up? You sound like you just got some bad news or something." He didn't respond. She implored, "Tell me. Is it something with the Bears? Something else? Hell, you know you can tell me anything, right?"

"Yeah, I know."

"Alright then, what's up? Come on Z. What is it?

"OK, I'll tell you. Just let me talk and don't interrupt. And promise me you won't get mad at Abel either, OK!?"

"Why would I ever get mad at Abel? What did he do?"

"He didn't do shit. I did it all. See, what had happened was Abel came by my house after my game with the Lions. I had a lot of shit on my mind and it was one of my worst games ever. Anyway, I was down in my feelings because of the game. I was down because I had got some bad news and I couldn't talk to you."

"So you're blaming me!? What happened? What was the bad news?"

"Remember when I said don't talk."

"Oh, yeah. Ok, I'm sorry. Go ahead."

"I wasn't blaming you but I needed someone to talk to and couldn't reach you. And when I couldn't get you it just fucked me up even more. Anyway, remember my uncle that came and stayed with my family when I was a kid?"

"Yeah, now that you mention him, I think so."

"Well I found out he got killed in a car accident."

"Oh, Baby!! I'm so sorry."

"Thanks. Anyway, after I found out it bothered me all day long and I ended up really fucking up in the game. I broke my yards receiving streak and lost over $200K in bonus money."

"Damn Z!! $200K. For real!?!"

"Yeah, well Abel watched the game and called me after it was over to see how I was doing. He knew I had a bad game and offered to come by and check on me and to cheer me up and.....Well I was really feeling sorry for myself about the game and my uncle and went home and smoked a blunt and drank a shitload of jack and coke and...."

"You know you never could hold your liquor."

"Right, but I didn't care about that."

"Well anyway, Abel came over and I asked him if he wanted a drink and to smoke with me."

"He can't handle his liquor either. What happened Z?"

"Well we smoked and drank and one thing led to another and...and....and we ended up hooking up and..........and I liked it. I liked that shit a lot. Damn P, I think I like him a lot!! Hell, I think I'm falling in love with him."

Precious was totally silent and didn't make a sound for a long time. She always knew that the distance that she created in their relationship could force Xerxes to find companionship with someone else. She never expected that the someone might end up being her best friend.

Xerxes wasn't sure if she was still on the line or if they had been disconnected. He asked, "P. Precious are you there?"

"Yes, baby, I'm here."

"So what do you think!?? Do you hate me? What's up!? I would never want to hurt you or us, but I was down in my feelings and......."

"Z, Z baby, it's fine. It's fine......"

"Fine!? You're not upset!? You must be about to tell me you got a new man or something. Hell!! Yell at me!! Curse me out!! Call me an asshole or a motherfucker!!Scream at me!! Do something!! Say something!!"

"I'm not gonna do any of that baby. I don't have anything to say either but I love you"

"You love me!!! After what I just told you!? Don't you have any questions? Want to know if I'm DL? Anything?"

Precious said, "I will always love you boo!!! Always!! And I don't have any questions. "

"Aren't you shocked or at least surprised?"

"I'm not surprised that you ended up with somebody else. I made this bed and I have to sleep in it, but I am shocked that you got with Abel. Honestly, I am relieved about that."

"Relieved!!! How!?! Why??"

"Yes I'm relieved. First, Abel is such a good man. I can understand why you might fall in love with him. Hell, I love him too. Second, I think y'all will be good together. Y'all are a really good match. Third, I'm gonna tell you why it didn't surprise me. I'm gonna tell you something that you probably don't know that I know."

"Oh shit, What!?"

"I already know the whole thing about you and your uncle."

"M-m-my uncle!?!? You know!?! How do you know about that!?"

"You talk in your sleep at least you used to talk in your sleep."

"T-t-talk in my sleep...."

"Yes. Especially after I gave you some of this good lovin'.'"

"Fuck you P!!"

"Hmmm. Funny, it sounds like that isn't really something you want to do anymore."

"You got jokes.............."

"Anyway, normally after we did our thing, you would usually fall asleep and after about fifteen minutes or so you just started talking."

"What did I say?"

"Well you usually talked about the same thing. You talked about how you grew so big you couldn't fit in the bunk beds with your baby brothers and sister and you finally got to have a room of your own. You talked about how excited you were because you finally had some privacy and how mad you were when you found out your uncle was coming to stay with y'all when he got out of the service."

"Damn!!! I didn't think nobody knew about that. I didn't even tell my folks. What else did I say?"

"You sounded excited when you described how your uncle told you about his job in the service and all the places he got to go. Then you sounded serious when you talked about how you woke up one night and your underwear was wet."

"Shit!!!"

"You were in a panic and wanted to run and tell your folks but your uncle calmed you down and told you you were having a wet dream. You described how he told you all about sex and what was happening to your body."

"Fuck, you know about all that too?"

"Yes, baby. He told you you were becoming a man and what that all meant. Then you started breathing really hard when you described how he relieved your tension by swallowing that nightstick."

"Nightstick!?"

"Yea, you know what I'm talking about. Anyway, after that first time and everytime you had a wet dream, he took care you and y'all kept it up until he moved out west."

"Damn. I said all that!?"

"Yeah."

"So what happened after I finished with the story."

"Well, like the typical man you fell sound asleep and snored all night long keeping me awake. It was like you couldn't doze off until you got that story out of your system and once you did, you could sleep straight through the night."

"When did I first start talking in my sleep and why did you never tell me!?!"

"The first time I knew about was the night I told you I got into Law School."

"That was the first time we ever..."

"Yeah, that was the night I first met and became acquainted with that nightstick!!'

"So why didn't you ever say anything?"

"Honestly, because I had forgot about it until you just told me about Abel and reminded me about your uncle. I had usually forgotten about it the next morning when we were together and you didn't say nothing so neither did I."

"So you really aren't upset or mad?"

"First of all, why did you think it would matter to me? If I didn't get mad when I heard about you and all of them extraneous bitches at Michigan...."

"Damn, you knew about them too!?!!?"

"Come on Z. You weren't the only one from Roosevelt at Michigan and you know them nosy, shit-talking bitches couldn't wait to tell me about everything you did."

"Damn, P. For real!! I'm so sorry."

"Baby, there is no need to be sorry. I have known you since the day before forever. I ain't going nowhere."

"But, I mean, I got with a dude!!! And he's your best friend besides me. Don't you think that is really fucked up!!"

"Baby!! Baby. I'm not mad. I made my decision about politics. I knew what could have happened. But I also knew that no matter what happened, I would always, always, always be a part of your life and you would always be a part of mine."

"You promise?"

"Yes, Daddy. I'm glad that if you and I couldn't make it together at least you might be able to make it with Abel. He is a good man and needs somebody like you. Don't hurt him."

"I won't."

"No for real Z!! Promise me you won't hurt him. He's been through a lot."

"I promise I won't hurt him. You know I still love you right?"

"Yes Baby, I know."

"You are the absolute best."

"Thanks for that Z. Bye baby. Love you too."

Xerxes was relieved. He had told Precious about the monumental changes that he was going through and was reassured because she still loved him and still wanted to be a part of his life. With Precious' blessing he was free to move into his new lifestyle with Abel and couldn't stop thinking about him. He had told Abel about his uncle and their relationship when he was a teenager. He didn't think anyone else knew about that until he talked to Precious. He knew Abel had to be special if he was comfortable sharing his most private secrets and innermost thoughts.

He was free to fully explore and experience the special attraction that he was developing for Abel. He was excited but also apprehensive because he had never tried to have a relationship with another man. He enjoyed their lone sexual encounter much more than he expected and knew that he wanted more. He was not promiscuous and knew that Abel was not either. He was determined not to run through a lot of sexual partners because he remembered how unfulfilling and unsatisfying those days of depravity and amorality were back in college. He did not want to go back to that lifestyle and wanted his life to be settled. He decided that since he wasn't going to be with Precious he needed to find out if he could be with Abel. He was determined to find out if a relationship was possible and wanted to know if Abel was open to it as well and sent him a text.

Xerxes: What up? Thinkin abt u. Wanna see you!!

He was apprehensive about the new world that he was stepping into and hoped that Abel would be a willing and receptive cicerone. He had vast experience pursuing women and was a master at all of the tricks he needed to employ to get any one he wanted. He was a neophyte in wooing a man and was ignorant about how to proceed. When he texted a female, almost any female, she would be ready, willing and waiting to do whatever he asked. He wasn't being vain or arrogant, too many women had been too compliant with his wanton desires before in his life. He was scared and afraid because he didn't know how to woo Abel and had no idea if he would even want to accompany him on his new life journey.

Xerxes was coming to terms with the tectonic shifts taking place in his life. He hoped Abel had similar desires and feelings and wanted to have a candid and honest conversation about their possible next steps together.

Abel was caught off guard when he read Xerxes' text admitting he was thinking about him. He had been focusing on being "just boys" again and worked hard to control his emotions. He still wanted a relationship, if one was possible, but consigned himself to cherish and protect their friendship if that was all that was available.

He anxiously replied.

Abel: We can hang. When? What you got in mind?

Xerxes: Sat 8 PM. I'll send a ride. Be casual.

Abel: Casual!? Wasn't gonna wear a tie and tails.

Xerxes: U got jokes. B comfortable. C U Saturday.

Abel: Cool. Looking forward to it.

Xerxes: Me 2. TTYL.

Xerxes smiled because the date and time for his first official date with Abel was set but he was nervous because he still needed to figure out what he wanted them to do. He thought about a movie or a sporting event but neither option was suitable for the type of conversation he hoped they would have. He thought about an intimate dinner at one of his favorite restaurants but didn't want the constant interruptions from fans or autograph seekers that always occurred when he appeared in public. He wanted a quiet place where he and Abel could concentrate on each other and finally decided a meal prepared and served at his place would offer the optimum amount of privacy.

Saturday morning arrived and Xerxes stopped by Mr. Sam's Cutz to see if Oscar could hook him up. The shop was filled with its regular collection of weekend characters and several patrons were engaged in a rousing game of spades. Xerxes told Oscar he was having dinner with someone special and wanted to look as good as he could. Oscar assumed that he was dining with Precious and said, "How is your girl? Tell Precious I said hello."

"I will"

"Tell her she's doing some good work in DC and we all appreciate it."

Mr. Sam chimed in, "Yeah Xerxes, tell your girl that Expungement Summit that she put on a while back was some really good shit."

Kwame added, "Yeah Man, that summit allowed me to finally get my record cleaned up. That and help from Mr. Sam. Now, maybe you can hook me up and get me a tryout with the Bears?"

Xerxes replied, "I don't want you to be trying to take my spot but I'll see what I can do."

Kwame laughed and replied, "Nah man, you're good."

Mr. Sam added, "My next door neighbor's niece got her record cleaned up at that summit too and she's opening a beauty parlor and nail shop down the street." He continued, "Some of us are going down after we close today to help her clean up so the contractors can get in."

Signifying Ray said, "Oooh, weee!! Imagine all the new loose pussy that's gonna be walking up and down the street when that shop opens."

June Bug shocked everyone in the shop when he chided Ray saying, "Loose pussy or tight, your old ass wouldn't know what to do with the pussy if it had your name on it!!" The shop roared with laughter. June Bug added, "Xerxes, I got my shit cleaned up at that summit too and I'm back in school taking night classes. Tell your girl I said thanks."

Xerxes complimented him, "Good man!! Good. Thanks. I will."

Oscar whispered to Xerxes, "She may not know it, but she is changing lives and changing this neighborhood. Tell her we all appreciate her."

Xerxes thanked everyone for their compliments and assured them all he would pass their good wishes on to Precious. He decided it made no sense to explain the changes in his relationship with Precious or announce the changes in his lifestyle. Oscar finished his shave. Xerxes got up from the chair and paid him and made sure to include a substantial tip. He bolted from the shop and grabbed a bottle of champagne on his way home hoping he and Abel would have something to celebrate.

Xerxes was nervous about his rendevous with Abel. He donned a pair of loose fitting, khaki-colored linen slacks and matched them with a light tan loose-fitting linen shirt. He wanted to be comfortable and hoped that everything about his impending conversation with Abel would be the same. He arranged for the cook to prepare a Caribbean inspired fish dish with a kale and fruit salad. He requested that she make Jamaican patties made of turkey instead of beef and he wanted her to add cal-loloo to the menu as well. He also asked if she could make a Jamaican Rum cake for dessert. He made virgin, Caribbean rum punch with fresh mangoes to accompany the island cuisine. He wanted the meal to light, fun and tasty and hoped the broad range of menu options and the effort he put into planning and executing their first date would impress Abel.

The driver that Xerxes sent to pick Abel up rang his doorbell promptly at 6:45 PM. He planned for Abel to arrive at his place right at 7:00 PM. The driver delivered Abel on time and as scheduled he rang the doorbell promptly at 7 PM. Xerxes greeted Abel at the door and welcomed him with a long, lingering embrace. Abel was in awe because he was not used to anyone expending so much effort on his behalf and was impressed by Xerxes' preparation and attention to detail. He told Xerxes, "What's up Big Sexy!! Thanks for the car and everything man. This evening has already been more than I expected."

Xerxes replied, "I just like to do special things for special people. Come on in and get comfortable. Don't make fun of my slave feet, but take off your shoes and get comfortable if you want. Can I get you something to drink?"

Abel joked, "Slave feet, right. Something light would be cool."

Xerxes said, "I got beer, wine, soda, juice, sparkling and bottled water and anything stronger you might want." Xerxes also said, "Oh, and I got a virgin Caribbean rum punch, if you think you are man enough to handle it."

Abel said, "I'm man enough dog. Give me a rum punch."

Xerxes gave Abel a half glass of virgin rum punch and joked, "It will put hair on your chest. I hope you can handle it."

Abel grabbed the rum punch and sipped it and told Xerxes it was good.

Xerxes described the menu for the evening and told Abel that he hoped that he was hungry.

Abel said, "Yeah man, I can eat."

He led Abel to the round table on his patio and motioned for the cook to serve the kale and fruit salad appetizer. The cook complied and also brought a plate with the turkey patties to go with the salads. Abel sampled the patties and the salad and raved about how good they were saying, "This turkey patty is hitting the spot and the salad is the bomb!! The kale mixes perfectly with the fruit. I love the taste it leaves in my mouth."

Xerxes winked and said, "I know something else you like in your mouth too." They both laughed. He apologized, "I'm sorry man. I want to be serious tonight."

Abel replied, "No worries man. I'm cool."

Xerxes asked Abel if he needed or wanted anything else.

Abel said, "No man, I'm good."

Xerxes thanked the cook, told her he would let her know when to serve the entree and excused her. Once they were alone, he told Abel, "I wanted to have this dinner so we could talk about this situation we are in."

Abel replied, "I didn't know we were in a situation man. You make it sound so serious."

Xerxes replied, "I am serious man. I'm not trying to be out here twisting in the fucking wind. Once I make up my mind about something, or someone, I like to act on it."

Abel asked, "So what did you make up your mind about?"

Xerxes said, "I talked to Precious. I told her what happened between us....."

Abel interruped, "What!?! You promised. Damn, does she hate me now!?!?"

Xerxes stopped him, "No man, she's cool with you and me. She told me something about me that I didn't even know she knew. She told me I used to talk in my sleep and she already knew about me and my uncle and when I told her I had got with you she wasn't surprised. Her feelings and your feelings were all I cared about. After I told her she said she was good. She said that if I couldn't be with her, she would be glad if I was with you. I wanted to talk to you to see how you felt." Xerxes continued, "I mean, I don't even know if you're seeing someone or if you have been seeing someone or whether you want to be with anyone, but I needed to let you know how I feel."

Abel said, "And how do you feel?"

Xerxes said, "Fuck man!! I'm smelling you. I like you. Shit, I like how we fit together. I like how my dick feels inside you. But more important than the sex bullshit, I can't get you out of mind. I think about your ass all the time. I want to see what we can do together. I want to see what we can do as a team, as a couple." He went on, "Hell, I don't even know if you would even consider being with a motherfucker like me, but I know I want to be with you!!"

Abel sat back from the table and took a deep breath, "Wow, man!!! I enjoyed being with you too. I enjoyed the friendship we were developing. I never let myself think that it could be anything more than what it was." He said, "You're a NFL super-fucking-star. You can have anybody you want. I never thought you would want me." Abel continued, "I have been wanting a relationship. A monogamous relationship, but didn't think I was ever going to find anyone." He added, "And certainly not with someone like you." Abel continued, "You are the perfect specimen. You are the kind of dude I have always dreamed about being with. But, why me?" he asked.

Xerxes said, "To be honest, a lot of it is what Precious told me about you. A lot of it is what I have gotten to know about you for myself since we been hanging out." He continued, "You ain't bringing a lot of shit with you that I know of. You have a fucking life plan and you're making that shit work. You are committed to what you put your mind to. Hell, I love how your lips feel when they are on my dick. I love how you feel when I am inside you. Most importantly, though I think we can make one another better." Sounding frustrated Xerxes said, "Fuck man, I'm rambling like a bitch. I love you dog!! I just love you!!"

A single tear fell from Abel's right eye.

Xerxes reached over and touched his hand. He said, "What's wrong baby?"

Abel said, "Those are the words I have always wanted to hear from someone. Those are the words I was hoping to hear from you." He asked, "So how do we get this thing started? Where do we go from here?"

Xerxes said, "Let's figure that out together. It sounds like we are both game to see where this might go, right?"

Abel nodded his head.

Xerxes said, "Cool. I think we should first be open with one another about our pasts and any baggage or situations that might come up. Then we decide how we want to deal with any shit that comes up going forward. We try to spend as much time as we can stand together without smothering one another." Xerxes continued, "And we commit to having as much fun together as the law allows."

Abel smiled, "I could not have said that any better. So, do you want to go first talking about baggage or do you want me to?"

Xerxes said, "I can go first. Mine is easy. When I was in college, I fucked a lot of women that didn't matter and that didn't mean shit. They saw me as a potential meal ticket and I just wanted a nutt. I always used protection and never got caught up. The only woman that I was with that I cared about was Precious. She was and is the love of my life and will always be a part of my life. We talked about that when I told her about us. She is realizing her dream, and I'm not mad about it, and she wishes me, I mean us, well. Other than my uncle when I was a kid, I have never been with a dude other than you." Xerxes said, "Your turn."

Abel asked, "So how do you know you won't find another dude that you want to be with besides me."

Xerxes said, "I know the difference between sex and love. I have only felt love for two people, Precious and you. I'm done. I don't have to look any further."

Abel said, "Ok man. My situation is a bit more complicated." He continued, "I used to kick it with this young dude named Cyrus." He added, "I recently realized that he was nothing more than a warm body to lay next to when I was feeling lonely or down. I was using him to tune me up when I needed it and he was using me as a sponsor." He added, I used to think sex with him was the best sex that I would ever have....."

Xerxes interrupted, "Used to?"

Abel said, "Yeah, I met this pro football player nigga with a big Wakanda ass dick." He laughed, "We got together one time and he turned me the fuck out." Abel said, "I haven't thought about anybody else since I got with him."

Xerxes smiled knowingly.

Abel went on to explain how he and Cyrus met and hooked up and how their relationship progressed from there. He told him he how he got busy with work and was not able to connect with Cyrus for a long while and how he got really upset and cursed him out. Abel pulled out his cell phone and played Cyrus' last message for Xerxes. He told him he had decided to end the relationship and planned to do so whether he and Xerxes got together or not. Abel admitted that he actually thought they were done already. He confessed that he had not talked to Cyrus since receiving the voicemail message but told him that he had recently begun to receive text messages and calls from him again.

Xerxes asked, "So be honest A. Do you want to get back with this cat?"

Abel said, "No baby. I was with him because I didn't think I could do any better. Now I know I can do better, but he is someone that I have known and been intimate with. I can't just drop it."

Xerxes said, "Damn!! That's just like you. Shit, caring and concerned about some motherfucker that has treated you like shit. I will be there for you baby while you clear this situation up. Just know, that I want us to work on the Abel and Xerxes situation as soon as we can".

Abel replied, "That sounds good as fuck."

Xerxes asked, "What sounds good as fuck?"

Abel responded, "The Abel and Xerxes situation. Let's make that shit happen as fast as possible."

Xerxes said, "You hold all of the cards. As soon as you can kick Cyrus to the curb, then you can have all this."

He stood up and flexed his muscles and the bulge in his baggy slacks conveyed his arousal. Abel smiled and his eyes darted back and forth between the massive bulge in Xerxes' slacks and his eyes. He walked around the table to where Abel sat and motioned for him to stand. Abel rose from his chair as Xerxes unbuttoned his slacks and allowed them to drop to the floor. Abel kissed Xerxes' chest and licked his navel as he fell to his knees. Xerxes was fully erect and Abel welcomed his massiveness into his warm and welcome mouth.

They never got to the rest of the dinner.

16

Abel was in his office checking e-mail and approving expense reports when his phone range and "202-555-1234 US Congress" appeared on his Caller ID display. He got excited because he hoped it was Precious but needed to multitask so he pressed the speakerphone button to answer the call. He was about to greet her with a bon mot but was shocked when he heard, "Morning, you punk motherfucker!!! How the fuck are you?" He recognized Precious' voice, but had never heard such contempt in her voice before.

He responded hesitantly, "M-m-m-morning Precious? Is that you? How are you?"

She replied, "Fuck you!!! Don't ask me how the fuck I am!! You obviously don't give a fuck about how I am. The first time I introduced you to Xerxes, what did I tell you?

"W-W-what did you tell me?"

"Yes, Motherfucker!!! I told you not to take my man didn't I?" she bellowed.

"Y-Y-yes. Precious baby are you OK. I have never heard you talk like this. Are you high? What's wrong?"

"What's wrong?!? Bitch, you stole my man. That's what's wrong!!"

"I'm going to beat your ass in the street. Come on Cletus!!"

Abel wasn't sure what to do or say and was quiet for a long

while. The phone was silent and neither he nor Precious said a word. Precious began to giggle, silently at first, but after a few seconds, she laughed out loud. Abel, still tense and unsure of Precious' disposition, hesitated but followed suit and began to laugh as well.

Precious said, "I just wanted to call to let you know that I am not mad about what happened with Xerxes. We had a nice long talk about him and what y'all did. I'm happy for the two of y'all and glad he can be with someone that really cares about him." She went on, "Xerxes is a good man and deserves to be with a good person. Someone that he can trust and someone that will have his back." Precious asked, "Can you be that person for him, Abel? He really needs that."

Abel replied, "Yeah, I think I can be that for him."

Precious continued, "Xerxes told me about what y'all did and he assured me that it was all his fault. He said he didn't plan it and had no idea anything would happen when you came over to check on him. He said he had a lot going on. I had just won my election and was leaving to come to DC right away without us having a chance to have a long talk about us which rocked his world and he found out that his uncle died and he had a bad game against Detroit or Dallas or somebody. "

She went on, "I guess it all came down on him at the same time and he was feeling sorry for himself and needed someone bad. I wasn't there to help him but I am so glad you were. Thank you."

"What are you thanking me for?"

"For being a good and true friend. Me and Z finally had a long talk. The long talk that we probably should have had when I told him I was going into politics."

"What do you mean?"

"Well, I remember when I told him my plans. I did all of the talking and never let him tell me how my decision affected him and us. I apologized for that."

"I realized that these were my plans and not OUR plans. I didn't give him a chance to have any input. I apologized for that too. When he told me about y'all, we finally had the talk we should have had a long time ago."

"What happened?"

"We both realized that we love each other and while we might not be able to be together as a couple for the rest of our lives, we really wanted to be together as friends. I told him that being together at the end was most important."

Precious told Abel how she and Xerxes grew up as friends and why they became so close. She also told him she knew about his relationship with his uncle because Xerxes talks in his sleep. She said, "Even though Z is strong, athletic, muscular and definitely masculine, in some situations, he is a grown-up boy. He hasn't ever had a lot of friends or people he could trust in his life so if you are going to be in his life, he has to be able to trust you. You can't just think you are that person, you have to BE that person."

Abel responded, "I have been looking for someone that I could trust and love and be with for a long time, you know that. I have been with guys in the past that were with me because of things I had or things I could do for them. My Momma always told me 'You can only trust love when you have nothing to gain from it' and I ain't found nobody yet that didn't have something to gain from being with me. He is the only person that I think really loves me for me other than you. In a lot of ways, Xerxes and I have been looking for each other all of our lives. I'm ready to be everything he needs me to be." He asked, "So Miss Girl, how do you really feel? You and Xerxes have been together forever. Are you sure that you are cool with this? I don't want to gain a man and lose you. Losing you is not worth it."

Precious replied, "Thanks baby. I appreciate that. Honestly, I had always thought that me and Z would be together forever. We had never talked about marriage or anything traditional, but I knew that he would always be a part of my life. When I made the decision to run for public office, I knew what I was getting into. I couldn't ask anyone else to take this journey with me because to get to where I want to go, I need to be free to make decisions quickly. I knew that the choices I was making might impact my relationship with the only man I loved. But if I didn't make the right choices for me, I would resent him and resent myself somewhere down the line. Me and Z will always be friends. I know that like I know I need air to breathe. But there ain't a lot of men out there who would let me spread my wings to see if and how far I could fly. He is letting me do that."

Abel said, "That is something that I like about him too. As I have gotten to know him when we work out, he is confident in himself and his abilities. His light doesn't dim or diminish when mine begins to glow. Most of the guys that I have dealt with in the past have been intimidated by me. They were intimidated by my accomplishments, my income, my education, my car, my house. All of the shit that I cannot and will not change. It is like having a dick that is too big. What can you do about it?"

Precious laughed, "You gay boys always go to the size of the dick, don't you?"

Abel said, "Whatever" and asked Precious how she was liking being in DC and being a politician. She told him, "I am loving what I am doing. I feel like I am making a difference. I am trying to get on the right committees and get my name out there. It's hard work and you have to learn how to recognize bullshit. You have to learn not to expend one ounce of energy or one second of time dealing with all the bullshit that comes your way." She added, "But I love it."

Precious continued, "I have already identified who my allies are. I know which ones of these fools came to Congress just to get on TV or to make money. But I'm doing my best not to be one of those." She said, "I want people to know that I was here and that I made a difference."

Abel asked, "What can I do to help?"

Precious replied, "Donations are always welcome." She continued, "I am developing my platform and my brand. I know what things I want to focus on. When I get that plan in place, I will be able to tell you what other types of support I will need."

Precious' tone became very stern. She said, "Xerxes really likes you. If you are not able to give him your all and you think that you can't accept all of him, then end it now. He has given his heart, I mean his whole heart, to two people – me and now you. I still love him. As Whitney Houston sang 'I will Always Love him'." She added, "And I will kill a motherfucker that ever tries to hurt him."

Abel replied, "I am afraid. I really love Xerxes. I think we could be the shit!! I have had so many disappointments in the past. I don't know if I can stand another one."

Precious replied, "I know boo. All I can say is I would trust Z with my life." Her voice trembled and Abel was certain she had begun to cry. She went on, "I think he would harm himself before he harmed me, and now you. It is going to take some time before you can trust him like that. Hell, I have known him since we were kids. All I am saying is be open to the possibilities. Don't let your fear prevent you from being with a really good man."

Abel asked, "Precious are you alright!? I promise you I will be open to the possibilities with Xerxes. Now stop crying before you make me cry."

Precious said, "Damn baby, we sound like a bunch of old hens. Can we lighten up the mood?" She continued, "One benefit of being with Z is the sex is amazing. I still remember when we got together the first time, I could barely walk the next morning."

"You are a crazy ass bitch, but when we got together, he took my breath away too."

"Pour me some tea Thing Man!! Give me the four-uno-uno and don't leave anything out."

"How much time you got?"

"I am good. My first meeting isn't for another hour or so."

"OK, Miss Girl. Get you some coffee and I will tell you everything."

Precious laughed and said, "Ah sookie, sookie now!!"

They laughed. Precious went and grabbed a Keurig cup of coffee and settled in to hear the details.

Abel said, "When I got to his place, he was dressed in tight, white boxer shorts. The sight of those white boxers and his dark skin made me weak."

"Were they the 2Xist fitted ones? The ones that showed everything?"

"Yes, Lawd!! It took my breath away when I saw how big he was!! I thought I would die. I didn't want him to see me looking at it, but I couldn't help myself."

"I know right. I used to feel that thing up against my back all night long when we were together. And it never seems to go down!!"

Abel described how he and Xerxes began to talk and how he had been drinking and fired up a blunt. He confessed that Xerxes asked him if he wanted to hit the blunt.

Precious interrupted, "Bitch you know you can't handle water let alone weed."

Abel replied, "I know, but I was being a good friend. He needed a friend. So I took a hit."

He told Precious that Xerxes asked if he wanted a shotgun and he admitted that he didn't know what it was. He described how Xerxes explained what it was and convinced him to try it. They both laughed when Abel told her that he immediately felt high. He said, "I started to choke and he asked me if I wanted a drink. I asked for a small jack and coke...."

"You were smoking weed AND drinking. I'm surprised you ain't pregnant. I know you gave up all of your cookies, didn't you?"

"Do you want to hear the story or what? We talked a little more and then he gave me another shotgun. Before I knew it, he was kissing me. Damn!! He has the softest lips I have ever felt and he kisses so good!!"

"Oh, Lord, I know that's right!! And he's got that evil tongue. It tastes and feels so good."

They both knew exactly what she was referring to and giggled.

Abel told her, "Before I knew it, he was on top of me. He was kissing me and it seemed like his mouth was everywhere."

"It probably was. Lord, I remember those days."

"I could feel the entire weight of his body on top of me. His dick kept getting bigger and bigger."

"And it's such a beautiful dick too."

"He slid inside me and I gasped. He was so big and long and hard and he kept going in deeper and deeper."

"Damn, keep talking!!"

"I didn't think he was every going to stop. I'm surprised that I didn't pass out."

"I would have kicked your ass if you passed out and missed out on all of that good loving."

"He began so slow and his rhythm was so smooth. He felt like silk inside me and he kept asking me if I was okay and whether he was hurting me."

"The first time we got together, he did the same thing with me."

"He kept stroking and moving inside me and each time he went deeper and my eyes started to roll back in my head. My head was spinning and I could feel myself getting so wet."

Precious said, "Wait!! Wet?!? What?!?!" She asked, "Boys do that too?" Every time he was with me, I thought we were going to drown."

Abel said, "Damn, you are so nasty."

Precious said, "Tell me more!!"

Abel said, "He came in one last thrust. I could feel him throbbing as his juices flowed inside me. He was breathing and panting so hard and almost bit my ear off."

Precious said, "Damn!! For real!!"

"I told him damn Daddy, that was some good shit and when he bit my ear, I released. We lay there for a few minutes marinating together."

Precious said, "Damn, now I got to go and put on another pad. You gay boys have the best sex. Bye Abel, I got to go now. On a serious tip though, be careful with Z and never lie to him. I love you, talk to you later."

17

Cyrus was pissed both because he had left such an offensive message on Abel's phone and because he never heard anything more from Maurice. He had finally healed from the ambush inflicted on him by Maurice's friend and was desperate to find a way to get his life back on track. He needed to persuade Abel to forgive him and take him back into his good graces. He knew if he was successful, especially after the horrible message he left, he would be back in control of their relationship again. He decided he would not rest until he had Abel back under his spell.

Cyrus always used sex to win Abel back when they disagreed in the past because he knew he couldn't resist his appeal. He had been in a sexual drought since his beatdown at Maurice's apartment and knew he could relieve his sexual tension and vanquish any resistance Abel might offer if he could get him back in bed. Cyrus knew having sex was all he needed to do to regain Abel's favor and was confident that once they reconnected he would have no problem breaking down any other resistence he might offer. He just needed to devise a way to cajole Abel to have sex with him again.

He needed Abel to be totally compliant and fantasized about punishing and dominating him when they did eventually reconnect. He pictured the two of them making love slowly and passionately. He visualized taking his time and tormenting Abel by withholdng his seed. He wanted Abel to beg him to release and smiled confidently as he pictured him in utter submission while savoring their love making. He knew he would only get one shot to "dickmatize" Abel and vowed that he wasn't going to blow it when it came.

Cyrus was determined to reclaim his comfortable and secure spot back in Abel's life. He realized that he needed to nurture and cultivate their relationship for a while before returning to his wanton lifestyle of indescriminate sex. He had to make sure that Abel was securely "on lock down" again before pursuing any new boy pussy.

He never considered that anyone else could possibly ever be interested in Abel. He figured that Abel had also been on a drought assuming that he had not seen or been with anyone since they were last together. He expected Abel to be anxious to see him and willing to do anything he wanted to satisfy him. Cyrus planned to use this unease to make Abel appreciate him more and realize what he had been missing.

Cyrus remembered how much Abel loved and worshipped his body when they first met. He decided he wanted to be bigger, harder and more toned when they reunited and devoted more time in the gym and worked out extra hard.

He knew he had fucked up and was willing to do anything he could to get Abel back. He was even willing to feign contrition or pretend to be remorseful and abandon his cocky and conceited demeanor if that would help sway Abel. Cyrus had always been unrepentent for his behavior in the past but decided that this time he needed to both apologize profusely for the vitriol and venom in his message and concoct a persuasive lie to explain to Abel why he left it. His lie would have to be plausible enough to convincingly justify why he was in such a foul mood and explain why Abel was the focus for all of his enmity. He knew Abel would never believe him if his prevarication wasn't absolutely perfect.

The first lie he concocted was to tell Abel he was drunk. He would justify his inebriation by saying something like, *"Abel, baby, I'm sorry for my message but I was mad and upset because you had been putting me off for so long for that Precious bitch. I was so pissed off I went out drinking by myself. You know I don't drink and I got fucked up. I didn't think your ass wanted to see me no more but you wouldn't tell me to my face. I was fucked up, my head was full of all kinds of bullshit and I took it all out on you. You know how much I love you. Will you forgive me?"* He realized, however, that Abel knew that he had never been a big drinker and concluded that he would not believe he had been drinking or was drunk when he castigated him.

Next, he conjured up a lie about a close friend that suffered a tragedy. He would say, *"Abel, baby, I'm sorry for my message but I had just found out my homeboy Khalil got killed in some bullshit. Me and Khalil grew up together in the Foster Care system and he was living that street life and got shot. I was so fucked up when I got the news and tried to call you to help me deal with it. When I couldn't get you, I got more pissed off and left that fucked up message. Please forgive me baby."* He remembered though that he'd told Abel he was always a loner when he was growing up in Foster Care. He confessed that he discovered at an early age that friends came and went like the wind when he was a boy and he learned not to get too close to anyone. Inventing a new imaginary friend would generate a lot of questions that he was not prepared to answer. He also realized sadly that the only "friends" that he ever had in his life were other guys he was fucking. He certainly couldn't mention any of them to Abel and quickly discounted this fantasy because he knew Abel wouldn't believe any lie he made up about a friend.

He finally concluded that it was best to fabricate a tale that was as close to reality as he could devise. He decided to admit that his life was collapsing around him and a lot of things were all going wrong at the same time. He would tell him, *"Abel, baby, I'm sorry for my message but my shit is all fucked up. I was coming home from the gym one night and some motherfuckers jumped me, beat me up and stole my money. I had just got some cash to get money orders to pay my bills and shit. They must have been watching me when I was at the ATM or something. Now I'm behind and don't know how i'm gonna get my shit back in order. I tried to call your ass after it happened, but you weren't nowhere to be found. I needed you man, but you weren't there for me. I was so fucked up and mad that I took it out on you. Will you forgive me?"* He mused that he would even pretend to cry as he told his tale hoping his performance would make Abel feel more sympathy for him. He surmised that feigning emotion and vulnerability would help make his dismay seem more plausible.

Cyrus liked this final fabrication best. He could exaggerate how bad his financial situation had become since the "robbery" if Abel believed it. He alone had the responsibility to determine when he got back on his feet so he could extort as much as he could for as long as he wanted from his empathetic paramour. He mused that successfully persuading Abel to believe his lie and convincing him to support him financially, would ultimately result in Abel compensating him for his bad behavior and disrespect. He relished the thought of making Abel pay for his indiscretion and decided he would focus all of his energy and effort into getting back in his life and gouging him for as much as he could.

Cyrus was gleeful about his created fantasy because it included elements of the truth and he would easily be able to answer any questions if Abel probed for more details. He actually had been beaten up albeit not by robbers. His funds really were low but that was because he had not been able to make money from his sexual exploits while he was recuperating. He felt no remorse about lying to Abel and was fully prepared to embellish his canard any way that he could to get what he wanted.

Abel was well off and financially secure and Cyrus used this as his justification for taking him for as much as he could. He was prepared to lie and tell Abel that he had exhausted all other possible options to try to solve his problems on his own, not wanting to involve or bother him with them. He intended to play on Abel's guilt by telling him that he reached out to him only after all his other alternatives proved futile.

Ideally, he wanted to blame Abel for all of his misfortune by suggesting that if he had been available when he called everything would have been OK. He justified his contrivance by telling himself that Abel should have known he couldn't survive without him. He wanted Abel to feel guilty and was confident that if he told his fable the right way, he could leave him with the impression that Cyrus' debacle was in reality all his fault. If he could show Abel how much he needed him and convince him he was lost without him, he would have him right where he wanted.

He needed to be certain that he had the details of his lie committed to memory so he practiced his story over and over again. He anticipated the questions that Abel might pose and prepared answers for them. He knew he would only have one opportunity to tell the tale so he had to make sure he told it the right way. He wanted Abel to be remorseful for being unavailable and knew exactly what buttons to push and what strings to pull to make that happen.

He spent days roll playing his conversation and practiced what he planned to say and how he expected Abel to respond. He replayed their fabricated conversation over and over in his mind until he was confidant he could answer any question or overcome any objection that might arise. He imagined their conversation going something like:

Cyrus: Hey Baby, you got a few minutes.

Abel: Oh, you're talking to me now instead of yelling at me?

Cyrus: Uh, yeah man. About that. I need to apologize for

that. A lot of shit was going wrong with me and I took it all out on you.

Abel: A lot of shit like what?

Cyrus: Well, I got robbed. I got my ass kicked. And I'm behind in all of my shit. All I could think of was calling you and......

Abel: Robbed!?! What happened!?!

Cyrus: It was a while ago. Back when I left that message. I was coming home from the gym one night and stopped by the bank. I needed to get some cash so I could get some money orders to pay my bills. These motherfuckers must have been watching me because they jumped me when I left the bank.

Abel: When? Why didn't you tell me?

Cyrus: I tried to tell you but you weren't no where to be found.

Abel: Are you OK?!?

Cyrus: I'm good now. Don't worry about it. It's been a while and I couldn't reach you when I needed you so I been trying to work shit out on my own.

Abel: I'm sorry baby.

Cyrus: No worries. It's cool. I will work it out. I just hope my landlord and some of these other motherfuckers don't yank my shit before it's too late.

Abel: Baby, I'm sorry. What can I do!?

Cyrus: Well first, don't ever disappear on me again. You know how much I need you and depend on you.

Abel: But, what about your landlord? Who are these other motherfuckers you were talking about?

Cyrus: Well I told my Landlord what happened and he said he would give me a few more weeks to get caught up. I will figure something out for them other motherfuckers.

Abel: Damn Cyrus, I'm sorry! What do you need?

Cyrus: Well, now I'm only behind by like about three months in my rent. It's about the same with my cell but I didn't want to ask you. This probably never would have happened if you hadn't ghosted me. I mean, I used to think I could count on you but.....

Abel: No baby, I want to help!! You can count on me!!

Cyrus: Are you sure?? I need to know you will be there for me. I mean, I love you but I also need to know you will be there when I need you.

Abel: Yeah. I'm sure. I can, I mean will be. What do you need me to do?

Cyrus: Well, like I said I'm behind a couple of months in rent and my phone and some other shit. Hey, instead of going over it on the phone, can we get together? I can show you everything I am dealing with and you can let me know if you can help.

Abel: Sure, we can do that. When do you want to meet?

Cyrus: I can come by later on if that's cool with you. I mean if your other man won't mind.

Abel: I ain't go no damn other man!!

Cyrus: Well, maybe we can order some food, go over my shit and just catch up. It's been a long time since we've been togther and this anaconda is missing you? I mean, you may not want it no more, but....

Abel: Damn!!

Cyrus: What's wrong?

Abel: When you said anaconda, I got excited. Now all I can do is think about it.

Cyrus: You should see it. It's thinking about you too and right now it's harder than trying to get them Kardashian bitches to stop fucking Black basketball players. But I didn't think you was feeling me like that no more.

Abel: What?? Why?

Cyrus: Well, you haven't been that easy to catch. You didn't seem to have no time for me no more. I just figured you found somebody new.

Abel: I'm sorry Daddy. You know how work can be. I ain't got no time to find somebody new. What time you want to connect?

Cyrus: You tell me and I will be there.

Abel: How about around 7?

Cyrus: Cool!! See you then. Make sure you are ready for me!!

His imagined conversation with Abel aroused him. He grew stiff as he visualized pressing his manhood against him when they met. He imagined loosening his sweatpants and allowing them fall to the floor putting his bigness on full display before he slowly and deeply penetrated Abel. He planned to fuck Abel good, long and hard. His objective was to erase any doubt or uncertainty that anyone else could satiate him as well. He wanted to remind Abel what he had been missing and to make sure that he never let Cyrus get away ever again. He wanted to make sure that when he was done, Abel was completely submissive and would be totally committed to him again.

Cyrus' had no lasting scars or bruises from his fight at Maurice's and his workout regimen resulted in a bigger and firmer body. He regained his swagger and felt that he was finally ready to reach out to Abel. He thought long and hard about what he wanted to wear and decided on a tight-fitting tank top and, of course, sweatpants. He imagined how surprised Abel would be with his harder abs, bigger arms and broader chest. He found an old pair of tighter and more revealing sweatpants and planned to wear them to their reunion. He strutted around his apartment lustily imagining how easily Abel would succumb to him.

Cyrus wanted to make a good impression on Abel when they did reconnect so he planned to get a fresh haircut once they agreed on a date and time to meet. He decided that once he secured the date with Abel he would drop by Mr. Sam's Cutz to see if his barber, Kwame, could hook him up.

Kwame had been Cyrus' coiffeur since he first became a barber at the shop. He was a recurring customer at Mr. Sams because it offered a large pool of potential sex partners with whom he could furtively flirt or covertly entice. He loved tempting the guys who were "on the downlow" or pretended to be straight by showing and hiding the massive bulge in his sweatpants while they unsuccessfully tried to divert their eyes. Teasing the patrons in the barber shop made his dick and it was one of Cyrus' favorite pasttimes when he visited the shop. He enjoyed that almost as much as he enjoyed feeling the pressure of Kwame's heavy manhood brushing against his arm when he innocently and unknowingly stood close while cutting his hair. Cyrus knew Kwame was straight but always positioned his arm just right to surreptitiously feel his bigness.

Cyrus had concocted a plausible story, coordinated the perfect outfit and worked his body into optimum shape. Once he and Abel set the time and place for their reunion, he would make sure he looked his best. He couldn't wait to use the remorse he expected and hoped that Abel would feel to wheedle as much as he could from him. He wanted to teach Abel to never abandon him or go silent ever again. He couldn't wait to reach out to Abel to put his plan in motion.

18

Xerxes convinced Abel that they should handle the 'Dear John' conversation with Cyrus together. He listened to the last message that he left and persuaded Abel that he needed to be present just in case anything got out of hand or something negative jumped off. Abel told him that Cyrus had never been violent before but welcomed his company and support.

Xerxes asked Abel, "Are you sure you want to end it with this dude? I can tap out and let you work this shit out with this motherfucker if you really want me to." He wanted to give Abel one last chance to be sure he wasn't forcing him to do anything he didn't want to do. He added, "I mean I know we been spending a lot of time together, but I want you to be sure. I don't want you to have no second thoughts. I want you to be sure before we get to the point of no return."

Abel replied, "No baby!! Not at all. I've been totally honest with you. I didn't have or want anything from him. And other than good sex, he didn't give me nothing." He continued, "Cyrus is like an old car that I need to trade in for a new model."

Xerxes joked, "Yeah, trade in for a newer, bigger and better model with more features, right baby?"

Abel laughed, "Most definitely!!"

Xerxes said, "OK, sexy. That's what I was hoping you would say. So how do you want to handle this situation?" He joked, "Do you want me to get some of my old teammates to kick his ass?"

Abel replied, "Hell, no!!"

Xerxes said, "I know. I was just joking. OK, whatever you decide, you know I got your back."

Abel smiled and they kissed. He said, "He's been texting me lately about hooking up. I think he thinks I still want to get with him. I will text him and set up a meeting at my house and we can tell him about us. Is that cool?"

Xerxes said, "That's cool as a motherfuckin' fan baby. Let's set that shit up yesterday so we can get this nigga' out of our life!!"

He pulled Abel close and kissed him long and hard and whispered, "I can't have some extraneous motherfucka, messing with my dude." He asked, "You are my dude, right?"

Abel smiled, "Don't you already know?" He added, "Let me text him and see when we can get this done."

    Abel: Hey man!! Need to talk. When are you free?

Cyrus was surprised to finally get a reply from Abel and was excited about the possibly of seeing him again and replied.

    Cyrus: I'm wide open man. I can work around you."

    Abel: How about tonight around 7?

    Cyrus: Mos def. B ready. Gotta make up for lost time.

He included several eggplant and peach emojis. Abel showed the text to Xerxes who pretended to snatch the phone feigning that he would send a harsh reply. Abel maintained his hold on the phone and sent a response.

    Abel: OK, see you at my place at 7.

Cyrus thought Abel's reply seemed stoic and dry but figured he must have been busy and put it out of his mind.

He wanted to be pumped up for his meeting with Abel and went to the gym to get a good workout. He finished his workout and headed straight to Mr. Samz Cutz to see if Kwame was busy.

The shop was very sparsely populated for a mid-week afternoon. Mr. Sam, Kwame and Oscar were the only barbers who had customers and only a few of the chairs in the waiting area were occupied. Signifying Ray and June Bug were engrossed in a game of checkers. Kwame was just finishing a customer and told Cyrus that he would be able to accomodate him as soon as he was done. Cyrus was glad that Kwame would be able to fit him in his schedule but disappointed because there weren't a lot of prospects to cruise while he waited for his turn in Kwame's chair.

Kwame finished with his customer and beckoned Cyrus to take a seat. He took a seat and carefully positioned his arms on the armrests of the chair hoping he would get a chance to feel Kwame's girth while he cut his hair. Kwame did not disappoint and Cyrus smiled imagining that he must also be going through a drought because he felt larger and heavier than he remembered. Cyrus was glad that he was shielded by the barber smock because he couldn't control his erection thinking about sex with Kwame.

Kwame finished his work and Cyrus left the shop and went directly home to prepare to see Abel. He was singularly focused on impressing him when they met so he showered, moisturized and dressed in the tight-fitting shirt and sweatpants that he had planned to wear. He took one final look in the mirror before heading out and was pleased because he looked exactly how he had imagined he would in his plan for their reunion. His triceps, biceps and pecs were bulging and glistening and the prominent print of his mahood was on full display. He packed an overnight bag and took it along because he knew Abel would find him irresistible and invite him to spend the night.

Cyrus was never very prompt and often kept Abel waiting when they went on dates or when he would visit, but this evening he arrived promptly at 7 PM. He pressed the doorbell but thought he might have gone to the wrong address when Xerxes opened the door and motioned him in.

Cyrus asked uncomfortably, "I'm looking for Abel.....Does Abel still live here?" He continued gaining confidence, "Is he here?"

Xerxes smiled and responded, "You're in the right spot man. Abel is running a bit late and asked me to let you in."

Cyrus asked, "So who are you? Your face is familiar. Are you a relative or someone like that? I know I have seen you somewhere before."

Xerxes said, "Yeah, I'm something like that. Can I get you anything?"

Cyrus couldn't control his attraction to Xerxes. He had always fantasized about being with another masculine, muscular guy and Xerxes met every criteria he had ever imagined. Most of the dates that he had were with lovers who pursued him for his body but didn't exert much effort to workout or build up their own. Abel was one of the very few guys that excited or stimulated him because he put forth as much effort to build his body as he did his business. Cyrus wanted to find out more about Xerxes and decided that he would devise a way to get to know as much about him as he could.

Cyrus said slyly, "Yeah big Daddy, what you got?" He eyed Xerxes lasciviously and began to openly and overtly flirt, seeming to forget that he had come to visit Abel.

Xerxes replied, "What you want? We got everything."

Cyrus said, "Why don't you surprise me."

Xerxes said, "Cool man. Cop a squat and I will make you something special."

Cyrus grew comfortable chatting with Xerxes and realized that he was exactly the kind of guy that he wanted to get to know better and more intimately. He had to find a way to surreptitiously get Xerxes' contact information so that he could arrange a date with him at a later time. He was pleased because he would reconnect with Abel and have a new playmate on the side as well.

He kept trying to remember how he knew Xerxes but was certain they had never had sex before because he would have remembered being with such a perfect specimen. Cyrus tried to be sly and coy as they bantered but Xerxes refused to divulge any information or details that Cyrus could use to identify him. Xerxes' phone rang and he excused himself to take the call. He and Abel had hatched a plan for him to pretend to receive a call. Their ruse included him telling Cyrus that Abel was enroute but was running late and still was about thirty minutes away. They knew he couldn't be trusted and wanted to see how far Cyrus would go in pursuing Xerxes while they waited for Abel to arrive.

Xerxes returned and said, "That was Abel on the phone. He got held up at work but is on the way. He told me to apologize for him being late and he said to make sure I take care of you." He continued, "It looks like we got a few more minutes to kill some time. You need anything?"

Cyrus smiled slyly and said, "Hmmm. He told you to take care of me, huh? He leaned back in the chair, folded his arms and sat with his legs wide open. "What you got in mind?" he added.

Xerxes sat on a chair opposite Cyrus, looked directly at him and replied, "What you want man?"

Cyrus ogled Xerxes surveying all of his muscularity and felt a stirring in his loins as Xerxes matched his gaze. He could see the outline of Xerxes' endowment in the fitted sweatpants he wore and got excited because he had never intentially been with anyone as large or larger than him. He imagined that sex between the two of them would be like two gladiators grappling in the Coliseum in ancient Rome or Greece and was unable to control or diminish the erection growing he was developing. He pictured them fucking like lust-filled animals but decided that sex was not a good idea, even a quickie, at Abel's house when he was soon to arrive. Cyrus said, "Nah, man. I'm going to behave myself. If we had more than just 20 - 30 minutes and Abel wasn't on his way, there is a hell of a lot we could do."

Xerxes was enraged because Cyrus' innuendo was so obvious but hid his growing distaste for him and asked, "For real?? Like what man? Give me an example."

Cyrus responded, "Let me get your digits man. We can hook up another time. I can show you better than I could tell you."

Xerxes said, "I am sure you can. But go ahead, tell me what you got in mind?"

Cyrus stood up showing the massive print of his rock hard dick and said, "I gotta go to the bathroom man." He pretended to adjust his bigness but made sure Xerxes saw how excited he was before doing so.

As soon as Cyrus left the room, Xerxes signaled to Abel, who had been upstairs secretly eavesdropping on their repartee, to sneak downstairs and hide out of Cyrus' view. Abel obeyed and positioned himself out of sight just as he exited the bathroom. Cyrus stood in the hallway outside of the bathroom looking directly at Xerxes still holding his erect penis and asked, "You see anything you like? We still got a few minutes before Abel gets home." Xerxes looked directly at Cyrus then diverted his eyes until he caught sight of Abel and replied, "Yeah man. Yeah man, I do."

Cyrus, still unable to see Abel, was excited thinking Xerxes might be ready to relent to his advances asked, "Oh yeah, What you see man?"

Xerxes looked at Cyrus for a moment and then turned his gaze back toward Abel and replied, "I see the man that I love."

Abel walked out from concealment when he heard Xerxes' profession of love, looked directly at Cyrus and asked incredulously, "So what's happening here?" Cyrus was aghast and clumsily and unsuccessfully tried to conceal his erection.

Xerxes said, "Your boy here has been trying to push up on me, while he thought you weren't home."

Abel maintained a cold stare trained directly on Cyrus and and asked, "Is that true? Is that what you've been doing?" He continued, "Don't lie. I can already see your dick is hard and you're trying to hide it. Did you really try to get busy in my fucking house while you thought you were waiting for me to come home?!?!"

Cyrus felt trapped for a moment but caught himself and responded, "Abel, you know my dick is always hard when I'm thinking about you. Why would I try to get with this dude in your camp when I know that you are on the way home......"

Xerxes interrupted, "This asshole has done everything but put his dick in my mouth. He came out of the bathroom with his dick in his hand. When he went in it was hard as cold peanut butter. He made sure that I saw it and has been trying to flirt with me from the moment I let him in." Xerxes added, "He has also been trying to remember or find out who I am, but I wanted you to be here before we told him."

183

Cyrus looked at Abel, "We?" Who is this motherfucker Abel!? Why was he here to let me in and you weren't? What's up? Who is he that you would believe him instead of me, your boy?"

Abel and Xerxes walked toward one another and when they met, embraced and kissed. Abel looked directly at Cyrus and simultaneously said, "That's part of the problem. You've been trying to be my boy and he is my new man."

Cyrus looked confused and perplexed. He asked, "Who is this motherfucker Abel, for real?"

Abel said, "His name is Xerxes and he used to be a player with the Chicago Bears. He is my new man. We've been hanging out for the last few months now and have decided that we want to make it permanent and exclusive."

Cyrus felt flushed and a rush of rage and jealousy engulfed his entire body. He had never been jealous of anyone before and couldn't understand why he felt this way about Abel. He asked, "So why would you invite my ass over here, if you got this nig-ger in your life?"

Abel said, "I wanted to make it clear to you that I have moved on."

Cyrus interrupted, "And you needed him here. For what, to keep you from falling back in love with me?" He grabbed his dick and continued, "You know you still want some of this."

Xerxes laughed and asked Abel, "Is this muthafucka for real? I can see I am going to have a lot of work to do on you if this is the best that you thought you could do."

Cyrus defiantly stared at Xerxes and said, "I will bust your ass."

Xerxes looked him directly in his eyes and calmly said, "Come on Cletus!! You don't want none of this man. Guaranteed. Plus,

I would never disrespect Abel's house by kicking your ass here."

Abel said, "Cyrus, I actually asked Xerxes to be here because your last phone message caught me off guard. I didn't know what you might do when I told you I have decided to move on and that I want to move on him. He convinced me that he should be here to make sure everything went OK."

Cyrus said, "So what are you saying Abel? Be clear about it."

Abel said, "OK, this is as clear as I can make it. I am seeing Xerxes now. It is probably best if you and I end any contact or communication. We're through!!"

Cyrus was visibly upset. He asked Abel, "So you're treating me like a business contract now. You didn't treat this dick like a contract when it was fucking you!! Shit, well fuck you then!! I never liked fucking your ass anyway. You old motherfucker."

Xerxes took a step toward Cyrus but Abel stepped in to block his way.

He replied to Cyrus, "Well, we won't have to worry about that anymore will we?"

Xerxes walked toward the front door, opened it and motioned for Cyrus to leave. Cyrus looked at Xerxes and looked back at Abel. He stood for a long while and asked, "What am I supposed to do now? I still want to be with you!! I don't want to go!!!"

Xerxes said, "Boy you better get out of here with that Jennifer Holiday Dreamgirl bullshit!!" He added, "You don't have to go home but you do have to get the fuck up out of here. I am going to be spending a lot of time with Abel from now on and I don't want to see your nasty ass nowhere around. I am going to treat him the way he deserves to be treated and he and I are going to be monogamous. I bet your dumb ass doesn't even know what that means?"

Cyrus took a step toward Xerxes and he steeled himself for an attack. Cyrus paused and remembered how his last encounter with a man more muscular than he was turned out and calmed himself. He looked at Abel as if to say, "Give me one more chance". Abel grabbed Xerxes' hand and kissed it. Cyrus walked past both of them and heard the door close as he walked out. He felt like when the door closed it was also closing on his life.

19

Precious had made a very important decision about her life and needed to have a very important conversation with Xerxes and Abel. She sent them both a text message.

Precious: Morning. How y'all doing?

Xerxes: Fine P, HRU?

Abel: Good. Morning Precious. How you doing?

Precious: Free later? Need to ask y'all something.

Xerxes: Should be. What time?

Abel: Yes. When?

Precious: How about around 8 PM?

Xerxes: 8 PM Chicago time or DC?

Precious: 8 PM my time.

Abel: That works for me.

Abel: OK. What's up? What you want to ask?

Xerxes: Yeah, why you being so mysterious?

Precious: I'll tell you tonight. It ain't nothing bad.

Xerxes: Cool. We'll talk at 8.

Abel: Have a good day.

Precious had made a name for herself in Washington and her impact was being felt all over the country. She learned how to shrewdly and adeptly navigate policy making and the legislative process in Washington and gained support amongst her democratic and republicans counterparts in the House. She successfully funded several projects back in her home district and her constituents liked and praised her for the work she was doing on their behalf. The polls indicated that she would have no real obstacle to win the democratic primary and she was almost assured re-election to another term.

She really loved being in the Congress and had no aspiration to move up to the Senate even though she had been asked to consider it by several influential supporters. She wanted to continue the work she was doing and felt that incumbency offered her the freedom and flexibility to focus on some of the other goals that she wanted to achieve in her life.

She realized that everything in her life was going the way that she had imagined it but one thing seemed to be missing. She wanted to have a baby. Her urge to be a mother started as a whim when she saw several of her staffers with their children during a recent congressional family outing. The children were well mannered, inquisitive and innocently exuberant. Their mothers and fathers beamed their approval.

Precious began to imagine herself as a mother and the more she thought about it the more she relished the idea. Her daydreams of motherhood and becoming a parent were clear and vivid. What was not as clear and evident was having a husband or getting married but her yen to be a mother was overpowering and growing stronger day by day. She hoped that she could explain what she was feeling to Xerxes and convince him to be the one to help her realize her dream.

Precious began researching invitro fertilization and artificial insemination. She wanted to know as much as she could about every conceivable method and procedure that would result in her gravidity. She needed to be prepared to answer any question or refute any objection that Xerxes might offer. She and Xerxes had always had a healthy and mutually satisfying sexual relationship when they were together but he was with Abel now and their lives had changed so drastically. She needed to be certain not only that he alone was receptive to her plans, but that both he and Abel were okay with her desire to get pregnant. She was about to make the biggest request in all of their lives and everyone needed to be on board.

Precious loved Xerxes and Abel too much and did not want to interfere with their relationship. She did not want to hurt either one of them and certainly didn't want to cause a rift between the two of them either. She was well aware of what she was giving up when she made her decision to go into public office and was very happy with her choices. She knew that Abel and Xerxes were happy in their new life together as well. She hoped that her request would not disrupt the comfort and tranquility in either of their lives.

Once she allowed herself to believe that the possibility of having a baby could be a reality, the concept of motherhood totally consumed her. Every night she fell asleep and dreamed that she and Xerxes had conceived a baby together. In her dreams, her pregnancy was perfect and painless and she delivered a happy and healthy baby. Precious blissfully awakened each morning brandishing a broad smile as she remembered her nocturnal imaginings and thought about her new perfect little angel.

One morning, however, she awoke and was tired, disheveled and distraught. She had tossed and turned all night because an unusually preposterous dream interrupted her slumber and displaced her normal serenity. She blamed the unsettling dream on the Ethiopian cuisine that she had enjoyed the night before. In her dream, she had somehow been impregnated by both Xerxes and Abel and gave birth to a set of twins. She vowed never to eat Ethiopian food again because her dream was so unsettling. Even though she knew that her nightmare pregnancy was purely a fantasy, it haunted her and began to return to her every night. Precious was intrigued by the possibility of having two babies from two fathers and thought about it more and more. She grew to like the idea and wondered if she might be able to convince both Abel and Xerxes to help make it possible.

She was confident that she would be able to sell Xerxes on the concept of fatherhood but had no idea how Abel might react if she asked him. She knew that he was gay but she also knew that he had been with women before in his life. Abel had told her about women that he dated in high school and college so she knew he wasn't one of those gay boys that had not ever had been with a woman or was afraid of the pussy. She began to believe that she might be able to convince him to try sex with a woman at least one more time.

Precious knew that Xerxes would jump at the chance to conceive in the natural way assuming he was open to the idea of becoming a father. She hoped that once she won him over that, between the two them, they could persuade Abel to go along with the idea as well. If she was able to convince Abel to accept the idea, she decided that she would be open to using artificial insemination if that was the only method that he found acceptable. She wanted to have a back up option in case she did not have any success convincing him to have sex but decided that she would be just as ecstatic if she was successful convincing him to go along with the plan.

Xerxes and Abel were curious about why Precious wanted to talk to both of them together. They couldn't wait for 7 PM to arrive so they could find out what was on her mind. The day elapsed excruciatingly slowly as minutes passed by like hours and seconds felt like minutes. They both watched the clock as the day droned by. In the middle of the morning Xerxes texted Abel.

Xerxes: You want to come over here for the call?

Abel: Sure that works.

Xerxes: Cool. We can grab dinner after.

Abel: You sure? We always get sidetracked.

Xerxes: Damn, you're right. I'll behave this time."

Abel imagined the broad, sly smile that appeared on Xerxes' face and responded.

Abel: You know you're lying.

Xerxes laughed.

Abel: I wonder what's up? Has she ever been mysterious like this before?

Xerxes: Nah, P is a lot of things but mysterious and shady ain't one. Must be serious but I have no idea what it could be. I hope everything is alright though. She is kicking ass in DC and I am so proud of her."

Abel: Yeah, IKR. I've been watching some of the shit she has been working on and she is a motherfucking force. I'm so proud of her. Let me get back to work. I need to get some shit done before I head to your place in time for seven. C u later big sexy.

Xerxes: I got your big sexy.

Abel: Maybe I'll come by early, so I can get some.

Xerxes: Now who's the one that can't be serious. I'm here all day. Come by when you can.

Abel pulled up to Xerxes' condo at 6:45 PM. He had not been able to get his work done to get away early as he hoped. In fact, he ran out of a meeting early just to arrive when he did. He parked the X5 and briskly walked to the door. Xerxes opened the door and welcomed him with a tight bear hug before he could ring the bell. He said, "What's up man? I thought you were going to try to come by earlier."

Abel replied, "I know. I had to leave a meeting early just to get here by now. My day kept getting busy. I wasn't able to leave any earlier."

Xerxes said, "No issues man. You're here now and that's all that matters. Come on in, I will text Precious and let her know that we are both here and she can call whenever she wants. Can I get you something to drink?"

Abel replied, "A water or soda would be good. I am going to wait to see what she has to say before drinking anything stronger."

Xerxes said, "Good idea, I will do the same."

Abel and Xerxes seemed nervous as they sat in silence alternately watching the television and their watches until 7:00 PM arrived. Right at seven, the phone rang. Xerxes wanted to take the call so that both he and Abel could hear so he answered the call through his Alexa home assistant. He said, "Hey P, is that you?"

Precious replied, "Yes. Are both of you punks together? Is this a good time to talk?"

Xerxes and Abel replied almost simultaneously, "Punks!!!"

Xerxes continued, "Bitch please!! What do you want?"

Precious said, "I was just joking with y'all." She continued, "You know that you are my two favorite men on the entire planet, right? And I would do anything for both of you, right?"

Abel and Xerxes both replied, "Right."

Precious said, "Well I have to ask a favor from both of you and it is huge. I wouldn't ask if it wasn't important and I wouldn't ask anyone else."

Abel interrupted, "Oh damn Precious, you need a kidney or some other kind of transplant. How do you know if we are compatible? What do we have to do to get tested?"

Xerxes interjected, "Yeah Precious, what's the deal? You got us worried over here."

Precious said, "I don't need a transplant and I am not ill." She added, "And I wouldn't take a gland from either one of you anyway. Lord knows what y'all have done to your organs." Precious went on, "What I want does require a medical procedure though." She said, "Do y'all hear that sound?

Xerxes replied, "What sound?"

Abel said, "No, Precious. I don't hear anything!"

She answered, "For real!?! Y'all don't hear that pounding sound?"

Abel and Xerxes heard nothing and looked at each other disbelievingly. They replied almost in unison, "No, what pounding sound. What are you talking about. We don't hear nothing pounding!!"

Precious interrupted, "Listen. It's my damn biological clock. I don't know why y'all can't hear it. It's ticking in my head like a fucking time bomb."

Xerxes said, "Really?!?" "Damn P, is it that bad?"

Precious said, "Hell yeah, it is that bad. It first started after I went to a congressional family picnic and saw all of my team with their children. They looked so happy. I thought it would just go away but it has gotten worse over the past few months. I think, no I know I would be a good Mom and I would like to have a baby. It's all I think aboutt and all I dream about. Hell, I need to have a baby and I want to have a baby now!!" She added, "In fact, I would like to have two babies. I want you two gay bitches to be my baby daddies!!!"

The silence was deafening.

Precious waited and waited and when she didn't hear a reply she asked, "Are y'all still there? Did y'all faint!?!"

Xerxes and Abel were simultaneously astounded and awe-struck at Precious' request.

Xerxes said, 'Yeah babe, we are still here." He said, "Hold on. We need a minute to digest what you just said." Another few moments of complete silence passed. Xerxes finally said, "So you want to have a baby? A baby by both of us? Have you figured out how you plan to make this happen? I mean, maybe you forgot but Abel is gay!!"

Abel replied, "Yes, Miss Girl. I'm strictly dickly."

Precious said, "I know. I know. I mean I thought about doing it the conventional way for a minute, but didn't want to screw up what you guys got going on. I also didn't know how Abel would feel about it. Y'all both know that if he ever got some of this good poosoir, he would drop you like a rock Z."

Her joke broke the tension on the call and they all laughed

nervously.

Abel said, "So let me get this straight, after all these years, now you want me to be straight!! Good luck."

Precious said, "Don't nobody want you to be straight. Well maybe I do want you to act straight for five minutes or however long it will take."

Abel replied indignantly, "I can guarantee it will be longer than five minutes....."

Precious interrupted, "Whatever boy!!! This has been on my mind for a minute. I have been researching IVF and other artificial semination procedures in case y'all didn't want to do it the natural way." She added, "I want to get impregnated by both of you at the same time and hope that we make two babies. That is how it happens in the dreams I keep having every night."

Xerxes interrupted, "Dreams? For real P!"

Precious, "Yes. Like every night I have the same dream of us having babies. I know I got some prime Grade A eggs so hopefully y'all can produce some good manseed to inject in them. I guess technically they wouldn't really be twins but I would want them to be born at the same time. I plan to stretch these walls one time giving birth and that's it. It would cement us all together as a modern family and we would always be linked together."

Xerxes looked at Abel and asked, "You have been awfully quiet Abel. What do you think?"

Abel looked at Xerxes and said, "I haven't heard you say how you felt about it either."

Xerxes said, "I got to digest it, but I would do anything I could for Precious. I know I want to be a Dad someday and I always thought that it would be with her anyway. I figured whenever we did do it we would do it with this big black anaconda but if we gotta do it some other way, then I am open to that as well......"

Precious interjected, "More like a black garter snake" and they all laughed.

Abel said, "Honestly, I had never thought about being a Dad. I mean, I have known I was into men since I was a young boy. But I love you Precious. I would help you out anyway I could." Abel went on, "Assuming that we do this, what are the legal responsibilities? How will we handle the parenting thing?" He asked Precious, "I mean how would this impact your congressional schedule?"

Precious said, "What century do y'all live in. Women work and have babies everyday. It wouldn't impact my schedule at all and I would agree to whatever arrangement you guys wanted to set up. We can find a way to make it work if we all want it. I can get a nanny here. We could get a nanny there. If you both are down with the idea, then we can do some research on both ends and figure out how we want to get it done. Are y'all open to it?"

Xerxes looked at Abel and said, "Hell yeah P, I'm open to it."

Abel looked at Xerxes and said, "Precious, I would do anything for you. The idea of being a Dad is sounding pretty interesting. My mama would love to be a grandmother and Lord knows she never expected to be one by me. She may finally be able to put out that damn candle that she has been praying to hoping I would turn straight every since I told her I was gay."

They laughed.

Precious squealed on the phone, "Thank you, thank you, thank you!!! I love you guys so much." She said, "I will send you the information that I have found so far on IVF and artificial insemination. I will find a clinic out there by you guys and the next time I am home, we can check it out. Once we get everything we need and all of our questions are answered, we can determine when we want to do it."

Precious began to cry. Xerxes and Abel grew concerned. Xerxes said, "Precious, what's wrong baby? Are you alright."

Precious replied, "I just realized that I might be about to become a Mom with the two men that I love the most on the planet. The two men that I would wish to spend the rest of my life with. And you guys are OK with how I want to get this done." She said, "I love you both so much." Precious continued, "I have one last request."

Xerxes said, "Uh, oh. Here it comes."

Precious replied, "No Z. I just want to ask, if we do get pregnant and there are two babies, we never find out which baby belongs to which one of you. What I'm saying is, we treat both babies as if they are all of our children. I don't want y'all showing favoritism to one or the other. The only circumstance where we would need to have any testing done would be in a medical emergency situation."

Precious asked, "Are y'all cool with that?"

Abel and Xerxes said simultaneously, "Yeah, we're cool."

Precious said, "I love you guys so much!?! We can chat about how and when we want to do this. I'll get back to y'all soon." She said, "Now y'all go fuck each other tonight like rabbits." She added, "When y'all are on daddy duty, y'all won't have no more privacy."

Precious hung up the phone. Xerxes and Abel sat silently for a long time looking at one another. Xerxes finally interrupted the quiet and asked Abel, "Are you sure about what we are about to do man?"

Abel replied, "Yeah Daddy. This is the type of relationship I always dreamed of being in. I thought I would eventually have a child with my significant other. I never thought about a female being in the mix because honestly I had thought about adoption."

Xerxes said, "And how do you feel about this IVF shit?"

Abel asked, "Do you want to do it the conventional way?"

Xerxes replied, "I don't want to do anything that would make you uncomfortable. I love Precious and I love being with her." Xerxes continued, "I have to tell you."

Abel asked, "What?"

Xerxes said, "Thinking of you being with Precious like that is a fucking turn on for me. I think it would be hot as shit, if she was open to it, for all three of us to be together. Shit, I'm getting hard now just thinking about it."

Abel said, "What!?!?" He continued, "You want me to be with a female?"

Xerxes replied, "It's not like I'm asking you to fuck an alien." He said, "I know you have been with a woman in your life before. This would be the last time."

Abel responded, "That might be hot. Me with Precious. You with Precious. You with me!! It could be hot."

Xerxes said, "Let's go upstairs and practice on the you with me option. I'm excited as fuck!!"

Abel replied, "I can see. I'm already there."

They left a trail of clothes as they raced to Xerxes' bedroom.

20

Xerxes and Abel thought long and hard about the life altering request from Precious. They vacillated between excitement and euphoria at the thought of becoming dads and fear and dread about the changes and responsibilities fatherhood would bring to their lives. Everytime Abel raised a question or expressed a potential concern, Xerxes quickly offered a rebuttal that helped to allay his fears. Precious did her best to calm their nerves as well by constantly providing updates on new information or discoveries that she had made. She also frequently checked with them to make sure they had not changed their minds. Abel was initially the least excited about the proposition but Xerxes' and Precious' assurances helped to calm his fears. Precious, Xerxes and Abel realized they were warming to the idea of becoming a "modern family" while they grew closer and closer to one another.

They texted incessantly and talked frequently about how they wanted the process to work and what each other's expectations were. Abel thought more and more about actually copulating with Precious and realized that the thought of it excited him. He reminded Xerxes that he had dated girls and enjoyed sex with women in high school and college. He reluctantly admitted that they told him that sex with him was unsatisfying. He said that a couple of the women he dated confessed that they thought he was poorly endowed and began to cheat on him with other guys. Abel conceded that he was so traumatized by their harsh pellucidity that he began to exclusively pursue relationships with men and gave up on women.

He already knew he had a sexual affinity for and attraction to men based on his adolescent experiences with Ira and the random guys he connected with in high school which made his decision to cease dating women easy. Abel was still attracted to women for companionship or friendship but never ardently pursued them anymore for anything serious because he still held the impression that he was unable to satisfy them sexually. He admitted to Xerxes that he was willing to try intercourse with Precious because he knew that she wouldn't debase or shame him.

When Precious learned that Abel was open to having sex with her she was surprised and intrigued. She was intimately familiar with Xerxes and what sex was like with him. After all, they had been together many times after their first encounter when she told him about her Law School admission. She had not allowed herself to even consider what being with Abel might be like. Even though they had worked together for several years and spent a lot of time together in meetings or conferences, they had never been unprofessional or acted inappropriately.

She knew he was gay so the possibility of the two of them being lovers never entered either of their minds. Precious had always found him to be handsome and she was impressed with how much more muscular and toned he had become since he began to work out consistently with Xerxes. She knew he was a good man though and grew to like the possibility of intimacy with him as she thought more and more about it. She smiled lustily as she realized that having sex with both of them at the same time would allow her to actually experience one of her long time secret sexual fantasies.

Precious shared her yen for motherhood and her desire to get pregnant with her gynecologist and together they developed a treatment plan and regimen to improve her chances of conceiving multiple embryos. She educated Abel and Xerxes on the details of the entire process and kept them abreast of all of her fertility treatments and medical appointments. They learned more than they ever thought they would need to know about ovulation, cervical mucus, cramps, pain, spotting an increased sex drive. They hoped to synchronize their schedules to coordinate with Precious' optimum fertility and even downloaded the Flo app and used it to track her schedule. They identified a weekend that was in perfect harmony for all of them and scheduled their babymaking tryst.

They all agreed that they wanted their weekend of coitus to be memorable, fun and relaxed. They decided that each one of them would choose an activity or diversion that they would all participate in over the weekend while they were together. Precious finished all of her work and notified her staff that she would be unavailable over the weekend. She packed a bag in the morning and left her office and headed directly to Washington's National Airport. Xerxes chartered a private jet to fly her home from DC and arranged for it to land at the airport in northwest indiana so she wouldn't have to deal with the hassle and congestion at either of Chicago's airports.

Abel's choice for their first activity was for the trio to spend a night at an underground, gay dance club that he sometimes frequented with Cyrus. He had not been in quite a while but loved the music and the energy from the crowd. He instructed Precious and Xerxes to dress comfortably and be prepared to stay out until the wee hours of the next morning. They met the private jet when it landed at the City Airport and grabbed Precious' bags and whisked her away as soon as she deplaned.

They jumped in Xerxes' Tesla and Abel punched the address of their destination into the navigation system. Xerxes dutifully followed the automated instructions to a secluded section of town filled with commercial lofts, wherehouses and large storage facilities. They parked the car in the middle of a nondescript street and walked up to a large, windowless gray metal door with no address or any other descriptive markings. Xerxes wondered if they were in the proper location or if they had arrived too early because the street was deserted and no music or revelry could be heard outside.

Abel assured them they were in the right location as he led them through the gray metal door and up a long flight of stairs. A small booth sat on the left side at the top of the stairs. A bald, bra-less perky young lady with heavily tattooed arms sat inside the booth and asked all three of them to present their ID or driver's license and announced that the entry fee was $15 per person. Abel covered the fee for all three of them and the young lady stamped the back of each of their wrists with a symbol that was only visible under a blue light.

They stepped through another large metal door just to the right of the booth with the bra-less sentry and were immediately bombarded with the rhythmic beats and booming bass of classic house music. The door opened into a large, open, dimly lit room filled with sofas and chairs covered in brightly colored cushions and overstuffed pillows. A cornucopia of joyful patrons representing every race, sex, age group and sexual orientation occupied almost every seat in the room. A sign above a doorway announcing TO DANCE hung over an alcove at the back of the open room and led down another long flight of stairs to the main dance room.

Abel led the trio through the open room and down the stairs. The music engulfed them as they descended the long staircase. The large open dance area had very muted lighting in each of it's corners. A large mirrored ball hanging from the ceiling reflected strobe lights emanating from the DJ booth and provided additional lighting as it spun around the room. Rows and stacks of large speakers stretched across the entire wall behind the DJ. Bodies gyrated wildly and danced freely to the rhythyms of the music pulsating at 150 beats per minute. Precious, Abel and Xerxes were swept into the dancing horde and they joined the masses as soon as they reached the bottom of the stairs.

The music was mesmerizing and hypnotic and the revelers danced as if in a trance. Madonna's classic theme "Vogue" blasted over the sound system and several dancers preened and posed in a fictitious battle to see who could out vogue the other in front of the table where the DJ stood. The crowd roared their approval with the vogue competition as Janet Jackson's "Throb" blended in imperceptably and the dance floor filled with party goers succumbing to the beat. Loleata Holloway's gay classic "Love Sensation" mixed in smoothly next and the crowd yelled and screamed their appreciation.

The DJ was on fire and it was impossible to discern when one song ended and another began. Precious, Xerxes and Abel danced as if they were possessed and joined the crowd of house heads who seemed to be intoxicated by the music. The club did not have a liquor license and the trio chose not to pharmaceut- ically stimulate themselves unlike many of the other patrons. They didn't know how long they had danced or how long they had been at the club but finally succumbed to exhaustion and hunger and agreed they had enough and scaled the long stair- case to leave. They struggled to resist the call of the music as they left the crowd still dancing, but made their way back out to the street and the waiting Tesla.

Precious and Xerxes raved about how much they had enjoyed the dance club and were shocked that they had never heard of it. Precious said that she was hungry and Abel suggested that they stop by the closest White Castle to grab cheap sliders before heading home. He told them that there was no better or more intriguing sight than the "street theater" in a White

Castle just before sun up. Xerxes drove to the nearest Castle and parked the car. They all went inside to place their orders. Just as Abel had predicted, the late night denizens of the fast food restaurant offered a humorous and entertaining show. As the trio ate their sliders, fries and sodas they were regaled by homeless men with solutions to the problems of the world and gigolos, pimps and prostitutes arguing over the proceeds from their illicit and amourous endeavors. Precious, Abel and Xerxes had their fill of the whimsical entertainment and got back in the car and headed to Xerxes' condo and fell asleep.

They arose just before noon and Precious announced that her selected activity was for them to enjoy a leisurely brunch together. She had heard about a new, black-owned farm-to-table restaurnat that had recently opened and suggested that they try it out. They all showered and dressed and Xerxes drove them to the crowded restaurant. He and Precious were met by adoring fans and grateful constituents and caused a huge confluence of people in the establishment's small foyer. Abel stood back and watched the crowd jostling to get the attention of his famous friends.

Precious chose the restaurant because one of her constituents opened it after receiving a community investment grant as a result of an inner city development program she initiated and heard that it was receiving rave reviews. The restaurant was named "Big Momma's House" and touted that all of their fare was delivered and prepared fresh each day. They wanted to soak up the sun on this unseasonably warm and bright February day so they opted to sit at a table on the ample patio. Once seated, they bantered with diners at other tables and signed autographs while waiting for one of the servers to come take their order.

The tables on the patio were patterned after large picnic tables with bench style seating. Each table had a large umbrella on top that could be opened or closed during the summer if the sun became too warm or oppressive. The tables were covered with white linen tablecloths and could seat parties of between two and eight diners. A basket of freshly baked bread, rolls and croissant was delivered to the table as soon as they were seated. Each table was adorned with a bouquet of fresh cut flowers as well.

Because the menu changed each day, chalkboards were strategically positioned throughout the eatery so that patrons could easily see and choose what they wanted to eat. The staff dressed in khaki slacks and white long-sleeve polo shirts with the "Big Momma's House" name and logo embroidered across the left breast. After they had been seated for a few moments, a server approached and greeted them. He asked if he could bring fresh spring water and highlighted the various flavors of mimosa the restaurant offered.

Precious asked, "So, which one do you like the best?"

The server replied, "I like the standard OJ mimosa myself but some of my coworkers rave about the mango." He added, "I personally haven't had that one, but everyone seems to like it."

The trio placed orders for three mango mimosa.

The server said, "I will get your water and mimosas started and come back and get your meal order."

Precious felt a bit naughty and decided she wanted to flirt with the server. She said, "Yes honey, you hurry back and take me away from these dirty old men."

The server who was probably in his early twenties but looked like he was a teenager was startled and replied, "Y-y-yes ma'am."

Precious continued, "You know you can get this anytime you

want."

Xerxes chimed in, "I think there are statutory rape laws in this state."

Precious replied, "I know, he may look young, but I can turn him into a man."

Abel joined in, "And spend the rest of your term in jail too Mrs. Robinson."

They all laughed. When the server realized Precious was joking, he laughed too.

The server returned with their drinks and took their orders. He was still nervous from Precious' attempts at flirting with him and tried hard not look directly at her when he served their beverages.

Precious ordered the seafood salad, which came with shrimp, scallops and crabmeat. It was one of the restaurant's signature dishes. Xerxes ordered the Caesar Chicken Salad and Abel chose the Lobster bisque with a friend oyster po'boy sandwich to go with it. They talked casually as they waited for their meals to arrive. Once their food arrived, they continued their banter in between bites of the sumptuous food. They all agreed that the rave reviews were appropriate and planned to return to the restaurant when they could.

Xerxes got to plan to last activity for the trio and had arranged manicures, pedicures and massages for all of them at a high end spa after brunch. He wanted them to be relaxed and refreshed before heading back to his place. He knew that a good massage always stimulated his libido and remembered how relaxed and amorous, Precious became after she visited the spa when they were together.

Xerxes wanted their evening of relaxation and pleasure to continue when they got back to his place after the spa and selected
several classic movies that they could binge watch together.
He wanted them to chill before they moved to the last phase of
their fantasy weekend together.

He arranged to have fun, tasty and healthy finger food set up in
his media room as they all settled in to the serene and pleasant
atmosphere. He raised the temperature in the house to make
it warm and cozy and made sure that anything that Precious or
Abel wanted was close and on hand. All they needed to do was
relax and enjoy one another's company.

After watching several movies Xerxes turned off the television
and switched to smooth jazz music and allowed the soothing
sounds to waft throughout the house. They had spent all weekend laughing and talking about their bond and how excited
they were about the next steps their lives were taking. Xerxes
dimmed the lights in the media room and throughout the
house and slowly walked over to Abel and gently kissed him on
the lips. The gentle kiss became more passionate and as Xerxes
and Abel embraced, Precious walked up behind Abel and embraced him.

They took the communal hug as a symbol that they were ready
to begin the last phase of their weekend together and all headed
toward Xerxes' bedroom suite.

Xerxes used an app on his phone to turn on the steam and the
warm water formed a mist on the glass walls of the oversized
shower. They undressed and walked into the shower together
and took turns lathering, kissing and caressing one another.
Xerxes and Abel gently massaged Precious' breasts and they
took turns washing and cleansing each other. Precious stood
between Xerxes and Abel as they embraced and kissed and she
took her turn kissing both of them.

They completed their sensual cleansing and Xerxes turned off the water. They stepped out of the shower and took turns drying each other's naked bodies. They liberally moisturized one another with shea butter and cocoa butter and moved from the shower to the bedroom. The dim lighting displayed a sensual outline of their three conjoined bodies on the wall opposite the oversized bed.

Abel could feel the start of an erection as Xerxes kissed him. He turned around to embrace Precious and began to kiss her. As Abel kissed Precious, Xerxes pressed himself against Abel's back. Precious allowed her hands to explore Abel's body and she grabbed Xerxes' arms as he hugged Abel from behind. Her hands slowly descended from Abel's chest down his waist until she touched his rock hard erection. She was startled and quickly removed her hand. Abel gently grabbed her hand and placed it back around his member.

Abel allowed his fingers to explore Precious' bare breasts and was excited by her large and firm areola. He gently kissed her nipples as Xerxes moved behind her and kissed her neck and back. He dropped to his knees and began to taste the moistness between her thighs. Abel and Xerxes were stimulating Precious' most sensitive and erogenous spots and she had never experienced such pleasure. She could barely stand as both of her favorite men devoured her like nectar.

The sight of Xerxes pleasuring Precious excited Abel more stiffening his erection. The moans and sighs from each of them filled the room and the onomatopoeia of slurping and sucking drowned out the smooth jazz music. Xerxes lifted Precious and gently placed her in the center of his bed. Xerxes knew that Precious loved scented candles during their lovemaking sessions and had placed lit, lightly scented candles throughout the room. The slight smell of sage and incense also filled the air.

Xerxes joined Precious on the bed but positioned himself dir-ectly over her head. He began to kiss her as she slowly began to pleasure herself. She carefully massaged the treasure between her thighs and immediately became aroused. Xerxes noticed the white, sticky fluid that covered her fingers and said, "Let me taste that P!!!" She obliged and allowed Xerxes to savor the taste of her moistness. Abel saw the enjoyment on Xerxes' face and grabbed him by his ears and kissed him so that he could enjoy Precious' essence as well.

Abel wondered if he might be able to stimulate Precious the same way that he enjoyed pleasuring Ira. He remembered the power that he had over all of the men on whom he had per-formed oral sex. He wanted to know if he could excite Precious the same way. He climbed on the bed and placed his nose on the treasure spot that she had been massaging. She shivered when his nose touched her. He marveled at the scent of fresh soap and cocoa butter and licked his lips. He gingerly tasted her golden spot with his tongue and Precious giggled nervously. He bit her softly and she squealed. Abel alternated between using his nose, his tongue and a slight bite and Precious went crazy. She writhed and squirmed on the bed as Abel tasted her wetness on his tongue. Xerxes noticed the glorious fluid covering Abel's nose and lifted his head and kissed him. He relished the taste of Precious' essence on Abel's tongue.

Xerxes gently whispered to Abel, "She's all yours man."

Abel slowly slid his erect penis inside Precious. She winced at first and asked him to be careful because he was larger than she expected. He felt her warmth and moistness and she moaned a sigh of approval and welcomed all of his hardness. Xerxes' man-hood was hard as a rock too as he watched his man penetrate his woman. He walked around the bed and stood behind Abel and rubbed his manstick against the warmth of Abel's ass. He badly wanted to slide inside him but resisted the desire to penetrate him.

Precious was enjoying her experience with Abel. His rhythm was slow but forceful. As his thrusts increased in frequency his breathing did as well. He whispered to Precious, "Is this okay for you?"

Precious replied, "Yes, daddy." "Give it to me!!"

Xerxes chimed in, "Give it to her A."

Abel was focused and realized that he was enjoying Precious more than he thought he would. His motions became intense and he knew that he would soon release. He yelled, "Precious, I'm cumming!!"

She replied, "Give it to me Abel." "Make me pregnant!!"

Xerxes said, "She's yours Baby."

Abel released a flood of his semen inside of Precious and yelled, "Oh Fuck!! Oh, my God!! Oh, Fuck!!"

Precious screamed, "I want it all Abel. Don't stop!!"

Abel finally regained his composure and slowly withdrew from inside Precious. He put his mouth close to her ear and whispered, "I love you. You crazy bitch, I love you."

Precious giggled and replied, "I love you too, you old queen."

As Abel pulled out and climbed off of the bed, Xerxes immediately took his place. He had gotten so hard watching Abel that he caused Precious to gasp as he entered her. She seemed startled when he entered her and said, "Oh, Z" I forgot you were here." She went on, "I don't ever remember you being this big and hard Z. Something must have you excited."

Xerxes said, "I just got through watching my baby handle his business. I didn't know that he could put it down like that."

Precious said, "I didn't either. I didn't know he had it like that."

Abel interrupted, "Y'all know I am still in the room right?"

They laughed.

Xerxes kissed Precious on her nipples. He slowly moved in and out of her. He wanted her to get comfortable with his extra firmness. She was still wet from Abel penetration. Xerxes was more excited than he had ever been before with her. Knowing that the lubrication for his sex with Precious had been provided by Abel drove him crazy. As he began his thrusts inside Precious, Xerxes felt the warmth of Abel's tongue on his ass.

Xerxes was startled and yelled, "What the fuck?!?!"

Abel responded, "I just wanted to taste you while you are pleasing Precious."

Xerxes replied, "That shit was hot. Keep it up man."

Precious moaned as she felt Xerxes inside her. She welcomed his size and his girth. Abel was larger than she thought he would be but he was nowhere near as large as Xerxes.

Xerxes was more excited than Precious had ever remembered him being before. He was simultaneously forceful and gentle and made sure that Precious was OK. He began a continuous rhythm that was memorable to Precious as they repeated the dance that they had done so many times before together.

Abel alternated between tasting and teasing Xerxes to kissing and sucking Precious' nipples. They all loved the synchronicity of their lovemaking. Their bodies and souls were in harmony and they made beautiful music together. The realization of Precious' fantasy was more than even she expected it would be and she exploded several times during her encounter with both of her men. She yelled, "Z, Daddy, it's so good!!"

Xerxes said, "I'm going to make you pregnant Mama."

Precious replied, "I'm already pregnant. I know Abel did his job. Please do yours Z. I want to feel all of your man juice inside me."

Abel said, "Give it to her Xerxes. Give it all to her."

Xerxes yelled, "Oh, Shit!!! I'm cumming. Shit!!!!"

Precious screamed, "I feel it Z. Yes!! Yes!! I feel it all."

Xerxes fell on the bed beside Precious. He was exhausted and spent. Abel fell on the bed on the other side of Precious as well. She lay on the bed in between both of them. They all lay on the bed marinating in their lovemaking and before long they all fell asleep.

21

Precious was convinced that she had been impregnated by both Xerxes and Abel at the moment of conception. When she woke up the next morning she sensed that something was different. She decided not to tell Xerxes or Abel what she felt and made up her mind to wait until she had definitive confirmation before letting either of them know.

They all were strangely quiet and seemed extraordinarily nervous the morning after their night of pleasure and bliss. Xerxes expected that they would be ravenous after their night of steamy and passionate coition and had arranged for the cook to prepare a huge breakfast of fresh fruit, homemade biscuits, bacon, waffles, grits and eggs. He hoped that they would rehash their night of lustfulness and discuss and plan the next steps on their journey to parenthood while they leisurely enjoyed the hearty meal. He imagined that they would lounge together all morning before they had to take Precious back to the airport so she could return to DC. The disquiet and unease that filled the air was in direct opposition to the exuberance and ebullience that Xerxes expected.

Precious showered and dressed quickly and ate a couple of pieces of bacon and had a few bites of the fresh fruit before announcing that she needed to return to Washington to work on her re-election campaign with her staff. Abel and Xerxes were startled by her abrupt request to leave. Xerxes confirmed that the charter flight could return her to DC earlier than expected and he arranged for a driver to get her to the airport as quickly as possible. When the driver arrived, they hugged her long and tight and insisted that she notify them when she got back to DC. They decided to return to bed after she left and spent the rest of their day making love.

Precious comfortably eased back into her hectic legislative, public appearance and re-election campaign schedule once she was back in DC. Days lapsed into weeks and she focused her efforts on supporting her constituents and preparing for her first re-election campaign. She was so busy that she paid little attention to the slight physiological changes that she began to experience. She awoke late one morning and dressed quickly needing to get to the office for early meetings with her staff and her campaign team. She bolted out of her apartment and darted across the street to catch the Metro. She luckily found an open seat on the near full train just as it was pulling out of the station. She settled in for her six station ride to Federal Center Southwest and realized that her period was late.

She had been working extremely long hours on a vitally important bill that would offer relief to citizens with exorbitant student loan debt and her campaign team was finalizing her plan and strategy for the upcoming primary. She had been so busy that she had't been able to focus on her health and well-being. When she realized she was late, she remembered that she had noticed a tenderness in her breasts and experienced slight nausea and minor cramps. She blamed her symptoms on over-work and not taking a break or making time to recuperate. She assumed that the fatigue she felt was caused by the rigors of her schedule and refused to succumb to any feelings of exhaustion.

She hadn't yet mentioned her desires to get pregnant to any of her staff and wanted to be certain of her condition before noti-

fying them, or anyone else. Precious was nervous and excited
at the same time and couldn't wait to confirm whether she was
pregnant or not.

Her menstrual cycle was meticulously predictable and she
could rely on it like clockwork. She knew to expect it every 28
days and felt that it was more accurate than the best and most
expensive Swiss chronograph. When she was late by only one
or two days, she was concerned but not overly distressed. She
attributed her lateness to the stresses of working on her bill and
the requirements of the primary re-election campaign. When
the one or two day delay stretched into a week, she decided
that she needed to take a pregnancy test to finally confirm what
she already knew and felt.

Precious stopped at the new Duane Reed Drug Store that had
recently opened in her neighborhood on her way home from
work and picked up a First Response pregnancy test. The First
Response tests were rated to have the best and most accurate
results among the leading over the counter choices. She figured that if the test came back positive, she would arrange an
appointment with her gynecologist to get confirmation. She
maintained her decision to wait until she knew for certain that
she was pregnant before informing Xerxes and Abel.

Precious' morning was full of meetings with her staff and her
campaign team. She met with her staff to get an update on the
status of the student loan relief legislation because announcing
it could be a boon to her campaign. She met with her campaign
staff to be sure they were prepared to imediately shift their
focus to the general election and her Republican challenger
as soon as the primary election was over. She also needed to
make several fund raising calls to high-dollar campaign donors
as well. She wasn't able to reach out to her doctor until just
before noon. The First Response test had shown positive and

she hoped to secure an appointment as soon as she could to verify it. She dialed her doctor's number and the Receptionist answered, "Good morning!! Dr. Nwadi's Office, how can we help you?'

"Good morning!! This is Precious Thomas. How soon can I get an appointment to see the doctor?"

"Good morning Ms. Thomas is this apppointment for a regular checkup? Or, is something else going on and you need to see the doctor right away?"

"I need to see the doctor right away. It's not urgent, but I still want to see her as soon as possible."

"Let me check something. Can you hold the line for a moment?"

"Yes" replied Precious.

The Receptionist returned to the line, "The doctor just had a cancellation for tomorrow morning at 9:00 AM. Will that work for you?"

"Yes, I will move some things on my calendar, but I will be there tomorrow morning."

"Good, Ms. Thomas, I have you down for 9:00 AM tomorrow. We will see you in the morning."

Precious could barely concentrate for the rest of the day. She attended meetings but was clearly preoccupied. Her staff had to repeat statements or ask questions several times before she responded. She was off all day long and her Chief of Staff pressed her to make sure everything was OK. Precious dismissed her concerns or questions and told her team to keep their focus on getting the bill done and out the door.

She was normally the last person to leave the office for home each day, but this day was anxious and rushed home. She surprised her staff when she grabbed her belongings and bolted out the door right at 5:00 PM. All she wanted to do was to get home and luxuriate in the tub. She wanted to soak in the warm, steamy water and think about how her life was about to change forever.

She wanted to call Xerxes and Abel and let them know what she suspected but forced herself to wait until she was certain. She would have a definitive answer soon after her appointment with the doctor and decided to wait until then to tell them. She craved a drink of wine or something harder to soothe her nerves but decided against it. She thought that since she felt she was pregnant she needed to be healthy for her unborn child, or children. She finished her bath, prepared herself a steeping cup of hot chocolate and went to bed early.

Precious slept fitfully and woke the next morning well before her normal awakening time. She bathed and dressed slowly. Her mind was heavy with thoughts of the news she expected to receive from the doctor. She called her Chief of Staff to remind her that she had an early appointment and would not be in the office until the afternoon and prepared a light breakfast of coffee, eggs, wheat toast and bacon. After breakfast, she washed the dishes, cleaned the kitchen and waited anxiously for the Uber that she had arranged to take her to her doctor's office.

The DC morning traffic was not as jammed or congested as it can normally be and she arrived at her doctor's office at 8:45 AM. She exited her shared ride, walked into the office building where her gynecologist was located and rode the elevator up to the doctor's office. She slowly opened the door to the doctor's suite and was warmly welcomed by the Receptionist who checked her in and immediately took her to one of the examination rooms. The Receptionist instructed Precious to undress and assured her that someone would be in to see her soon. A Nurse practitioner told Precious that she would be the first patient seen by the doctor while she took her temperature, weight and blood pressure.

Dr. Nwadi entered the examination room a few minutes later. The doctor's flawless and smooth ebony complexion was just a shade darker than Precious'. She was much shorter than Precious but the five inch heels that she wore made them stand almost face to face. The doctor wore an impeccably tailored bright red suit with a crème colored blouse underneath. She wore a Delta Sigma Theta sorority pin on her left lapel. The doctor's medium frame was perfectly proportionate for her height and weight. Her thick, silver-white hair was fashioned into large, long and regal braids which were adorned with colorful ribbons of red, gold and green. Her Kenyan accent was clear as she greeted Precious, "Good morning, my sister!! How are you this morning?"

"Good morning doctor. I think am well, but I hope that you will confirm that for me."

"So what brings you in this morning on such short notice? We need you up on Capitol Hill doing the important work that you have been doing."

"Thank you doctor. I am doing the best I can." She began to cry, "I took a pregnancy test at home a few days ago. It was positive. I want you to confirm it for me."

The doctor asked, "But why are you crying my sister? Bringing another life into this world is a beautiful thing."

"I'm sorry. I'm just so happy and so hopeful. This is something that I want so bad."

"Ah. I see. Well, my dear, let us get this testing done so we will know for certain if you should be joyful."

The doctor explained that since Precious' home pregnancy test registered a positive result, she would administer several more sensitive tests to confirm. She explained that she would run another, more sensitive urine pregnancy test and that would administer a blood test as well. She apologized when she told Precious that she would need to perform a pelvic exam as well but explained that she wanted to be exhaustive in her examination. Lastly, she said that she would also take a sonogram to see how far along Precious might be if she was indeed pregnant.

Dr. Nwadi said, "All of this will take about an hour and a half. Do you have that much time?"

"I have taken off the entire morning. I am all yours."

"OK, my dear. We will do the urine test first. Someone will be here to take care of you. Once all of the testing is done, you and I can chat again. Is that OK?"

"Let's get it done. Yes, that's OK."

As soon as the doctor left, a Nurse practitioner came and led Precious to a bathroom just a few doors down the hall from the Exam Room. She handed Precious a urine sample cup and asked her to fill it. She was instructed to place the cup in a sample receptacle in the bathroom and to return to her Exam Room when she was done. Precious complied and left the sample.

When she got back to her room, another practitioner came to take a sample of her blood. She told Precious that blood tests were used less often to determine pregnancy than some of the other tests she would be taking but that Dr. Nwadi wanted to be completely certain of her condition. Precious told the Nurse that everything was fine and that the doctor had explained everything that was being done. Precious never liked needles, but complimented the Technician on her tenderness and gentleness. As soon as the Technician completed the blood draw and left the room, another practitioner entered the room and escorted her to the room for her pelvic exam.

Precious had never, ever enjoyed a pelvic exam and the possibility of being pregnant did not make this particular examination any more enjoyable, exciting or pleasant for her. The technician was a gentle as she could possibly be but also had to be as thorough as possible as well. Once she was done, she led Precious back to her original Examination Room.

The last two tests that Precious had take, the ultrasound and a transvaginal sonogram would inform the doctor how far along Precious' pregnancy had progressed. The sonogram was most important because it could determine if Precious was going to have more than one baby. She was led into another room and asked to lay on the examination table. The Technician told her that she would apply a translucent gel to her belly and a guide a wand over her stomach to get a picture of the baby. She shivered when the cold gel was applied and giggled as the technician guided the wand over her belly. She refused to look at the monitor and directed the technician to not tell her anything that she saw.

After the sonogram and ultrasound were complete, the Technician directed Precious to get dressed and return to her original Exam room. She handed Precious a towel to use to clean up any remaining gel from the last two procedures. The Technician told her the doctor was reviewing the results of all of the tests she had taken that morning, except for the blood test, and would be in to see her shortly. She told her the results from the blood test would take 2 – 3 days to process. The technician asked if Precious wanted water or anything and after she declined, left the room.

Precious dressed as quickly as she could and found her way back to the exam room. She sat nervously waiting for the doctor to return pretending to peruse a magazine. Dr. Nwadi tapped slightly on the door and opened it very slowly. She stepped into the room and looked directly at Precious saying, "My sister, we have the results from all of your tests today, except the blood test. We won't have those results for another day or so.

There is a bit of a surprise in what we saw."

"Surprise!? Dr. what did you find. Is everything OK?"

"My dear Precious, we found that not only are you have a baby, but you are having two babies. My dear, you are pregnant with twins."

Precious screamed. "Oh Doctor, are you sure?!?! Please tell me that you are certain. I so was hoping that there would be two babies!!"

Dr. Nwadi replied, "Yes, we detected two healthy fetuses. It is too early to tell the sex at this time, but you are having two babies."

Precious cried, "Doctor, you don't know what this means to me. Oh, thank you, thank you, thank you. Is there anything special that I need to do? Any special care that I need to follow?"

"We will put together a pre-natal care program for you. Congratulations, my dear!!"

"Oh, no doctor. Thank you!! Thank you for putting me in your schedule with such short notice and thank you for being so thorough!!"

"Hopefully you and the father will be able to participate in one of your upcoming appointments. It would be nice to get him involved in this process as early as we can." The doctor laughed, "I mean he has already been involved, but you know what I mean."

Precious laughed to herself as well. She was amused when the doctor said "The father". She said to herself, "Boy doctor have I get a surprise for you."

Precious left the doctor's office. She was ecstatic and nervous. She wanted to scream out loud and wanted to hug everyone she saw. Her life had changed forever and she wanted to shout it from the rooftops.

22

Xerxes and Abel made love all morning after Precious left to return to DC. They asked her if she wanted them to accompany her to the airport, but she indicated that she wanted to be alone. They were voracious from their lovemaking and went to the kitchen to see if any food was left from the breakfast that the cook had prepared. Xerxes said, "You looked like you really enjoyed yourself with P last night. Do you mind if I ask you a question?"

"Sure baby, you can ask me anything you want."

"After seeing you put it down last night, are you sure about this? You looked like you were really into it with her. Do you ever wish you could be with a woman? I don't want to get in your way man."

Abel reached over and touched Xerxes' hand. He said, "I was able to perform with Precious last night because you were with me and you wanted me to. I was excited because you were watching me and I wanted to turn you on." Abel asked, "Did it work?"

Xerxes responded, "Fuck yeah!!! My dick got hard as a brick watching you stroking her last night." He added, "Hell, I'm getting hard right now just thinking about it."

Abel said, "Good. I want you to think of that when we are together from now on. I want the thought of me inside Precious to make your dick hard while it's inside me."

"Damn, baby." "You want to go back upstairs."

"No big Daddy. Let's save that for later." He added, "We got to do something else other than just fuck all day."

"Yeah, I guess you're right. But I'm going to wear that ass out tonight."

Abel got serious and asked, "What if it worked? What if she gets pregnant? Are you, are we ready for that?"

"Honestly man, I am excited about it. I would love to be a Dad. I would love for P to be the Mom. It would be icing on the cake if we were both Dads."

"I never, ever thought that I would be a Dad. I was never interested in or attracted to any woman that I would want to be the Mom of my kids. Damn, now I am excited about the possibility."

"Our child, our children, if we have them, will be well cared for. We have to make sure they are well educated and not spoiled. I hate spoiled brats."

"I know what you mean. I remember all of the spoiled rich, white girls I used to get with in college. They all thought that just because they had money, they could treat me any kind of way. They could get me to do anything."

"What was that like for you?"

"It seems like I was on a continuous fuck man. These white bitches would do anything to get some black dick. I used to hate them asking about my BBC."

"BBC?"

"Yeah, big, black cock." He added, "These white bitches took it up the ass. They would let three, four or five of us fuck them at the same time. They were relentless. And if you acted like you didn't want to be with them, they would offer cash, cars, trips, drugs." He added, "They used to hate me because I would never fuck without a hat on. I wasn't never going to marry no white hoe. Shit, I was not going to have no babies by no white bitch. My mamma would kill me. She used to tell me "If she can't use your comb, don't bring her home". He added, "It was just an easy fuck for me."

Xerxes added, "Precious had to know. She didn't seem to be upset or to care. I think she knew what is was like being a football player. But she never ever asked who I was with or what I was doing. She always asked about my classes and how I was doing in school." Xerxes said, "She always wanted me to be better and do better so after a while, I gave it up for her. I guess I started to think that it was so empty and wasteful."

Abel said, "She is a special woman, isn't she? But what if she is pregnant by both of us? How do we make that shit work?"

Xerxes said, "We just make sure that we are the best dads and friends that we can be to each other and the babies. I think her idea about not finding out who the father is might be a really good idea."

Abel said, "Yes. That way, we won't treat them differently." He added, "So do you want a boy or a girl?"

Xerxes said, "A boy of course. I need somebody to continue this legacy. What about you?"

Abel replied, "I think a boy, but I would be happy with either one." He went on, "I never thought I would have either one. It's hard out here for a Black Man. He is going to have to deal with being black in this racist ass country."

Xerxes interjected, "They both will."

Abel said, "Yeah, I know. But it is harder on a black boy than a black girl. The system is set up to put us down and keep us down. If I wasn't a business owner and you a former football player, we would probably see it even more." Abel said, "I used to hear about it from Cyrus. He would tell me about how the cops would stop him just because it was a Tuesday sometime. He hadn't done anything except for be in the wrong place at the wrong time."

Xerxes interrupted, "Are you still thinking about that mother-fucker?!?"

Abel said, "No, baby. Not at all. I haven't thought about him in a long ass time. But the possibility of bringing a male child into this world brings back all of the shit I had to face when I was setting up my business. All of the problems I had finding funding and dealing with racist ass lenders for financing." He added, "We gotta make sure we raise them right if they are boys. Black boys are three times more likely to have a relationship with the criminal justice system than white boys. We have to make sure that we protect our kids, if we have them, from this bullshit."

Xerxes said, "That's the kind of shit I wanted to do with my foundation." He added, "I want to make a difference in all children's lives. Especially now that I, I mean we, may be fathers."

Abel said, "I'm with you baby. Let's make that shit happen."

Xerxes asked Abel, "What do we need to do to get this off the ground? How do we get it started?" He said, "Now that I know what I want to do, I want to put my energy behind it. I can probably get some of my old teammates to participate as well." Abel said that setting up a not-for-profit organization was something that he would normally rely on Precious to help him do but agreed to do some investigating to see how it might be done.

Xerxes thought that establishing a relationship with one of the local schools might also be a good way to start the ball rolling. He wondered if it was possible to fund a perpetual scholarship at Roosevelt high school. He wanted to do something to make sure that graduating students could afford and were able to go to college. He wanted to make sure that potential scholarship recipients met specific and stringent attendance and scholastic criteria to be considered for an award. Xerxes knew the person that LeBron James had worked with when he set up a similar scholarship at his alma mater in Akron, Ohio and they agreed that they needed to contact him.

Abel smiled with admiration as he noticed the excitement in Xerxes' eyes when he talked about the scholarship. He knew that the scholarship or foundation would secure both his and Xerxes' legacies. He knew that they would be able to support a lot of the neediest students in the area for a long time with their largesse and his eyes began to moisten.

Xerxes said, 'Baby?!? What's wrong baby? Why are you crying."

Abel replied, "I'm sorry Daddy. This is exactly the kind of thing that I always wanted to do with a man. This is what I always hoped to do with my man." He added, "And you want to do it. You want to do it as much as I do."

Xerxes said, "Of course I want to do it baby. But why are your crying?"

Abel responded, "I don't think I could ever love you anymore than I do at this moment. I am glad that I am with you."

Xerxes got up and walked over to where Abel was sitting. He leaned down and kissed him gently on the lips. Abel returned the kiss and stood up and put his arms around his shoulders. They kissed again and embraced each other. They stood in the kitchen in a long passionate embrace.

Xerxes asked, "So are you sure you want to do this with me?" He added, "After today, I am all in with you." Xerxes said, "This is your last chance to change your mind. After today, I am never going to let you go."

Abel looked Xerxes directly in his eyes. He said, "I'm already yours Daddy. I have been since our first night together. I thought you already knew."

Xerxes kissed Abel passionately and they felt the heat from their embrace. Abel could feel the size and hardness of Xerxes' erection on his stomach and put his arms around Xerxes' shoulders. Xerxes picked him up right there in the kitchen and lay him down on the table. He dropped his athletic shorts and removed Abel's boxer briefs all in one motion. Abel was already moist with anticipation and Xerxes entered him smoothly and deeply. They consummated their relationship and love right there on top of the table.

The cook walked into the kitchen to clean the dishes and prepare for lunch. Seeing the conjoined pair on the table, she secretly retreated to another part of the house smiling as she left. She knew that Xerxes had finally found the right person for him.

23

Precious texted "(>.<)(>.<) and TWINS" to Abel and Xerxes and immediately dialed Xerxes' phone. He recognized her ringtone and answered the call using the speakerphone. Precious screamed "Wake up bitches!!! We're pregnant!!!" She continued, "Z?!? Z, is Abel there with you?!! Wake the fuck up!! I got some news."

Xerxes nudged Abel and stirred him from his slumber. The beep on their phones from Precious' text and the excitement and joy in her voice roused them both to full attention.

Xerxes responded groggily, "Morning P. What's up baby?!? What did you say?"

Precious yelled, "Take your dick out of Abel's ass or mouth or wherever it is!! I'm pregnant!!! I am definitely pregnant and we're having twins!!! Can you believe it?!?"

Xerxes shook Abel as he sat upright in the bed, "Wake up A!! Wake up man. Precious is pregnant. She's having twins!!"

Abel slowly awakened and realized what he was hearing, "W-w-what? Who the fuck is that making all that noise this early?"

Precious said, "Come out of that big dick coma Abel." She squealed, "Your old, gay ass is about to be a Daddy." She asked Xerxes to switch to FaceTime so they could all see one another.

Abel sat up as well and yelled, "What?!? Those powdered eggs of yours actually worked!?!?"

Xerxes roared with laughter, "Get her baby?!!"

Precious replied, "Not today Bitch!! What is more remarkable is that both of you horny bastards had any good swimmers left. I know y'all spend every day and night wasting baby juice on each other." She added, "The doctor says the babies are fine."

She continued, "When I got up the morning after y'all raped me I felt different and already knew I was pregnant...."

Abel interrupted, "Uh, you can't rape the willing. I seem to remember you attacking me....."

Precious stopped him, "Anyway, I didn't want to say anything until I knew for sure. I guess that is why I was acting so funny and left to come back to DC early that next morning. I took a pregnancy test when I got back and it was positive. I went to the doctor a few days later and she confirmed it. And she told me I was having twins!!!"

Xerxes asked, "So how far along are you? Do you know what we're having yet?"

Precious replied, "The doctor said about eight weeks now. She wants to meet the father. I didn't have the heart to tell her that I had two baby daddies. I'm afraid that she is going to think I am a whore with two daddies..."

Abel interrupted again, "Well, you are a whore."

Precious replied, "Whatever Abel. I can still kick your ass if I have to." She added, "It would be nice if y'all could be a part of some of the pre-natal stuff. The doctor wants me to attend some birthing classes and shit like that." Precious asked, "Can y'all work that into your schedule?"

Xerxes said, "I can be there whenever you want or need me to be?"

Abel said, "I can rearrange my calendar to get there too.When do you need us?"

Precious replied, "The doctor gave me a whole schedule. I wanted to give y'all the happy news first. I can send you the schedule by text. Maybe y'all can alternate weeks or something? That way, one of y'all will be here throughout the whole pregnancy. As I get closer to the delivery date, both of y'all can be here then."

Xerxes and Abel said, "Sounds like a plan."

Xerxes said, "I can probably come first since A might need more time to work out his schedule."

Abel said, "Cool, that works for me. Precious, is there anything that you need right now? Are you good?"

Precious replied, "Yes Abel baby, I am really good. The doctor says I am healthy and so far, the babies are doing well." She added, "I told my staff and they won't even let me lift a paper clip. I have someone who rides to work with me in the mornings and someone who goes home with me in the evening too. Yes, baby I'm really good."

Xerxes said, "P, we have to bring you up to speed on what's been going on here too. Abel and I have committed to one another and to being good Dads. We are also funding scholarships to support other kids to have as much opportunity as our kids will have." Xerxes said, "Baby, you would be proud of us. This is the kind of thing that I always wanted to do. I'm so glad and fortunate to be doing it with people that I love."

Precious began to cry. Abel asked, "What's wrong Precious? Why are your crying." He asked sarcastically, "It's not baby hormones or nothing like that is it?"

She replied, "Fuck you Abel!! These are not hormones. She added, "This is almost too good to be true. This is happening just the way I dreamed that it would. I'm having a baby with my two favorite guys. I couldn't ask for anything more."

Abel asked, "So Precious, what does it fell like? I mean, what is being pregnant like for you?"

Precious said, "Well, I am still the sexiest bitch on the planet. I mean, I have not really begun to show yet. And when I do begin to show, y'all still better tell me I'm sexy." She said, "I had some morning sickness for a few weeks, but I was able to handle it OK. I can't seem to stand certain foods or smells that I used to love. Like don't put an avocado in front of me right now, but other than that, I am good."

Precious went on, "I am trying to be as active as I can. Lord knows, I don't want to gain more weight than I have to." She interjected, "Z, after I drop this load, you are going to have to put me on a serious workout program. I am going to get my body back if it kills me."

Xerxes said, "I got you baby. We will get that body back in shape right away." He added, "What else do you need? Do we need to start to getting stuff for the baby? I think that whatever you get there, we need to duplicate here. I hope we will get a chance to spend a lot of time with this little munchkin."

Precious said, "Look at you?!?! Coming up with good ideas on your own." That makes a lot of sense." She said, "I will start a list. My staff wants me to have a huge baby shower. And rest assured when I want to get out and get my freak on, y'all will definitely be doing Daddy duty."

Abel joked, "Get your freak on!! With who?!?"

Xerxes added, "Yeah P, me and A are going to cockblock you from now on."

Precious took a serious tone and said, "Whatever. Before I let y'all go there is one thing we need to discuss."

They asked in unison, "What?"

Precious replied, "Well I am a public figure and the fact that I am pregnant is going to make the news. People are going to want to know who the father is." She added, "I wouldn't put it past one of these stupid ass Repugnicans to make a big deal about me not being married but if they ask who the father is, what should I tell them? Most people won't be able to get their mind around me having two baby daddies. I can read the headlines already."

Abel interjected, "No worries Precious. You should tell them that Xerxes is the father."

Xerxes asked, "What? Why? Are you sure?"

Abel replied, "Yes, I am sure....."

Precious interruped, "Abel I can name you or Z, but I don't think naming both of y'all makes sense. I am not ashamed of you or anything if that is what you think. I just want us to know and be ready for whatever may be coming down the road."

Abel said, "I know you're not ashamed and I understand what you are trying to do, but saying Xerxes is the father makes the most sense." He added, "I am a gay man and don't want to cause any scandal and no one will believe that the baby is mine anyway. Hell, no one would think I would even know where to find the pussy. Let alone, know what to do with it once I found it."

Precious replied, "Hell, not only did you find it, you definitely knew what to do once you got to it." She apologized, "Oh, sorry. I just had a flashback."

They all laughed.

Xerxes said, "I understand why you have to name someone. If Abel is cool with you telling the media that I am the father, then so am I." He went on, "One question though. Will there be any problems with A showing up at some of the birthing classes."

Precious said, "No, I don't think so. People know that we were together and that you are an ex-football player who does TV and sports now. They also know that Abel and I have a long friendship from my attorney days. I can just say that he is helping me out while you are on assignment."

Precious asked again, "Abel are you sure? I don't want you to think that you are playing second fiddle or anything."

Abel replied, "No Precious, I am good." He asked, "I don't remember if you said you knew what we are having yet. Did the doctor tell you?"

Precious replied, "I wouldn't let her tell me. I want it to be a surprise. I want to find out when they get here."

Xerxes interrupted, "So no gender reveal parties or anything like that?"

Precious said, "No. No damn gender reveal party. Sounds like Abel has turned you into a flaming, party-throwing faggot already." She asked, "Y'all remember our deal. We won't ask the sex or who the father is unless we have to find out in a medical emergency, right?"

They both responded, "Deal."

Precious asked, "Anything else you gay boys want to know. We have been talking for almost an hour now. I know y'all probably need to fuck again soon or something."

Abel and Xerxes looked at one another and when they looked at Precious, she could see how embarrassed they were. She chided, "See y'all can't even look me in the eyes. I will get the pre-natal schedule to you in a few and I will let you know if the doctor needs or wants anything else."

Precious' tone got very serious, "I love you punks. Thanks for helping an old fag hag like me realize my dream."

Xerxes said, "P take care of yourself. You are carrying precious cargo."

Abel said, "I love you Precious."

She said, "I love you back to the moon and beyond." She hung up the phone.

Xerxes hugged Abel. He said, "We are about to be Dads." This is really happening."

Abel kissed him and said, "I love you big Daddy. There is no one who I would rather be a Daddy with than you."

Xerxes kissed him back. Abel turned his back to Xerxes and they both fell asleep with smiles on their faces.

24

Precious was fortunate enough to find a new Mother's exercise class at a recently opened community center that was within walking distance to her apartment. She had been able to successfully coordinate a schedule with Xerxes and Abel so that one or both of them was always able to attend the pre-natal classes with her. She had finally begun to show and Xerxes jokingly started calling her "D" instead of P. It was Abel's turn to join her for the class this week but his flight was delayed. He texted Precious to let her know his flight had landed and he would join her as soon as he could.

The community center had been an amalgamation of contiguous individual small store fronts that closed when they were unable to afford the skyrocketing lease rates in the rapidly gentrifying neighborhood. The displaced shops included a hair salon, a fast-food carryout restaurant, a shoe repair shop and a small, family owned dry cleaning concern.

The pregnant wife of a well connected Capital Hill Lobbyist bought the space with a community development grant and converted it into a facility offering a myriad of services and support to women in the local area. Precious found out about the center from a staffer who supported one of her congressional colleagues.

One of the shops that comprised the center had been divided into several small rooms that were used as individual huddle rooms and supported one-on-one consultations or small group meetings. Another shop had been converted into two large spaces that were used as classrooms that offered personal and professional development training seminars. An area along the front of the center that looked out onto the street had been remodeled into cubicles, offices and a conference room for staff meetings. The pre-natal classes were held in a large, open space just behind the office area. Floor to ceiling mirrors covered three of its four walls. A locker room with showers, a steam room and private cubicles with massage tables was located behind the open room. Ceiling fans hung like spinning metal stalactites twelve feet apart throughout the entire facility and helped regulate the temperature in the center especially when the popular pre-natal classes were in session. Precious joked that with a room full of pregnant mothers and in the heat and humidity of Washington, DC summers, the space could get as "hot as fish grease" without the fans. A large stack of colorful, padded mats were stacked along the wall at the back of the room.

Precious arrived at the center early and positioned her red mat near the center of the room on the second row from the instructor. She was warming up and stretching while she waited for Abel to join her. She always arrived early because the center and the services it provided were so popular and in such heavy demand that every new Mother's exercise class filled to capacity as soon as it was announced. The classes attracted a broad cross section of women who represented every race, creed, color, income, socioeconomic and educational attainment level.

Precious wore asphalt grey lululemon Align yoga pants with a matching long line energy bra. She added a pair of grey Skechers Arch Fit athletic shoes to top off her look. The other women in the class often complimented her because she always wore color-coordinated outfits that perfectly fit her growing body. Her hair was pulled back away from her face and tied with a grey scrunchy.

She wasn't sure if any of the other women in the class knew that she was a member of Congress and went out of her way to be as cordial and friendly as she could. She was careful not to flaunt herself or her station and tried to be as friendly and outgoing as possible. Precious never had many close girlfriends as a child because they were either jealous of her relationship with Xerxes or thought she wasn't pretty enough because of her dark skin. At Spelman, she focused so much on her studies that she neglected socializing and made few friends there as well. Politics forced her to be interesting and engaging and she used those skills to interact with the other Moms in the class.

Most of the women who regularly attended the pre-natal class with Precious were joined by male companions. A handful of women had female friends who accompanied them instead of men. Precious initially caused a stir when Xerxes joined her in class one week and Abel showed up to support her the next. Two particularly rambunctious expectant mothers in the class, who never had anyone to accompany them, took every chance they could to ridicule and humiliate Precious because of it.

Once, when Xerxes joined Precious for a class, she overheard the two women talking about her before the class began. She walked into the lockeroom and heard one of the women say, "Shequita girl did you see that fine motherfucker over there with that skinny black bitch!?! "He could be my baby daddy anytime!!"

Shequita replied, "Yes, girl. He is fine!!! I don't know why he is here with her when he should be with me?"

Precious slipped in and out of the locker room without being noticed and told Xerxes what she had heard. She recounted what they said and how they described her. She felt him tensing as she spoke but grabbed and massaged his arm to calm him. She told him, "Z, baby don't worry about it. Let them say whatever they want. They are probably just jealous because neither one of them has a man or anybody here to help them."

Xerxes replied, "Yeah, I guess you are right, but I don't like them coming for you like that."

Precious joked, "Let me drop this load and I will take on both of them bitches. You know these whores been all up in my face about you since we were kids. I ain't had no fight yet, but you about to be my Baby Daddy and I got some pent up hostility now!!!"

The thought of Precious fighting anyone over him caused Xerxes to roar with laughter. She had never exhibited jealously or shown envy of any kind even when he was having indiscriminant sex with any and everyone he could back in college. He was still laughing loudly when Shequita and her friend exited the locker room but abruptly stopped as soon as he saw them. The two harpies must have sensed that they were the focus of his amusement because the one named Shequita exclaimed loudly, "They better not be talking about us."

The Instructor heard Shequita's bluster and quickly started the class to diffuse the brewing altercation. She led the expectant mothers and their partners through a series of exercises that included pilates, barre and yoga. Shequita and her friend attempted to help one another complete the warm up stretches but were panting breathlessly by the time the actual class began. They strained and labored to keep up with the instructor for the remainder of the hour long class and were spent and could barely breathe by the time it was over. Any energy they hoped to use to castigate or berate Precious had evaporated.

Abel finally arrived just as the class was about to begin and quickly joined Precious on her mat. He greeted her with a warm hug and a peck on her cheek and complimented her on how good she looked in all grey. Shequita and her friend had purposely positioned themselves directly behind Precious and began their impolite chorus of snide comments as soon as they saw Abel. Shequita grumbled, "This bitch can't figure out who her baby daddy is? She bring a different nigger up in here every class."

Abel overheard the comment and quickly turned his head to stare at Precious' tormenters. He leaned over to Precious and whispered incredulously, "Are they talking about you?!? He asked, "Do they fuck with you like this all of the time?"

Precious replied, "Yeah. It mostly happens only when Z is with me. I think they like him or wish they could get with him or something. Hell, I don't even listen to it no more. They usually just say shit to try to provoke me, but I ignore them. They're just jealous. I've had to deal with jealous bitches all my life when it comes to Z."

Abel said, "Yeah, but you don't need that kind of stress, especially right now. Don't make me have to beat these bitches down if they keep fucking with you."

Precious said, "No, Abel, please don't. Just leave it alone!!"

Sensing that her tirade was making Precious and Abel uncomfortable, Shequita continued, "I know she know we talking about her. She better not say nothing."

Abel said, "Oh, no she did-n't!! I can't let these bitches carry you like that. They obviously don't know that I will fight a girl. I'm about to get them right together up in here."

Precious implored, "No, Abel. Don't do nothing. Don't say nothing!! I can't have this blow up and make it in the news. It might affect my campaign."

Abel said, "Oh, damn. That's right!! OK, Precious. I'll let it slide just for you."

Precious' detractors were unable to continue their attacks during the rest of the class. The instructor led the soon to be Moms through their strenuous workout regimen and they needed all of their energy to keep up. As soon as the class was over, Precious quickly grabbed her mat and returned it to the back of the room and sprinted into the shower room to freshen up before leaving with Abel. Shequita and her friend were still recovering from the arduous class and lingered on their mats. Abel turned to them and said, "So I heard you and your girl talking about my friend....."

Shequita interrupted, "I know she didn't send you over here to fuck with us did she!?!? I'll beat her ass....."

Abel interrupted, "No, she absolutely did not send me over here. She doesn't even know I am talking to y'all at all and would probably be mad if she did. In fact, she told me not to say nothing to y'all!!"

Shequita asked, "So if your girl didn't tell you to come over here, what the fuck do you want then?"

Abel replied, "I honestly just want to know why y'all are coming after my girl like that? I mean what did she ever do or say to cause y'all to come for her like that!?" He continued, "Hell, it's only three black women in this whole fucking class and y'all are coming after her. Why would you embarrass yourselves in front of these Karens and Beckys like that!! The white women get along. The Asian women get along. The Latinas get along. What the fuck is wrong with you bitches that y'all can't get along with my girl." He asked, "Do y'all even know her name or anything about her?"

Shequita retorted, "I don't need to know her name. I just know don't like the bitch."

Abel said, "That don't make no damn sense and it makes y'all sound as stupid as fuck. I mean y'all are really fucking with her. She is already nervous and scared because this is her first pregnancy. Y'all ain't doing nothing but adding stress to her situation. Why!?!" He went on, "For real, why? It can't be only because you just don't like her. Did she ever do anything to y'all? Ever said anything bad to either one of you?!"

Shequita and her friend looked at one another and said, "No, she ain't never even said nothing to us but Hi. I just don't like the way she look. She always showing up in her matching outfits and shit. I don't like the way she talks. Always sounding so proper!!......"

Abel interrupted, "What!!!! You don't like how she looks or how she sounds. What is she supposed to do about how she looks or how she sounds? That is some elementary school bullshit. So y'all are cool with embarrassing yourself and acting like these other motherfuckers expect us to act. When are we going to stop attacking one another and making each other the enemy? They're already laughing and talking about all of us behind our back."

Shequita said, "I don't care what they think. Hell, I don't know them....."

Abel interrupted, "But you don't know my girl either. You don't know if she can help you with something or if y'all can help her. Y'all don't know what she might be able to do for you because you haven't taken time to get to know her.

Shequita said, "I don't want to take the time to get to know her. She come up in here with her new clothes and designer bag and hair always in place. She looks like she ain't never had a bad day in her life."

Abel said, "Man, if you only knew. She has come a long way from where she started. So just because she looks like she got her shit together, it didn't happen overnight."

Shequita said, "Well......."

Abel interrupted, "Well nothing. Y'all need to also know that the same negative energy y'all are channeling toward my girl is running through your baby too. Y'all going to give birth to some evil ass little munchkin and it'll be because of the negative vibe you're putting out now. When that evil little motherfucker is beating your ass one day, I hope you remember how you treated my girl."

Shequita's friend finally chimed in, "And bitch you know you don't need another evil little bastard. Hell, you got three of them little assholes already."

Shequita replied, "Shut up bitch. My babies ain't bad."

Shequita's friend answered, "Bitch stop lying. You know you call them little motherfuckers Bebe's Kids behind their back."

They all laughed.

Abel softened his tone and added, "This is a hard ass class. I know it's hard for my friend and she has somebody here to help. I don't know how y'all do it and y'all ain't got nobody here to help you either. It must really be hard to be pregnant and not have any help. My friend told me that she feels so lucky to have me and my best friend to support her. She said she wouldn't know what she would do if we weren't with her. Hell, she said she might not have even gone through with having the baby if we weren't with her. She thinks y'all are really strong to be doing this on your own."

When Abel told them that Precious thought they were strong

Shequita and her friend softened. He continued, "She is so nervous because this is her first pregnancy." She told me that this can't be your first pregnancies because y'all seem so confident and experienced."

Shequita asked, "She said that about us?"

He said, "Yeah, she said it." He continued, "Man, y'all could really coach her and help her get through this instead of putting her down. What was your first pregnancy like? Were you scared? Did you have anybody to help you?"

They both shook their heads No.

Abel said, "OK, let me get this straight. Y'all want to give my girl a hard time and stress her out and don't have no good reason other than she is a sister, you don't like how she looks and she ended up in the same class y'all are taking? Damn, sure makes a lot of sense to me."

Shequita's friend softened and said, "We ain't mean no harm. We was just fucking with her. We couldn't fuck with these white bitches and we was just having some fun."

Abel replied, "Yeah y'all think it was fun but she didn't know it and couldn't understand why y'all were coming for her like that. She thought y'all really didn't like her and couldn't undertand why. Hell, she's real good people and I bet if y'all got to know her y'all would get along really well. And I know I would certainly appreciate it if y'all did."

Shequita was so excited to have a man, any man, show her any appreciation or positive attention and said, "Damn, you're good!! Ok, we can try to chill out on your girl for you handsome. We can look out for her but we gotta get something out of it. What are you going to do for us?"

Abel didn't want to be indebted to either of them and asked hesitantly, "Uh, I don't know. What do y'all want?"

Shequita said excitedly, "I want that big muscle-bound mother-fucker that comes to class with her sometime. Can you hook me up with him. He is fine as shit!!"

Abel replied, "I think I might be able to arrange something for after y'all have your babies. I know you ain't trying to get with him now, right??"

Shequita said, "I'm a freak, but I ain't that damn freaky. If I get with that big motherfucker now my baby will have a head shaped like Gumby or something with him ramming that big old dick inside me. I can wait."

The friend chimed in, "Yeah, Lord knows you don't want an-other crazy looking baby. You got too many of them already" and laughed out loud.

Shequita replied in a deadpan tone, "Not today bitch. Not today."

Abel said, "OK, Let me see what I can do." He added, "I'll try to hook you up with my boy if y'all could look out for my girl if me or my buddy arean't ever able to make it to class and she is here by herself."

Shequita replied, "Sure baby, we got your girl. Let me give you my digits so you can hook me up with that fine ass man."

Abel replied, "Sure. I will give them to him and tell him what we talked about. I will make sure that he hollers at you the next time he is here too. Is that cool?"

Shequita couldn't contain her excitement and yelled, "Yes. Hell yeah!!"

Abel replied, "Y'all are the best. I'll let my buddy know that if we can't make it that y'all got things under control."

Shequita replied, "Thanks sexy. We got you and we got your girl too."

Precious emerged from the shower room and was surprised by the broad smiles that Shequita and her friend directed her way. Abel introduced them and Shequita said, "We got you little mama. Let us know if you need or want anything."

Precious and Abel walked out of the center and she asked him, "What did you say to them? What caused such a drastic change?"

He replied, "I promised them a date with Xerxes after they have their babies." He added, "But you have to tell him though."

They couldn't contain their laughter as they got out to the street.

25

Precious' campaign team scheduled her election victory party at the Genesis Center downtown. It was the largest venue in town that served as a convention center, sports arena and concert venue depending on the event for which it was reserved. The cavernous sports arena could be partitioned into separate smaller spaces that accommodated large and festive group events. Many of the local high schools used the venue for proms and other celebratory functions and it was often reserved for church services, revivals or trade shows. Precious' team reserved one section of the arena space and planned for and expected a crowd of about 300 – 500 supporters and well wishers.

Her staff arranged and coordinated all of the events and activities for the festive celebration and invited her largest financial supporters, representatives from the local and national news media and several political and entertainment personalities. Her staff also made sure that as many of her constituents who wanted to attend were able to join the celebration as well. They spared no expense for the lavish ceremony including an extravagant and sumptuous buffet and assured the crowd would be in a festive mood sponsoring an open bar. Large video monitors were arrayed throughout the venue so that revelers could watch the election returns in real time as they came in. Precious' only request to her team was that the event be spiritual, cheerful and convivial.

Her staff arranged for a young and progressive minister to open the celebration with an inspirational and uplifting prayer. The minister had become a local celebrity who was a well known for implementing revolutionary programs in his church geared toward transforming the youth and people in the community that needed the most support. He founded a program to help inmates begin their education while incarcerated and supported them with scholarships and stipends to continue when they were released. He also led a job training/apprenticeship program to help his congregants secure skills and ultimately well paying jobs in new and emerging technologies and industries. Precious planned to announce support for his job training initiative at the event and made sure her staff included him on the agenda.

The minister was followed by a mass choir comprised of students from schools all across Precious' congressional district. Her staff wanted to showcase her commitment to the youth within her constituency and amassed a group of over 100 singers. They performed a medley of contemporary and traditional gospel songs and spirituals but brought the crowd to its feet with their rendition of the Gospel music classic "Jesus Is Real". Precious' hopes that the night would be a real celebration instead of a tiresome and tedious political rally filled with long bombastic and boring political speeches was definitely coming true.

Her Campaign Manager walked onstage after the choir to announce the results of the election and to notify the assembled throng that Precious' Republican challenger had called to officially concede. The crowd cheered long and loud upon hearing that the results were confirmed and Precious' victory was official. Precious was introduced by one of her congressional colleagues, who had also gained national notoriety, by listing several of her significant accomplishments including specific legislation that she had authored. The crowd welcomed her to the stage with rousing and prolonged applause as balloons, streamers and confetti rained down on her from above.

Precious wore a sparkling red dress that perfectly complimented her pregnant body with a plunging neckline. Her
breasts had significantly increased in size and she decided she
wanted to bring them out for the night and show them off. Her
hair was pulled back from her face and fashioned in stylish
twists and she looked flawless. The applause from the crowd
showered over her like a spring rain. She was glowing and
her smile was radiant. She was exultant and grabbed Xerxes
and Abel and embraced them tightly. They both looked re-
splendent in their stylish black tuxedos accessorized with red
pocket squares to match and compliment Precious' dress. The
three of them had been inseparable throughout the night and
received compliments on how attractive they all looked.

Precious slowly walked to the center of the stage and stood for
several moments basking in the adulation. A remixed version
of Whitney Houston's rendition of the Chaka Khan classic "I'm
Every Women" blasted over the sound system throughout
the room. She began her speech by acknowledging the young
minister, the choir and her campaign manager. She recognized
all of the dignitaries who were in attendance and praised her
campaign staff for all of their assistance and support. She
profusely thanked her Capital Hill staff and commended her
Republican opponent for his effort and professionalism during
the campaign. She saved her most effusive and heartfelt praise
for Xerxes and Abel and finally began her prepared remarks.

She felt trepidation when a slight trickle of liquid dribbled
down her legs and she detected the slightest hint of sweetness
in the air. She remembered that these were two of the early
signs of delivery from her pre-natal training and decided that
she needed to shorten her remarks just in case her fears were
realized. She thanked everyone for their support and unob-
trusively asked her Campaign Manager to return to the stage.
Her Campaign Manager knew something was amiss because

Precious was scheduled to annouce her key initiatives for her next term. The crowd, surprised by the shortness of her speech and excited to return to the celebration, cheered loud and long. Precious whispered to her Campaign Manager, "I think my water just broke. I am going to get Xerxes and Abel to take me to the hospital." She added, "Can you cover the highlights of my next term and I will call you later to let you know how things go!!"

Precious slowly and cautiously walked offstage. Xerxes and Abel noticed a look of discomfort on her face. Abel asked, "Precious are you OK? You don't look so good." Precious calmly said, "Can you take me to the hospital? I think we are about to be a family. I think my water just broke."

Xerxes stuttered, "W-w-w-what do you need us to do? I will get the car. A, can you take care of P?"

Abel said, "Sure baby. Precious what do you need? Do we need a wheelchair? Are you OK? Does it hurt?!? Do you need me to carry you?"

Precious said, "Boy No!!! Calm the fuck down, both of you!! Just help me to the car."

Xerxes bolted ahead to get the car. Fortunately, Precious was the VIP attendee so his car was parked right up front and handy to retrieve. He bolted through the door of the Genesis Center and when he got outside he told the Valet Attendant that he needed the black Tesla. Xerxes implored "Hurry up man!!! We gotta get to the hospital."

Precious and Abel walked out just as the Valet pulled the Tesla up to the front entrance. They slowly and carefully eased Precious into the front passenger seat and Abel jumped in the back seat directly behind her. Xerxes bolted out of the parking lot as soon as Abel was secure and sped to Methodist Hospital.

The hospital was only a few blocks away and Xerxes arrived in less than ten minutes. Precious called Dr. Mbaku, the local gynecologist to whom Dr. Nwadi had referred her, to let him know that she was going into labor and was on her way to the hospital. Simultaneously Abel called ahead to let the hospital know that they were on the way with an expectant mother who was ready to deliver. When they arrived, he jumped out of the car and ran inside to get help before Xerxes could bring the car to a complete stop. Abel dashed through the Emergency Entrance and ran to the registration station yelling, "My friend is about to have her baby!! Can someone help us?" A lanky attendant who looked as if he was half asleep or bored jumped up and grabbed a wheelchair and followed Abel back to the entrance.

Xerxes parked the car in the Emergency Entrance driveway and walked around to help Precious get out. He had gotten her out of the car just as Abel and the attendant arrived with the wheelchair. Abel and the Attendent eased Precious into the wheelchair while Xerxes parked the Tesla and joined them a few minutes later. They pushed her inside the hospital to the registration desk to check her in. The Attendant asked, "Ma'am, what is your name and how far apart are your contractions?"

"Precious Thomas and my contractions are about ten minutes apart right now. My doctor is Dr. Mbaku and I called him to let him know what was happening and that I was coming to the hospital. He said he would be on his way."

The attendant said, "OK, thank you" and prepared an admitting band and placed it on her wrist. An orderly appeared and took Precious to the Triage Room where a Nurse connected a fetal monitor to her belly to keep track of the babies' heart beats. The nurses also monitored Precious' contractions to determine how far apart they were and checked her cervix to determine her dilation.

Her confidence disappeared while she waited in the austere
and stark room and she grew more nervous with every moment that passed. She had only been in the pristine room for a
minute or two but seconds passed like hours and it felt like she
had been there an eternity. Her contractions lasted longer each
time they occurred and increased in frequency. She felt as if she
had been abandoned and wanted to cry out for Xerxes and Abel.
She began to cry just as Dr. Mbaku walked into the Triage Room
to introduced himself.

Dr. Mbaku was a tall man with a smooth, caramel complexion.
He had an easy smile and perfectly white teeth. His large hands
grabbed Precious' and he greeted her warmly. His soothing
demeanor comforted her and made her feel at ease and her
tears stopped. He had salt and pepper hair that was styled in
a close-cut fade. He had a full beard and mustache that were
both perfectly shaped and trimmed and surrounded a pair of
large luscious lips. The doctor wore dark blue slacks and a light
blue shirt with button down collars. A brightly colored bowtie
was apparent over the top of his white doctor's coat. Precious
chuckled at the thought that she might attempt to flirt with
the doctor if they met under different circumstances.

Dr. Mbaku had a heavy Ghanian accent and said, "Hello, Ms.
Thomas. I am Dr. Mbaku. Our friend Dr. Nwadi asked me to take
good care of you while you are here. It looks like you are about
to bring two new African Kings or Queens into this world. Do
you have any questions that I can answer for you?"

Precious said, "No, doctor. I just want this to be as painless and
as fast a possible." She joked, "I'm not built for pain."

Dr. Mbaku replied, "Well, these two new little people will get
here on their own time. You and I are just here to guide them."
He asked, "If things get too painful, do you want me to administer an epidural?"

Precious said, "No, I want this to be as natural as it possibly can be." She added, "Now if I start to speak in tongue or something like that, you do what you gotta do."

Dr. Mbaku laughed, "Well, I haven't ever had anything quite like that happen yet, but I will keep it in mind." He went on, "Is there anyone that you would like to be in the Delivery Room with you? Is the father here?"

Precious said, "Yes, they both are."

Dr. Mbaku hesitated for a moment and then said, "There may not be enough room for both of them. Do you want to select which one you want in the delivery room with you?"

Precious replied, "If both of them can't be there then I don't want either one of them in there."

Dr. Mbaku said, "Yes, Ma'am I understand." He added, "Let me go and update them on your decision. The next time you see me, we will be delivering your babies."

The doctor summond an attendant and directed her to move Precious to the Labor and Delivery Room.

Dr. Mbaku went to the Waiting Room to find out Abel and Xerxes. They both stood up and walked toward him when he asked who was waiting for Precious Thomas. He told them hat Precious was being moved to the Labor and Delivery Room and that her contractions were becoming more frequent. He told them that the delivery room could not accomodate both of them and Precious made the decision that neither of them should join her since there was not enough space for both of them. He assured them that there was no need to worry and confirmed that Precious and the babies were doing well. He told them that he expected labor to begin at any time and directed them to another, more secluded waiting area. As he turned to walk away, he told them that they would be fathers by the next time he saw them.

Abel looked at Xerxes and said, "Damn, I guess this is really happening man!!"

Xerxes replied, "Yeah. I hope P and the babies are good."

Precious eyes blinked as she was wheeled into the bright, white, sterile Labor and Delivery Room. She was distracted by the brightness of the lights and the blips and beeps that emanated from the machines, monitors and other equipment all around the room. She did not immediately see Dr. Mbaku but heard three distinct voices when she was positioned in the center of the room. The voices belonged to the Anesthesiologist and the two attending nurses who were in the room to assist the doctor with the delivery. Everyone was dressed in all white and wore face masks and hair coverings. They all introduced themselves and told Precious what role they would each play in her delivery.

Precious looked up directly into several large, bright lights as the Anesthesiologist positioned himself just to the right of Precious' head. He told her to let him know if she experienced too much pain and assured her that he would administer something to help make her feel better. The two nurses stood on both sides of Precious and kept checking monitors and IVs and constantly made sure that she was comfortable and doing well. She told them that other than a dry mouth she was doing and feeling fine. One of the nurses gave her a few ice chips and Precious thanked her.

Dr. Mbaku walked into the operating room clad in complete surgical gear and asked the staff if everything was OK and if they were ready. The nurses responded that everything was nominal. He asked Precious, "So soon to be Mamma, how are you doing?"

"I am doing fine."

"Are you ready to do this?"

"Yes doctor."

Dr. Mbaku said, "Ok, I will monitor you, but if the pain becomes unbearable, let us know."

Precious said, "Yes, doctor."

Precious began labor as Dr. Mbaku monitored her progress and guided her through the delivery. His operating room demeanor was pleasant and soothing and he kept Precious abreast of everything that was happening along the way. He told her when to push and for how long and let her know everything that he was doing and what he saw.

Precious was progressing well and if she was experience any extreme pain or discomfort, she hid it well. She moaned a bit and groaned slightly but pushed dutifully when directed by the doctor. The nurses wiped her brow of perspiration after each push and offered additional ice chips to ease her xerostomia. The doctor told her that the baby was almost here and instructed her to give one final push. She complied and the doctor grabbed the newborn in his large left hand and severed the umbilical cord with his right. He handed the wailing babe to one of the attending nurses who cleaned it and placed it in the waiting neo-natal bassinet. Dr. Mbaku assured Precious that the baby was perfect and suggested that she rest for a moment, reminding her that she would have to do it all over again.

Precious was still sweating and panting from her labor but followed the doctor's guidance and rested for a few moments. The nurses dabbed away perspiration and gave her more ice chips. The doctor asked if she needed a few more moments to rest before starting the second delivery and Precious said, "No doctor, let's get this done and over."

The doctor's soothing tone returned as he directed Precious to push again. He told her how the delivery was progressing and directed her to push and rest alternately. The Anesthesiologist asked how she was doing or if her pain was too harsh. Precious replied that she was fine and just wanted to get things done. The doctor asked the nurses about her vital signs and they told him that she was doing fine. He instructed her to push again for one final time and the second baby was delivered as well. Dr. Mbaku held the second baby in one hand and snipped the umbilical cord with the other, just as he had done before, and handed the second twin to the nurse so it could be cleaned up as well.

The doctor praised Precious on her deliveries and asked how she was doing. She was exhausted and sweating but not in any real pain or discomfort. The nurses wiped her brow and cleaned her up. When she was ready they placed the twin cherubs on her breasts so she could meet them for the first time. She smiled widely and cried.

The nurses complimented her on delivering two beautiful and healthy babies while they continued to monitor her vital signs to make sure that she was doing well.

Dr. Mbaku said, "Congratulations Mamma. Your babies are perfectly healthy and you are doing fine. I don't think there is much more for me to do here. We will get you up to your room and let you rest. If you will excuse me, I need to go tell your young men that everything went fine and that you are well. After I talk to them, I will send them up to your room."

Precious whispered, "Thank you so much doctor. I appreciate everything you did for us."

Dr. Mbaku walked out of the delivey room and headed directly to the waiting room to talk to Abel and Xerxes. He removed his face mask as Xerxes and Abel stood up and walked toward him. Dr. Mbaku looked at both of them and told them that Precious was doing well. He told them that the babies were healthy and doing fine and that the delivery had been worry free. He let them know that they would be able to see Precious in a little while, if they wanted.

Xerxes and Abel were euphoric. They were ecstatic. The hugged one another and hugged Dr. Mbaku too. Xerxes said, "I am going to be Big Daddy. A, you can be little Daddy" and laughed out loud.

Abel replied, "I definitely am not going to be no damn little Daddy. I will come up with my own name." He added, "Speaking of names, we never did talk about baby names with Precious. I wonder if she has thought about it?!"

Xerxes chimed in, "That's right A. We don't know if she had a boy, a girl or both."

They looked at Dr. Mbaku and asked simultanously, "So doctor, what's up? What did she have!?"

Dr. Mbaku smiled.

ABOUT THE AUTHOR

James "Doc" Holliday

After nearly forty years as a sales leader in corporate American, James Doc Holliday finally got a chance to tell a story. His first draft read like a business memo but he ultimately found his voice and A Modern Family is the result.

Born in Gary, Indiana and raised there and in Mississippi, he was educated in the Gary Community School corporation, which in the 1960's was one of the best public school systems in the nation. After graduating from Gary Roosevelt High School, the lifelong Panther matriculated to Purdue University and DePaul.

Work and employment allowed Doc to live in the midwest, the east coast and the west. He says, "I always thought I had a story inside me. But never got a chance to focus any energy until after retirement. This is the first of what I hope will be many stories that I want to tell. I finally have the time to do it."

A Modern Family is not the story that I started to write. I had a completely different story and outline in my mind. As the words began to flow, the characters took over. Precious was only supposed to be a minor character, but her personality shown through. Cyrus was supposed to have more of a prominent role but Xerxes outshown him. While not what I intended when I first put pen to paper, I am so excited that Precious and Xerxes fought through and forced me to tell their stories.

www.ingramcontent.com/pod-product-compliance
Lightning Source LLC
Chambersburg PA
CBHW060909250626
47159CB00008B/2929